Incident at Elder Creek

Anna Furtado

*Quest Books
by Regal Crest*

Tennessee

Copyright © 2016 by Anna Furtado

All rights reserved. No part of this publication may be reproduced, transmitted in any form or by any means, electronic or mechanical, including photocopy, recording, or any information storage and retrieval system, without permission in writing from the publisher. The characters, incidents and dialogue herein are fictional and any resemblance to actual events or persons, living or dead, is purely coincidental.

ISBN 978-1-61929-306-9

First Edition 2016

9 8 7 6 5 4 3 2 1

Cover design by AcornGraphics

Published by:

Regal Crest Enterprises
1042 Mount Lebanon Road
Maryville, TN 37804

Find us on the World Wide Web at
http://www.regalcrest.biz

Published in the United States of America

Acknowledgments

First and most important: Thank you readers who give deeper meaning to every word by your reading them. However, this book wouldn't be in your hands without the following people, who also deserve many thanks: Beta readers Natalie Farias, Earlene Meyer, and Nancy Nunes—you ladies rock; publisher, Cathy Bryerose, and editor, Patty Schramm, without whose dedication and expertise this story would never be made public. Ann McMan: your cover embodies this story in art and gives readers a beautiful first impression.

Dedication

To the spirits of the old mining town of Columbia, California, who, during a visit several years ago, whispered in my ear, insisting they had a story to tell.

Chapter One

TUCKER STUMBLED AWAY from the saloon struggling to stay upright. Her eyes refused to focus. It took several tries, blinking and opening them wide before she made out blurred details as she gazed up and down the street. The town looked deserted, the street dark. She heard a dog bark from a few streets away, piercing the eerie quiet. As she glanced at the bar behind her, she wondered if she dared go back in. Best not to chance it, she thought. Through the window, she noticed the small nightlight lit behind the long bar, reflecting off the wall mirror mounted behind the liquor shelves. The place looked closed.

How did she get through that door? Her spinning head wouldn't let her puzzle it out. She brushed debris from her shoulders and tried not to lose her balance while taking a few tentative steps. As she made her way down Elder Creek's empty main street, she tried to pretend nothing was amiss. But something was definitely wrong.

She felt as if she'd too much to drink, yet not quite the same as being drunk. Everything hurt, but she didn't remember being in a fight. She wasn't about to give in to how she felt. All she wanted was to get back to her room at the hotel and lie down. She'd figure out what the hell happened to her later, after she slept.

As she approached the hotel, she glanced around again but stopped because the movement of her head made her dizzy. Still, she saw enough to know nothing looked out of place. The mercantile nightlights were still lit. Mouser, the old black cat with one white paw, who lived in the store, lay curled up in a basket in the window, fast asleep. The faded cardboard sign next to him read "Closed." Through the imperfect old glass panes, Tucker made out the silhouettes of the neatly lined up merchandise bins.

In the next block, Joe Dawson's beat up old green Toyota pickup sat in front of the Elder Creek Bank, the bed stacked high with junk he collected and would yield him a few bucks to keep him going another day. She imagined Joe somewhere close by, foraging in the dark. He did his scavenging in the wee hours of the morning sometimes. He was a strange, solitary duck who collected the detritus of people's lives. It suited him.

She raised her head to the heavens, willing her vertigo not to return. The stars in the sky twinkled overhead telling her everything should be right with the world, but she wasn't so sure it was. As she stood on the wooden sidewalk, her stomach felt a little off, and she tried to remember when she ate last. Maybe she picked up food poisoning. Maybe—or maybe not.

She pushed on toward the tiny National Hotel and her room there. One thought prevailed in her mind. She needed to lie down.

As she passed under a still glowing street lamp, she examined her knuckles. They were bruised and discolored, but they didn't appear to be swollen. When she turned her palm over, she saw an angry redness. A burn? No wonder her hand hurt. A couple of small blisters raised the skin to bubbles. She stopped again and flexed her fingers. She felt some soreness, but she doubted anything was broken.

She tried to remember.

Only murky images without form or meaning swirled in her mind. No matter how hard she tried, nothing clear materialized. As she started out toward her destination again, it took every ounce of energy to lift one foot in front of the other. She forced herself to trudge on. Only one more block, she told herself.

The early morning chill felt good against her throbbing hand. Dark tendrils of her wavy hair, loosened from the ponytail she sometimes wore, blew in the breeze against her cheek. She knew her hair would be even more of a mess than it felt if it weren't for her ever-present black felt cowboy hat perched firmly on her head. The thin flannel western shirt she wore barely gave her body enough protection against the coolness. Did she leave her jacket somewhere? She couldn't remember wearing it the last time she'd left her room.

Her jeans pressed against a painful area of her thigh every time she stepped out, but she tried not to yield to it and limp. Since she didn't know what happened to her, she didn't want to let on anything was wrong to the night clerk at the hotel.

She didn't have to worry. He barely glanced her way as she came through the door and stepped across the hotel lobby.

The college kid from the next town over in Portero worked the overnight shift. His head was always in a book. Without knowing what she looked like, but conscious she felt a bit of a mess, she took comfort because her appearance didn't alarm him when he gave her a ghost of a smile as she entered the lobby.

The old hotel didn't have an elevator. The pain in her leg made it difficult to take the stairs, but she managed. Finally, blessedly, she reached the door to her room. As soon as she unlocked it, she fumbled for the "Quiet Please" sign to tell housekeeping not to enter and hung it outside. With the door locked behind her, she fell into bed, exhausted, after only removing her hat. Even though she felt bone-weary, sleep evaded her now, her mind churning.

What happened to her? She didn't have a clue. Try as she might, she couldn't conjure up any identifiable images. When had she last been in this room? At four o'clock in the afternoon—yesterday afternoon, she reminded herself—she finished a chapter in her new novel and headed for the bar. After that, her memory failed her.

She tried again to grasp for a thread, any recollection of recent events from after she reached her destination in the afternoon. Did she reach the bar at all? She didn't know. It took too much energy to pull anything more from her mind. Weariness overtook her and she slept at last.

TUCKER SAT IN the dark, staring at the golden liquid in her glass. A scalding hot shower and a few sips of the Baker's Bourbon soothed her after sleeping the day away. She'd woken at seven in the evening, sore as hell, still with no memory of what happened to her. She took another sip of Baker's and concentrated on the smooth liquid as it slid over her tongue and down her throat while trying to make sense of last night's events.

She recalled making her way to The Charlie, as they called The St. Charles Saloon. Entering the bar was her last memory from the previous day, or so she assumed. She intended to stop in for a beer and visit with her long-time friend, Jackie O'Malley, who owned the place. But she didn't remember Jackie or the beer, and her brain felt like wet cement. If it hardened, she'd be in big trouble.

The clock next to her computer on the small desk read eight-thirty now. Outside her window, the sky looked like black velvet. She needed to get some writing done but motivation escaped her. A persistent fog clouded her mind. The word *forget* rattled around in her brain over and over. She snarled in disgust and stared at her computer from across the room, willing its presence to give her incentive to get up and work. It was useless. She knew no words would come to her worth the energy to get up and walk over to the desk.

She reached for her phone instead. When Jackie answered,

Tucker didn't bother with fanfare. "Were you at The Charlie yesterday afternoon about four o'clock?"

"Well, hello to you, too, Tucker. And to answer your question, no, I wasn't there. With Tracey trained and working for me now, I can actually take a day off occasionally. So I was blissfully at home relaxing for the first time in about two weeks."

Tucker knew Tracey, but Tracey was not the person behind the bar when she walked into The Charlie yesterday. Ah, a new realization, she thought. Maybe her miasma would finally clear. As she listened to Jackie, a face materialized in her mind's eye—a bodiless head, akin to the Great and Powerful Oz. A name followed. The source of her new knowledge escaped her. She couldn't understand how it related to the prior evening's events, either. "Do you have somebody named Nigel—Nigel Dunbar—working for you?"

"No. I don't even know a Nigel Dunbar. Why?"

Tucker hesitated. "I—I'm not sure," she said.

"Tucker, you sound weird. Are you okay? And who is this Nigel Dunbar?"

"I think it may be kind of a long story, Jack. I'm not even sure I know all the details."

"Well, if you want to tell me what you do know, I have time. I don't need to be at work until opening tomorrow. Have you eaten?"

Silence.

"I thought so. Get over here and I'll make you something to eat."

"I don't know, Jackie. I have work to do."

"Then why aren't you doing it instead of talking to me? Something's bothering you. I can tell. Come over. We'll talk while I throw something together. You need to eat something."

Tucker sighed. "What shall I bring?" She didn't have anything to offer in her hotel room, and all the Elder Creek businesses were closed for the evening, except for the saloon. If Jackie needed something, she'd have to drive into Portero.

Jackie broke into her thoughts. "I don't need a thing. Just bring yourself. Do not stop anywhere. Do not pass go. Do not collect two hundred dollars. Well, if you find two hundred dollars sitting in the street, bend down and pick it up, for heaven's sake, but don't stop for anything else. I'll expect to see you in five minutes."

"Yes, ma'am." Tucker disconnected and stared at the phone. How was she going to explain whatever this was to Jackie when she didn't understand it herself? Her best friend would think she'd lost her mind. Maybe it was true. Maybe she was more like her mother than she knew. She'd always harbored the fear she'd be like her someday. Mentally unstable. Unpredictable. Battling with depression on good days and succumbing to it on bad ones. Maybe she should call Jackie back and tell her she changed her mind. No. It would never work with Jackie. If she did call her back to cancel, Jackie would be at her door before Tucker hung up the phone.

She slugged the rest of the Bakers down and slammed the glass against the surface of the tiny side table, vowing to pull herself together. She'd go to Jackie's and her friend would help her figure out what happened to her. Jackie was always there for her in the past. She would be now.

"SINCE I'VE BEEN talking about it, it's starting to come back to me, Jackie."

Tucker began by describing the only thing she remembered. She knew she walked into The Charlie, but something was different. She recalled thinking some kid must have been tinkering with the piano against the wall opposite the bar because she heard strains of "Oh, Susanna," but when she looked over, she saw a clean-shaven man playing the piano. He wore a faded red and white striped shirt accessorized with black sleeve garters. A bowler hat sat atop his head. Under it, shoulder length hair streaked with gray curled over his ears. Fuzzy, mutton-chop sideburns extended down his cheeks from his hairline. When she glanced at the bar, thinking she would ask Jackie if she hired a piano player to give the saloon more ambiance, she looked into the cold, steel gray eyes of the scruffiest, mean-faced guy she'd ever seen. His two-day whiskers darkened his jaw. Greasy, dark hair hung to his shoulders in strings, and he wore a shirt with a banded collar, which might have been white at one time, but now looked dingy and smoke colored, dappled with cinder-hued stains. The dim light in the bar made details behind him difficult to decipher.

She stepped toward the bar and he grimaced at her. She assumed it to be an attempt at a smile, but she knew he didn't mean it. He asked her what she was drinking. When she said she'd have a Blue Moon, he gave her a strange look. She clarified by adding, "beer," and he responded with a surly laugh and told her they only sold home brewed ale, none of that sissy big city stuff. She ordered what he offered, and it took every ounce of her willpower not to spit her first mouthful back in the bartender's face. It tasted bitter and warm. She took another small sip and asked the man if he was new to the bar. He said he'd relocated to Elder Creek shortly after the Reddman Mine opened in 'forty-nine. His use of the mine's official name surprised Tucker. Nobody called it "The Reddman Mine" anymore. They called it simply "the old mine" when she was a kid. Some of the older people still called it "Big Red," but they never referred to it by its official name.

Big Red closed over a hundred and fifty years ago when the gold veins petered out. As the miners scrabbled to pick out the last few flakes of gold they found ten years after opening, a tragic cave-in occurred. Stories ran rampant with rumors of anywhere from one to fifty miners dying. An accurate number proved impossible because accounts varied so widely and records proved scarce and unreliable. Then, there were the rumors of strange goings-on—ghosts—people said. In reality, the mine remained dangerous, and as a result, they sealed it not too long after it closed.

Everyone in town knew the stories, but no one really knew truth from fiction. If this guy came to Elder Creek since the mine opened in 1849, she got the feeling she wasn't any longer where she thought she was—or at least *when* she thought she was—or he was way older than he looked.

Not possible, Tucker realized.

Jackie listened to Tucker's story without comment until Tucker finally said, "I have no idea what happened after that, although it's obvious something did. Next thing I knew, I found myself outside The Charlie's doors and barely able to stand and walk. I actually ended up on my hands and knees for a minute. I pulled myself up using one of the support poles on the boardwalk. I was sore as hell—still am as a matter of fact—and I have blisters on my hands like I touched something hot, so I know it wasn't a dream."

She showed Jackie her palm. Jackie winced at the sight of it.

Tucker added, "I don't know how I found out the bartender's name, but I did. Someone must have told me." She repeated it, hoping more would come to her: Nigel Dunbar. Nothing.

Jackie stared at Tucker for a few seconds before asking, "What kind of story are you working on these days?"

Tucker wrinkled her forehead in confusion. "What? Why?"

"Because I'm wondering if you're working on a story about

Elder Creek or another '49er town. Maybe you were sort of day dreaming all this. You know, like a lucid dream or something. You know how wrapped up you get when you're writing."

"I was not dreaming. I have no idea how it happened, but I was definitely not asleep. Anyway, I'm working on a story about a school teacher in the Colorado territory. It has nothing to do with a mining town and it has nothing to do with Big Red or Elder Creek. Dunbar said he came to Elder Creek shortly after the mine opened. The mine closed in 1870. If he's still alive, that would make him nearly a hundred and seventy or eighty years old. Impossible, wouldn't you say?"

"It certainly is, but I have no idea who this Dunbar is, Tucker. He certainly doesn't work for me." Jackie tapped a finger on the table. "I wonder if you'll ever remember the rest of the story. Maybe it means something."

"Hard telling, but if it does, I'm not sure I'll have any idea what it might be."

"Well, maybe more will come back to you later, Tuck."

Maybe it would and maybe it wouldn't. It didn't matter because Tucker didn't intend to repeat the experience.

She decided to leave out the part about possibly having a price on her head. How she knew it, she didn't have a clue. Besides, it would only alarm Jackie and make her ask more questions, and Tucker suspected she wouldn't have any answers for them.

AFTER THEY FINISHED dinner, Jackie switched on the television to the news. The lead story flashed on the screen, an update about a young woman missing from the town of Portero, about eight miles from Elder Creek.

During the commercial break, Jackie said, "It's kind of scary that something like that's happened so close to us."

"It's true. I imagine people are pretty unnerved by it. I don't know what the world's coming to with all the killing going on and people going missing."

"It's happening more and more, isn't it?"

Tucker agreed.

They focused their attention back to the screen as the news resumed. When the news turned to politics, Jackie switched the TV off. "Sometimes politics almost makes me sicker than killing and kidnapping does."

"I know what you mean," Tucker said.

Tucker insisted on helping Jackie clean up the kitchen. It felt good to do something physical, to think of the mechanics of doing mundane tasks. When they were done, Jackie claimed she needed some exercise and she wanted to walk Tucker back to the National.

Tucker said, "I suppose it won't do me any good to say I'm a big girl and can get back to the hotel by myself."

Jackie lifted an eyebrow, but said nothing.

Tucker sighed. She always enjoyed Jackie's company, and right now, Jackie's presence made her feel more grounded. She chuckled and said, "I withdraw the comment."

As Tucker put her leather jacket on to leave she said, "By the way, Jackie, I can't find my denim jacket. I might have left it at the bar. Will you check on it?"

Jackie gave her a look of concern as she put her own coat on. "I'll look in our lost and found box tomorrow," she said as she held the door open for Tucker.

The walk helped loosen Tucker's sore muscles and cleared her head a little more. As they headed up Main Street toward the hotel, fragile autumn leaves crunched under foot, reminding Tucker of the brittleness she felt inside.

"Have you decided what you're going to do about the house?" Jackie asked.

"Do? What do you mean?"

"Well, Leah asked me about it. She wondered if she should be looking for a new place to live since you're back in town and staying at the hotel."

Tucker stopped. She looked at Jackie, eyes wide. "I wouldn't put somebody out of their home for my own convenience, Jackie. You know me better than that."

"Well, it is your house."

"I know. But like I said, I wouldn't put her out. I'm thinking I might want to buy something else and keep mom's house for a rental anyway. I've been looking around. I—I'm not sure what I want to do yet. I'm thinking I might buy some property and put a log home on it or something. I heard there's some land for sale up on Tenderfoot Hill. You know I love it up there. I might go take a look. Anyway, I'm definitely not throwing Miss Hudson out."

"I'm sure she'll be relieved to hear it. She also told me she's not sure what she should do about the rent. She said she used to mail you a check when you were in Phoenix, and she wondered if she should drop it off at the hotel or not."

Tucker sighed. "I guess I'd better stop by to see her tomorrow."

"That's probably a good idea, Tucker. It's time you two met, anyway." Jackie gave Tucker a look she didn't quite understand. In her frame of mind, though, she decided not to ask Jackie about it. She didn't need anything else to worry about.

They walked on in silence. Yes, Tucker would have to have a conversation with the old woman who lived in her childhood home, her mom's house until she passed away a few years ago.

For goodness sakes. I'd never put her out of the house. She's probably got it all decorated with doilies and lace. She's been an ideal renter, paying like clockwork. She's got a good job as the school librarian over in Portero, too. The kids probably love her like a grandmother.

Tucker said, "How's she fitting in with our little community? I heard she volunteered to serve on the committee to revitalize the town. She'd probably be a great help with the research because of her line of work."

"It didn't take long for her to become one of us. As a matter of fact, it feels like she's always been here. She's a lovely person. We've become pretty good friends."

As they strolled on in silence, visions of her friend sitting among Leah Hudson's lace and doilies, drinking tea from fine China cups poured from a matching teapot materialized. Maybe they wore hats with big flowers and lots of frou-frou netting on them. The image tickled Tucker, and she found pleasure in knowing Jackie befriended the woman. Maybe Tucker would like her, too. Frilly things weren't Tucker's style, but if Jackie liked her, there must be something affable about her.

When they reached the hotel, Jackie said, "I'm glad you're back, Tucker. I've missed you. I was thrilled to hear you decided to come back and head up the committee to convert the town into a living history site. We need you. Elder Creek needs you, and I need you back in my life."

Jackie hugged Tucker and strode toward home. Tucker stood at the entrance to the hotel, watching her until the darkness swallowed her up. "I'm glad to be home, too," she whispered. "I only wish I knew if I should be concerned about losing my mind or not."

THE NEXT MORNING, Tucker approached the house on Yankee Hill Avenue and an unexpected wave of emotion washed over her. Memories flashed before her in quick succession: growing up in the house with her mom, coming home from school and finding her mother curled up in bed, depression overtaking her ability to function. It wasn't always like that. Sometimes, when she felt better, her mom was fun, nurturing, kind, a real parent to Tucker. But when depression overtook her, Tucker took over as caregiver in the relationship.

Later in life, medications helped her mom, but they affected her personality. The balance teetered. They adjusted. Life went on. In the end, mental issues didn't take her mom's life. Instead, her heart gave out.

Tucker grieved and moved on. She was living in Phoenix with a girlfriend who eventually proved to be unfaithful. So with the house rented to Leah Hudson, Tucker stayed in Phoenix until she realized there was nothing more there for her, and when the call came asking her to head up the revitalization project, she packed up and came back to Elder Creek, knowing she was ready to return home.

She reveled in having a reliable renter in the house. She probably would have found it difficult to live there now, anyway. She looked forward to something new on a plot of land she called her own, one with some space around it and plenty of room to breathe. As she climbed the steps of the porch, she acknowledged Miss Hudson would have a home for as long as she wanted to stay, maybe for as long as she lived, depending on how many years she had left.

Before she raised her hand to knock, the front door swung open. The woman standing there took Tucker's breath away. Blonde waves framed her face. Tucker watched as the other woman registered surprise. Wide eyes stared back at Tucker— eyes so blue they looked like a clear, bottomless sea.

Who was this beauty, Tucker wondered? A friend of Miss Hudson's? A housekeeper? A relative, perhaps?

"H-hi," Tucker managed to stammer. She cleared her throat, willing her nervousness to disappear, only partially succeeding. "I'm Tucker Stevens. I'm looking for Miss Hudson." She craned her neck, trying to look into the living room around the young woman. "Is she home?"

The woman's surprised look vanished. She thrust her hand out toward Tucker. "Tucker, it's great to meet you. I'm Leah Hudson. Please, call me Leah."

Tucker stared at Leah's hand. When she finally overcame her own surprise, she wiped her hand on her jeans before grasping Leah's.

"I—I'm pleased to meet you. You—I mean, I—you—you

aren't who I expected." Oh, for goodness sake, I'm a blithering idiot.

Leah lifted an eyebrow. "Who were you expecting?"

"Um—" Tucker looked down at her cowboy boots and scuffed a foot against the painted porch board. "I guess I was expecting someone, well, maybe a little older?"

Now Leah lifted the other eyebrow. "Do tell. Why would you think that?"

"Well, um—" Tucker removed her ever-present cowboy hat. For some reason, she felt like she needed to do so in Leah's presence. She rolled the brim around in her hands, glad for something to do. When she finally looked into Leah's eyes, she saw them sparkle like bright blue crystals, full of mischief.

Leah's expression changed again. This time she feigned a look of disdain. "Oh, not the old lady librarian image. You can't be serious."

"Well..."

"You do know that's a horrible stereotype, don't you?"

"Well..." Every time Tucker said it, her voice squeaked a little higher. Her cheeks burned. "I'm sorry. I formed this picture of you from the rental application. You know, your job at the school, wanting a quiet place to live instead of living in Los Angeles. The application didn't allow for a date of birth, because of discrimination and all. I'm—I'm sorry."

Talking is good—maybe. It's helping me get over the initial shock—and the instant attraction pulling at places I'd rather not think about right now. Good grief, what's happening to me? My libido's out of control and I'm losing my mind. Great. Just great.

Leah laughed. Tucker felt butterflies flutter in her stomach. She knew she would love Leah's laugh until she died—possibly from embarrassment—which might be any minute now.

Tucker suddenly realized Leah opened the door without her knocking. "Uh, were you on your way out? I'm sorry. I delayed you."

"It's okay. I was on my way to check the mailbox. It can wait. Why don't you come in?" Leah opened the door wider and stepped back to allow Tucker entrance into the hallway.

Tucker hesitated as she looked past Leah. She wasn't sure what she was looking for, maybe more old memories, which might prevent her from entering. She felt nothing but the joy of meeting this lovely woman, though, so she thanked Leah and stepped inside.

Some of the furniture looked different. The pictures on the

walls were different. Nice. Pictures of forests and waterfalls. One of the ocean—near Mendocino, maybe—and there wasn't a doily in sight. Tucker heard Leah in the kitchen, adding ice to glasses, pouring the offered lemonade. Tucker spoke up from her seat on the couch in the living room, ensuring Leah heard her.

"I hope you're happy here at the house, Leah."

"I am. I love this place." More clinking, then she added, "I moved a few pieces of furniture out to the shed. I hope you don't mind. I didn't bring much with me, but I brought in a few things of my own."

"Not a problem. I'm glad you've made yourself comfortable. The house looks nice."

Leah entered the room carrying two glasses and offered one to Tucker.

"Thank you," Leah said.

"And you like working at the school in Portero?"

"Yes. I love the kids. They're so much more—" Leah searched for the right words, "—innocent and eager to learn. It's so refreshing. The children in LA have to grow up so fast. I think something happens when they aren't allowed to mature at the slower, more natural rate like the kids in this area are able to do. And I'm much happier myself. This is exactly what I was looking for when I came up from LA."

"Looking to get out of the rat race, right?"

"Correct. Looking for something a little more sedate, calmer. Elder Creek is perfect. I love the foothills. They're so beautiful and peaceful."

The deep blue of Leah's eyes mesmerized Tucker as she listened to Leah.

Leah took a sip of her lemonade and Tucker realized she had stopped talking. Tucker cleared her throat and said, "Well, Jackie told me there was some concern about my wanting the house back. Let me assure you it's not true."

Tucker saw Leah breathe out. A sigh of relief, no doubt.

"Thank you for letting me know. I was a little concerned. As you said, I've made myself very comfortable here. I've found a piece of the contentment I was looking for."

"Only a piece?" Tucker asked.

"There may be something more to enable me to have everything I've dreamed of, but for now, I'm good. What about you? What will you do? I'm sure you don't want to spend the rest of your life at the National Hotel."

Tucker chuckled. "You've got that right. I'm in the process of making plans. I don't quite have them all worked out yet, but I'm working on it."

"I hope the hotel isn't too expensive."

"No. It's not a problem. They gave me a good discounted rate since I came back to work on the revitalization project. I'll stay there until I find what I want. I'm thinking about a nice plot up on Tenderfoot Hill if I can get it. I think I might put a log cabin on it."

Why did she feel the need to pour out her dreams to this woman? She didn't know her from anyone, but she was so damn easy to talk to. The thought made her nervous again.

She cleared her throat and said, "I probably shouldn't bore you with all this. I wanted to make sure you knew you're welcome to stay in this house for as long as you like—and I'm sorry about the misunderstanding—about the librarian thing. Um, I can't tell you how sorry I am."

Leah laughed. The butterflies fluttered in Tucker's stomach again. She felt uncertain. Was it because of her discomfort with her earlier gaffe about Leah's age?

When Leah spoke, Tucker wasn't prepared for her next remark.

"It was a rather unfortunate assumption on your part, Miss Stevens, but I'll tell you what. I'll let you make it up to me. Meet me at The Charlie for dinner. You're buying."

Tucker felt a thrill run down her spine. Then, she felt something else—terror. Was Leah asking her out? This beautiful, amazing woman wanted to have dinner with her? Tucker Stevens? The bumbling idiot who assumed she was a doting old lady who decorated her house with doilies?

"I'm sorry," Leah said. She looked down at the floor, her cheeks tinged pink. "It was probably inappropriate of me. I'll take it back if you want. Let's pretend I didn't say it."

"No! I'd love to make it up to you—with dinner, I mean."

Tucker's heart pounded so loudly, she was sure Leah heard it. Maybe it didn't matter if she was an idiot. She was an idiot Leah, apparently, was interested in. She certainly wouldn't deny she found her attractive and easy to be with.

What the heck. Might as well. "What time shall we meet?"

Leah's face brightened with a big grin. "How about six o'clock? Does the time work for you?"

"Fine," Tucker said. "Shall I meet you there or would you like me to call for you up here?"

"Don't we have a meeting this afternoon at the city hall?"

"Oh, I nearly forgot."

She was certain Leah possessed the ability to make her forget everything.

"You're on the revitalization committee. Shall we go over to The Charlie afterward?"

"I'd like to, Tucker. I'd like it very much."

The butterflies slammed against Tucker's stomach, harder this time. Leah smiled at her and brought her lemonade glass to her lips. Tucker picked up her glass and slammed down the drink as if it were pure whiskey. It didn't calm her nervousness, not like the real thing would have.

She looked into the deep blue of Leah's eyes. It didn't help the butterflies at all.

Tucker croaked, "I'd better—" She stopped and cleared her throat, then tried again. "I'd better get going. I have some preparation to do for the meeting. I'll see you there."

Leah smiled. "Yes. You certainly will."

Tucker tried to keep her hand steady as she stretched toward the table and put her glass down. "Thanks for the lemonade—and for the invitation. I'm looking forward to it. Dinner, I mean."

She got up and started toward the front door. Her legs felt weak, but she managed to keep from weaving like a drunkard. Leah walked with her.

Tucker put her hand on the doorknob and said, "Again, I'm so sorry about my blunder."

The mischievous smile returned. Leah laughed but said nothing. She picked up something from the hall table and handed it to Tucker. "The rent check," she said and laughed at Tucker's repeated apology.

Tucker stuffed the check into her shirt pocket and tried to keep the pained look from her face. "I will make it up to you."

She stepped out onto the porch and watched Leah lean against the door frame, arms crossed. She looked so sexy, so far from Tucker's original image of Leah Hudson.

"Indeed, you will," Leah said. A hint of teasing framed the phrase. Her eyes twinkled when she said it.

As Tucker walked down the porch steps toward the street, she thought, *you are losing your mind, Tucker Stevens. You're crazy—and now you're acting crazy smitten. This can't happen. If something's truly going on in your head, how can you even think of getting involved with someone like Leah Hudson? She's way out of your league, even on a good day.*

TUCKER PUT HER hand out to open The Charlie's door and felt sparks jump from the metal push plate to her fingertips. She shook off the pain. The scowling face of Nigel Dunbar loomed in her mind. Should she even try to enter the saloon? The back of her neck prickled with fear. She hoped when she walked through the door she found Jackie behind the bar and not some stringy-haired, unshaven miscreant.

She raised her hand to the door again, slowly. This time, there were no sparks. She let out the breath she'd been holding and shoved the door open. Trepidation filled her until she saw Jackie, and she breathed a sigh of relief. As she took a step toward the bar, Jackie poured a mug of Twigs root beer and smiled.

"How's it going, Tuck?"

"It's going well now that I see your shining face."

She gave Jackie a strange look and shrugged one shoulder, trying to indicate the underlying meaning—no Nigel Dunbar and the accompanying unidentifiable distress and anxiety he brought her meant everything was fine for the moment.

"—and a mug of my hand-crafted root beer," Jackie smirked as she pushed the large, frosty tankard of the dark, foamy liquid in front of Tucker.

Actually, Jackie didn't brew the root beer herself, but it was local. She was instrumental in getting the Bartlett brothers set up to go large-scale, which allowed her to take some credit for it. Tucker took a healthy swig and gave a satisfying groan. Jackie's smile widened.

Jackie stood watching Tucker. "Anything exciting going on, Tuck?"

"No. Nothing I'm aware of. I just finished doing my prep for this afternoon's meeting. I hope we don't meet with too much resistance to the proposed opening of the mine. Doing mine tours will be good for the town."

"True, but with the old rumors and fears about something bad associated with the mine, a lot of unease has stirred people up with a vengeance. You can't believe it's going to be easy."

"Probably not. That's why I've been working so hard on my proposal. I've got some statistics from other towns where they do this kind of thing, and the rise in income when they started doing mine tours is impressive. Hopefully, it will help facilitate the process."

Again, Jackie stared.

When Tucker said, "What?" Jackie gave her a weak smile. "Jackie, if you've got something on your mind, just say it."

More silence as Tucker watched Jackie chew on her lower lip. "I talked to Leah."

"Oh, yeah. I hope she's feeling better about the house. I tried to reassure her."

"She's fine about the house. Happy, actually. It's *you* she's having a reaction to."

"Me?" Tucker didn't mean for the sound to come out so shrill. She coughed, hoping to restore her normal timbre and took a deep breath. Her voice sounded normal again when she said, "What do you mean 'me'?"

"She likes you."

When Tucker gave her a quizzical look, Jackie wiggled her eyebrows.

Tucker harrumphed. "Surprising, since I did something stupid and admitted to her I thought she was an aging librarian."

Jackie laughed out loud. A few patrons turned in their direction, but quickly returned to their own conversations. "She told me about your little faux pas. Quite the Don Juan, aren't you? Way to charm a girl, Stevens."

"I was at her house as her landlord. I didn't go there to ask her out."

"And yet you're having dinner with her later." Jackie raised her copper colored eyebrows until they reached the edge of her untidy bangs.

"Dinner is only to make it up to her — about my little misstep. It was her idea." Who was she kidding? Jackie would never fall for her excuses. Jackie always saw right through her.

"Mm hmm."

Tucker leaned across the bar closer to Jackie and spoke in a whisper. "Look, Jackie, I'm not sure what's going on — you know — in my head right now." She pointed to her temple. "So the last thing I want is to get involved with someone when I'm not even sure I'm —" she hesitated, " — you know, mentally stable."

Jackie slapped the surface of the bar with her open hand. "Oh, pooh. You're fine, Tucker. You have to stop dwelling on the past." In a whisper, she added between clenched teeth, "You are not your mother."

Tucker stared down into her root beer. When she looked up at Jackie, she smiled knowingly. "You like her, don't you? Admit it. You like Leah. You have a girl crush on her and you're not even gay."

"Yes, I like her. She's a great person — and you, Tucker Stevens, like her, too. It's written all over your face. You may as well accept it and surrender. Stop looking for excuses."

Jackie was fierce when she knew she was right. Why not? What did she have to lose by admitting she was attracted to Leah? Jackie already knew it anyway.

Tucker blushed when she said, "She's—beautiful." She continued with a growl. "And if you breathe a word to Leah, or to anybody, for that matter, Jackie O'Malley, I will strangle you."

A shiver ran down her spine when she said it. It was a figure of speech. She meant nothing by it. "I—I didn't mean—you know what I mean."

Jackie tapped the back of Tucker's hand, resting on the surface of the bar. "Stop being such a worrywart, Tucker."

"Just keep it to yourself, okay?"

Jackie put her hand over Tucker's. "Tuck. It's okay. Your secret's safe with me."

As Tucker finished the last of her root beer, Jackie glided over toward a group of tourists who wanted to pay their bill. Tucker watched as she handed them their change and sent them on their way to explore the town. The Charlie was empty now, except for the two women who came in while Tucker and Jackie talked. They looked like they would stay a while. Jackie came around from the back of the bar to serve them their drink order then sat on the stool next to Tucker.

Tucker pushed her mug around in the little pool of water forming from the frost on the glass. She looked at Jackie and said, "Tell me about Leah."

"Well, as you know, she's been here for about three years. She's the *old lady* librarian at the high school in Portero."

Tucker took in a breath to protest Jackie's chiding, but Jackie held up her hand to stop her, telling Tucker she meant nothing by her remark and continued. "Apparently, she used to visit here as a child. That's how she knew about Elder Creek. She told me she remembered fond summer vacations here. When she discovered an opening at the school in Portero, she applied and got the job. Folks tell me she's good with the kids, good at her job. I don't know much else. She comes in occasionally and we chat. I'd call her a friend, but we're not what you'd call close. Maybe we'll both get to know her better now."

Tucker looked at Jackie, an expression of alarm on her face. "What's that supposed to mean?"

Jackie laughed. "Oh Tucker, don't look so scared. I only meant now that we'll all be seeing more of each other while we work on the revitalization project together, we'll both get to know a little more about Leah."

Tucker jumped at the chance to change the subject. "Speaking of the project, will you be able to come to the meeting?" Tucker pulled out her phone to check the time and added, "I'm going to have to get over to the meeting hall in a few minutes."

"I'll be there. Tracey's on duty in about fifteen minutes."

As if on cue, Tracey walked into the bar from the back and waved. Jackie waved back.

"See. All set."

"Good." Tucker put her phone back in her pocket and pulled out a piece of paper. "I saw the mayor before I came over here. He gave me a list of people who might be opposed to the mine opening. He didn't want me to get blindsided at the meeting." She handed over the list. There were only three names on it. "What do you think?"

"Well, I'm thinking Doris and Phil Ackerman aren't going to be that much of a problem. They'll bitch and moan a lot, but it's what they do. It's not like they'll stand in our way. I'll talk to them to get a feel for what they're thinking, but I suspect it will be the same as always—once a curmudgeon, always one."

Tucker chuckled.

"And Leah? Is she on our side? About the mine?"

"Leah's fine about it, I think. Don't forget, she doesn't have the history the town's old-timers have."

"By the way," Tucker said, "is she a sister?"

Jackie looked confused. "I don't think so. She goes to the Methodist church now and again, I believe."

"Not a nun, you doofus, a sister. You know. Is she gay?"

"Oh." Jackie looked surprised. "I don't know. We've never talked about it. I've never seen her with anybody. But, you know, since I'm not gay, I don't have that radar thing."

Tucker laughed and shook her head. "It's called gaydar."

"Yeah, that."

Tucker took the paper back from Jackie and thumped it with her free hand. "Well, what about Joe Dawson? Why's he so opposed to Elder Creek pulling itself up by the bootstraps? Is he a curmudgeon, too?"

"I wouldn't call him that. I'm not sure about him. He never voiced having a problem until a few weeks ago, and then he started to get very vocal about it. Do you want me to talk to him, too?"

"No, why don't we see if they show at the meeting. Then we'll take it from there. I might take you up on feeling these three out later, though. Right now, I'd best get over to city hall."

"I'm right behind you. Let me check in with Tracey and I'll meet you over there."

As Tucker walked out The Charlie's front door, Dunbar's face flashed through her mind. He wore a threatening sneer, causing her to shiver. She shook the vision off. She couldn't give in to wild phantoms with all the work she needed to get done.

THE NOISE IN The Charlie surged to a crescendo as Tucker sat opposite Leah perusing her menu. Apparently, Jackie instructed Tracey to reserve them a table tucked back in a corner of the saloon.

Tucker spent the past few minutes sneaking glances at Leah over her menu. Leah read with intensity as she studied her choices as if the food options were part of an important historical document. Her concentration delighted Tucker.

Leah lifted her eyes from her menu to meet Tucker's, and she raised her voice enough to be heard above the din. "Something wrong, Tucker?"

A smile slowly materialized across Tucker's lips. "Not a thing."

"Why were you staring?"

"I wasn't staring."

"Then, what were you doing?"

"Appreciating."

Inwardly, Tucker groaned. *No, no, no!* her brain screamed. *No flirting! This is a business relationship. She's your tenant. She's on the city revitalization committee—and quite frankly, you don't know if you're losing your mind or not. So. No. Flirting.*

Leah gave her a long, sultry look, then glanced back down at her menu. One corner of her mouth curved upward as she said, "I see." She scanned the page again.

Sweat beads formed on Tucker's forehead as she fought for something else to say—preferably something that didn't sound like she was trying to charm Leah out of her sexual favors.

While keeping her eyes on her own menu, Tucker tried to sound nonchalant as she spoke. The first word got stuck. She tried again. "So, how did you think the meeting went today?"

"Pretty well. Too bad there are some dissenters, but I guess it's bound to happen. It shouldn't be too difficult to bring them over to our side and convince them of the benefits of opening the mine, though."

"The Ackermans may be easy, but I'm not so sure about Joe Dawson. He may be a hard nut to crack."

"Surely he'll want Elder Creek to succeed at this project. Everybody will gain from it. He will, too."

"How do you figure the town junk man will benefit?"

Leah pursed her lips as she thought. "Recycling?"

Tucker cocked her head to one side.

Leah continued, "You know, he should have lots of plastic to cash in if he picks up all the water and soda bottles people leave behind. There will be aluminum cans, too. He'd make a killing."

"You don't think we should put in recycle bins so the city can get the benefit from them?" Tucker pulled out a small notepad from her shirt pocket to write a note about city recycling.

"Maybe the city can award him the contract to do the recycling. That way, the city gets the money, and he can profit from it, too. We need to start doing better in the recycling department anyway. It's an opportunity to have the townspeople start separating out cans and bottles, also. We're way overdue for it. Maybe the city should hire Joe as the recycler for the whole town."

"Hmmm. I'm not sure Joe would go for that. He's kind of a loner—likes working on his own, doing his own thing. I think schedules, routes, and reporting to someone at city hall isn't exactly something he'd like. But I'll talk to the mayor about it and see what he thinks. Maybe a bit of the revitalization budget might be apportioned for recycling downtown and start small. It'd be an important part of keeping everything clean and can raise the consciousness of the citizens and get them ready to go city-wide with the effort later." Tucker made another note.

"I'm surprised you don't do that in your phone."

Tucker looked up. "What do you mean?"

"Your notes. If you did it in your phone, you'd be able to ditch the notepad and pencil."

Tucker's cheeks tinged pink as she realized Leah must think her a country bumpkin.

"Well. Um. I've always carried a notepad, ever since I was a kid. I'd jot down thoughts, questions and story ideas, random stuff like that."

"Oh, yes, Jackie told me you're a writer." Leah paused before asking, "What do you write?"

And there it was—The Question. In some circles, the answer came easily. Among others, it was tricky.

"Um. The four books I have published are about women

in the Old West."

Leah rested her elbows on the table, joined her hands, and placed her chin on them. "Really? Tell me about them."

And there's the second part.

As if on cue, Jackie materialized at their table, saving Tucker from answering.

"Hi, folks. Sorry it took so long to get to you. We're kind of busy tonight. What can I get you?"

Jackie's rusty colored hair fell in front of her eyes in wisps. She looked a little frazzled.

"What are you doing here? I thought you took the night off," Tucker said.

"I did. Tracey called me in. Look at this place." She whirled her pencil in a circle, indicating the room as if with a magic wand able to bring the chaotic commotion around her under her control. "I'm not sure what's going on, but there's no way Tracey could handle this all by herself."

Tucker looked around. Almost every seat was taken—an odd occurrence for the dying town on any evening, even on a weekend night.

"Perhaps the message is getting out about your delicious food, and don't forget *your* great root beer." Tucker glanced back down at her open menu and didn't give Jackie a chance to respond to her sarcasm. "I'll have the Cowboy Burger with everything, French Fries, and a Blue Moon." Tucker closed her menu and handed it to Jackie with a grin.

Jackie smiled at Leah and said, "Leah, what can I get for you?"

"I think I'll have the Chicken Caesar, with extra Parmesan, please. And I'll have a Blue Moon, also."

As Jackie took Leah's menu, she glanced over at Tucker and smirked. Tucker gave her a stern look, willing her not to say anything sophomoric about her and Leah having dinner together. Jackie winked at Tucker and walked away, causing Tucker to blow out a sigh of relief.

Tucker looked over at Leah and said, "I pegged you as a white wine kind of woman."

Leah laughed. Tucker thought she'd give her anything she asked for when she heard her laugh like that.

"There's a great deal you probably have me *pegged* for, which may or may not be true, Tucker Stevens. However, there's only one way to find out what those things may or may not be."

"What way is that, Miss Hudson?"

"You'll just have to spend more time with me."

This time, Tucker knew her cheeks didn't merely color pink. Her whole face burned. She knew she was bright red. She couldn't even blame it on the beer since they didn't have their drinks yet. She found an excuse to prod the conversation in a more professional direction readily enough. "Well, we *will* be working on the revitalization committee together," Tucker mumbled.

She'd done it. She'd managed to make Leah laugh again, and it sounded wonderful. She sat with Leah, a smile on her own face, until Jackie returned with their meals and frothy glasses of beer on a large, round tray.

She plunked everything down in front of them and said, "I hope you don't think I'm being rude, but we're so busy tonight, I don't have time to chat."

"Not a problem," Leah responded. "We've got lots to talk about. We're getting acquainted." She batted her eyes at Tucker.

Jackie looked from Leah to Tucker. Tucker's face reddened again. Jackie raised an eyebrow at her before excusing herself to attend to another table where a small group hailed her from a recently vacated table.

"So," Leah said, "you were telling me about your writing."

Damn, the reprieve is over.

"Well, the one I'm working on now is about a woman who worked as a teacher in Durango after the civil war." Tucker hoped her vague information would be enough to appease Leah, however, her theory proved wrong.

"Go on." Leah stabbed some of her salad and took the contents of her fork into her mouth. After she swallowed, she said, "Is she an *older* woman? A librarian, perhaps? Maybe in her dotage?"

"Um. No. She's actually in her twenties." Tucker decided to ignore the obvious tease. "The teacher meets a Pinkerton detective who's after a fugitive from back East. The teacher has information about the whereabouts of the guy, but isn't sure she trusts the Pinkerton agent, so there's tension there." She didn't want to mention the detective was also a woman, and the tension was something other than a personality conflict.

"So how did you get interested in writing Westerns?"

"I think living in this town growing up probably gave me my initial interest. My field of study in college was cultural anthropology. Put that all together and you've got the books I write with an emphasis on the West in the 1800s."

"So tell me more about this book you're writing," Leah said.

Tucker hoped her next remark would put a stop to this topic of conversation. "Well, I don't want to tell you everything in case you want to read it someday."

"I probably will. I have read your others already."

"You have?"

"Yes, you know, read them."

"How could you do that?"

Leah's expression changed. "I *am* literate, you know."

"Of course. I didn't mean to imply—"

"Tucker, Jackie lent me your books a couple of months after I settled in. When I leased the house and saw your name, I thought it sounded familiar. You'll be surprised to learn I also know how to Google." She got that twinkle in her eye, telling Tucker she was teasing again. "So I did. Google you, that is. Then I asked Jackie about you, and she told me you were one and the same famous writer. She asked me if I was interested in borrowing her copies of your books. I said I was, she did, and the rest is history, as they say. I thought they were wonderful."

"You did?" Tucker's voice squeaked again. Good grief, she needed to stop doing that.

"Well, I would think you already knew that." Leah's laugh tickled her again, making the discomfort worth it.

"I—I'm glad you liked them."

"Of course I liked them. Why wouldn't I?"

"Some of them aren't everyone's genre." Even though Jackie told Tucker Leah was interested in her, it didn't make her a lesbian. Maybe she was curious. Maybe she wanted to be titillated. Maybe she was one of those people who got starry-eyed over someone who was published—or maybe she was only looking for a friend. Another possibility, she reminded herself.

Leah reached across the table and put her hand over Tucker's. It took every ounce of self-control for Tucker not to jump out of her seat when the electricity ran up her arm, down her spine and came to rest between her legs.

"Tucker, I recognized your name because I've seen your books advertised at the lesbian literature sites online. I don't always read historical epochs or non-fiction tomes. Sometimes I like to relax with *our* literature."

Tucker noted the emphasis on "our" literature. She blew out a breath. Leah's face glowed in the dim light of the saloon. She just came out to her. Not only that, it was obvious her interest progressed way beyond the realm of friendship.

Tucker felt sure of it now.

How on earth could she handle this? She shouldered the revitalization project, her own book project, now Leah obviously sought some kind of relationship with her—and she might possibly be losing her mind. How in the world would she manage to muddle through this particularly difficult phase of her life?

Tucker finally came to the conclusion she only needed to take one step at a time, get through this dinner with Leah Hudson. Tucker admitted it wouldn't be difficult. Leah was fun. Tucker liked her teasing and she loved her laughter. Maybe taking this one step at a time was the way to go. Maybe everything would be all right. Maybe.

THE LIGHT OF the television in Tucker's hotel room flickered with changing scenes. The only other glow in the room came from the small bedside lamp. Tucker sat on the bed, pillows stacked behind her back, surrounded by pages of notes and reference research from the meeting earlier in the evening. As she sifted through the papers, she tried to wrangle some order out of the chaos, but success eluded her. Other jumbled thoughts competed for her attention and the distraction of the television finally won her over.

She tapped the volume button on the remote to adjust it to a barely audible setting to hear the news program. The local Portero reporter talked about the missing girl's family growing frantic. The reporter looked serious and spoke with urgency in his voice. The young woman remained missing for almost a week now. The police lacked leads. He emphasized the tragedy of the situation and pleaded for the public's help. They flashed a picture of the blonde, blue-eyed twenty-something young woman on the screen.

Visions of Leah crowded out the television images as they went to commercial. Leah's dancing eyes loomed in Tucker's mind, those eyes sparkling as she and Tucker engaged in animated conversation at The Charlie over dinner. Tucker could almost hear Leah's laughter and her teasing tone. Her playfulness made Tucker smile. Then the ghost of their conversations quieted, replaced by snippets from the revitalization meeting earlier in the day. Tucker muted the television and returned to her notes.

As she spoke to people before the meeting began, welcoming them, catching up, she saw Joe Dawson circulating, chatting with those in attendance, working the room. She realized she'd seen

Joe and Jackie talking briefly and wondered what his motives might be. Maybe he finally decided to be social, but being amiable wasn't exactly Joe Dawson's way of doing things. Engagement might indicate mischief-making and sabotage.

Tucker glanced up and saw the news winding down. The topic switched to sports. Her eyes grew heavy as she sat mesmerized by the screen. Nothing piqued her interest enough to crank up the volume.

She gathered up the pages strewn across the bed, held the disheveled pile over the side and let them fall to the floor. She switched off the light on the nightstand and left the image of a nighttime talk show host mouthing words, lulling her to sleep in the flickering light. It only took a few minutes before she dozed off.

Chapter Two

TUCKER WOKE UP to sun beaming through her window. She cursed under her breath for forgetting to draw the drapes, but when she turned toward the light, she didn't see the heavily lined, room-darkening hotel shades she expected. Instead, dingy white sheer curtains hung from a cord strung tight across the top of the window frame. She felt her eyebrows furrow together involuntarily as she tried to figure out how the window dressing differed so drastically and she not notice.

She wondered what time it was, but when she looked at the nightstand beside the bed, the digital clock was missing. Nothing occupied the small table but a kerosene lamp and box of matches. She stumbled out of bed and headed for the bathroom. She'd need to wake up more to make sense of this. When she opened the bathroom door, she mewed in surprise. Instead of a bathroom, she found a closet. Only a long canvas duster and her black felt cowboy hat hung from thick nails pounded into the wall to act as hooks. She staggered back and spun toward the window.

On the street below, she saw two people approach from the south end of town wearing costumes as if they were in an old West movie. At yesterday's revitalization meeting, they discussed wearing authentic period garb, but she didn't think people would rush right out and outfit themselves.

The din of metal and the squeak of leather accompanied the crunching of wheels on a street Tucker now realized should have been paved, but wasn't. A stagecoach drawn by a team of four horses clattered toward the hotel and, as it reached the front door, the driver pulled back on the reins and yanked the long, wooden handle beside him as he yelled "whoa" a few times. The horses slowed to a stop as did the stagecoach behind them. After securing the reins, the man stood up and shook red road dust from his hat and long leather coat and swung himself down to the ground like he'd done it a million times before.

Tucker wiped her hand across her face trying to make sense of the scene. She watched as the stagecoach driver opened the door to the coach, and stuck his hand inside to help someone out. A woman emerged dressed in the frilliest, laciest outfit Tucker ever saw. The edges of a bright blue hooped skirt were trimmed with layers of white lace, giving the dress the appearance of a finely decorated cake. As it materialized through the doorway, the fabric shimmered brightly in the morning sun, almost glowing. The woman wearing the garment bent forward to clear the low doorway. She wore a broad-brimmed hat, the same color as the dress, that bore the same extravagant decoration. She held tightly to the driver's hand as he guided her to the wooden step between the doorway and the ground. Once her feet were firmly planted on the thick-planked sidewalk, the woman raised her head, the large brim moving out of the way to reveal her face. She met Tucker's gaze through the second-floor window. Tucker's mouth fell open. Leah smiled up at her.

LEAH DIDN'T ENTER the hotel. Instead, Tucker watched from the window as she walked south, down the street toward The Charlie. She disappeared under the wooden overhang along the street. After a certain point, Tucker lost sight of her, so she determined she needed to get dressed and get outside to figure out what the scene below meant. Had everyone lost their minds — or was she the one who slipped over the edge?

Fear rippled up her back until it reached the base of her skull. If she truly lost her mind, she'd better face it. In order to do that, it was crucial to figure out why things looked so different from her window — and she really needed to find the bathroom.

When she stopped at the front desk in the small lobby of the hotel, she found a mousy, graying man sporting a mustache and a neat, short beard. He peered over wire-framed glasses as she approached. She wondered about the college kid she expected to find at the desk, but the need for a bathroom pushed her to get straight to the point.

"Bathhouse is down at the end of the block. If you prefer privacy, we can bring a tub up to your room later tonight, but it'll cost you fifty cents."

Maybe later she would need a bath, but right now, she needed a toilet. She realized she might be phrasing her request wrong and tried again. "I need to...you know, relieve myself."

The man gave her a strange look and shook his head. "Outhouse is out the back." He gestured with his thumb toward a hallway beside the desk. The corridor led toward the back of the building.

Outhouse? "We're certainly getting into the spirit of this whole living history thing, aren't we?"

He looked confused. She decided it best not to pursue the

conversation. Anyway, she needed to use the facilities urgently, no matter how rudimentary. She thanked the man and sped down the hall, looking for a sign saying "outhouse" or, perhaps, "damsels in distress" or something indicating a restroom. She found nothing but an unmarked door at the end of the hall. When she pushed it open, she found herself in an expanse of field. She felt disoriented—again.

She turned back to look at the hotel. Then, she whirled toward the field. This couldn't be right. There should be a street behind the hotel. And on the other side of the street, there should be a row of houses. None of that existed. A few trees dotted the landscape here and there, green with leaves beginning to change with the coming of autumn, and, off in the distance equivalent to a city block, a tiny wooden structure sat under a tree with no leaves on it whatsoever. A path, only wide enough to accommodate one person, worn down through the dried field grass, led directly to the tired-looking structure.

Tucker said aloud, "An outhouse? Come on. Isn't this going a little too far?"

She stepped onto the path and headed straight for it. What choice did she have?

TUCKER EMERGED FROM the putrid smelling privy, relieved, so to speak, and with one purpose. She needed answers and she needed them now. Since she only recognized one person—the one she'd seen in the street from her room—she decided she'd look for Leah. Maybe she'd get some straight answers from her. In order for her to find them, she'd have to figure out where Leah went after she left the front of the hotel.

She headed for Main Street and stomped off in the direction she'd seen Leah going when she alighted from the stage. As she passed one business, the aroma of breakfast food encircled her, and visions of sausages and eggs made her stomach clench with hunger. Maybe it'd be better to get answers on a full stomach.

When she peeked into the doorway, wafting with the breakfast aroma, she hesitated. It didn't look like any restaurant she was used to and this should have been the bookstore anyway. She cocked her head and eyed the place again. All the tables in the room were occupied, but a couple she didn't recognize, wearing period dress, got up and called out goodbyes to some of the other diners, who all responded to them. As the man and woman exited the building, the man tipped the rim of his hat when he passed Tucker. The woman gave her a reserved smile.

Tucker stepped inside.

There wasn't a book in sight. Nor were there any other wares for sale. A woman stood at an old-fashioned wood stove at the rear wall with her back toward Tucker. She wore a simple gingham print dress with a large bow at the back. Her copper colored hair was tied back in a bun at the base of her head. When she spoke, her voice sounded familiar.

"I'll be with you in a minute," she said, plating up food on thick china. When she swung around, plate in hand, Tucker gazed into the jade green eyes of Jackie O'Malley.

"HAVE A SEAT," Jackie said, gesturing with her chin to the recently vacated table. "Be right with you."

She deposited the plate of food in front of a man dressed in a suit and thin-stringed bow tie. A bowler hat sat on the chair to his left.

Tucker was stunned. She watched Jackie's movements as she waited for the tingling sensation coursing through her body to subside. How could this be happening? Were Leah and Jackie both in on some hoax she, the head of the Elder Creek revitalization committee, wasn't privy to? What the heck was going on?

Jackie glanced back at her as Tucker stood rooted to her spot. When Jackie lifted an eyebrow at her, Tucker maneuvered almost involuntarily toward the empty table and plopped down on the wooden seat. As Jackie approached, Tucker whispered, "Jackie, what the heck is going on?"

Jackie raised both eyebrows this time and said, "Jackie? I think you have me mistaken for someone else. Name's Olivia. Olivia Justice. Pleased to meet you." She thrust out her hand.

Tucker didn't take it. Confusion washed over her as if dumped, cold as ice, from a vat above her head. "Jackie, stop this. It's me, Tucker. You know me. And who's Olivia Justice?"

Olivia pursed her lips. "Look. I don't know who you think I am, but evidently, I'm not this Jackie. If you want breakfast and you have the money for it, I'll get it for you. Otherwise, I'd suggest you go down the street to the church. They usually have food for people who can't afford it."

"Jackie, come on. It's me, Tucker."

Olivia's scowl told Tucker she was having none of this. "Do I need to get the sheriff?"

"What? No. Jackie—" Olivia's look of warning told Tucker she wouldn't receive another before she got thrown out on her ear. "Jack—uh, don't you know who I am? For god sakes, we grew up together." The desperation she heard in her own voice made her woozy.

Olivia stood there for a moment with a stern look on her face. Finally, she softened a little and said, "Look, I'm not this Jackie. I don't know why you would think I was someone with a boy's name, but it's neither here nor there. I'm not who you think I am. My name is Olivia and this is my establishment. If you come in here, you get served one of my three meals. Ten cents for breakfast and fifteen for lunch and dinner. Now stop calling me Jackie and put your money on the table, or I'll have to ask you to leave." The look on Olivia's face changed to one of pleading. "Please, don't make trouble and I won't either."

Ten cents for breakfast? Wasn't that taking things a bit far? How was Jackie—Olivia—whoever she was—going to make a profit charging those prices? If the whole town operated this way, everyone would be bankrupt in a month, but at this point, she merely needed to figure this out without alienating anyone who might be able to give her information, or who bore the potential to be a friend. Antagonizing this woman probably wasn't a good idea.

"I'm not out to make any trouble—Olivia, is it?" Olivia accepted her statement with a tentative smile and Tucker continued, "Yes, I'd like something to eat." Tucker fished in her pocket for her money clip. Instead of bills, she found a handful of coins. She pulled them out. They looked different. She squinted at them as they sat in her palm. They looked old. Oh, most of them were still shiny, but the designs on the faces of the coins weren't today's money. She recognized them as coins she'd seen pictures of in advertisements in magazines, the kinds of coins people collected. She blew out her breath. At least the denominations looked like something she knew. "Ten cents for breakfast, you said?"

"That's right, ten cents."

Tucker handed her a dime and smiled weakly. "Can I see a menu?"

Olivia cocked an eyebrow and blew out a breath. The stray hairs on her forehead blew upward then settled back down. "Look, whoever you are—"

"Tucker. My name's Tucker."

"Tucker, this isn't the big city. Maybe you're used to a menu and fancy choices where you're from, but in Elder Creek, we're pretty simple. I cook breakfast in the morning. Eggs, maybe some cured ham or sausages if I have them, which I do right now. Some potatoes, a piece of fresh-baked bread. It's what you get for this." She held up the dime between her thumb and forefinger. "If you want it, I'll get it for you. If you don't, you can have this back and be on your way."

Tucker stared at her for a second or two then said, "Thank you, Olivia, I'll take it."

Olivia finally smiled. "Coming right up, Mister Tucker," she said as she headed for the stove.

This wasn't the first time someone mistook Tucker for a male. She knew her body to be androgynous and her face angular. She let out a sigh. She'd better play along until she figured out what the heck was going on. The question occurred to her again as it did more than a few times in the past hour, wondering if the town had gone completely mad — or was the problem within her own mind?

BY THE TIME Olivia returned with Tucker's breakfast, most of the other patrons finished their meals and left. As Tucker ate, she watched Olivia go from table to table, removing breakfast dishes, wiping down surfaces, and cleaning crumbs off chairs. When she completed those tasks, she swept the floor of any remaining debris.

Tucker soaked up the last of the golden-yellow egg yolk on her plate with a hunk of the hardy sourdough bread Olivia served and said, "Getting ready for lunch now?"

Olivia stopped sweeping and concentrated on Tucker. "Just about," Olivia said.

She sounded so much like Jackie she could pass for her twin. Tucker decided to risk making the observation. "You look and sound exactly like her, you know."

"Who?"

"Jackie. I'm sorry if I offended you by mistaking you for her. She's my best friend."

Olivia stared for so long, Tucker's face started to redden. Finally she answered, "Then, I'll take it as a compliment, shall I?" Tucker thought she heard a hint of an Irish accent, which third generation Irish-American, Jackie O'Malley, no longer possessed.

"Yes, you should. She's a fine woman. She runs a business herself."

"Ah, I see, so, another resemblance to your friend."

Maybe she'd better not mention Jackie owned The Charlie. What if the place didn't exist wherever, no, *whenever*, she found herself now? Perhaps Jackie didn't exist. Maybe Leah did. Maybe she didn't. She decided she might as well take another gamble since a truce of sorts was in force.

"Can I ask you a question?"

Olivia looked wary but motioned for Tucker to continue.

"Do you know a woman named Leah? Leah Hudson?"

"No. Can't say I do. Where's she from?"

"Well, most recently, she's from LA." She realized her blunder when the look on Olivia's face changed from mild interest to consternation. "I mean, Los Angeles."

After the look Olivia gave her, she thought better of adding Leah lived in Elder Creek. Olivia would probably think she was making up stories since she said she didn't know Leah.

"Don't think I've made her acquaintance. I've been here in Elder Creek all my life, even when I was young and there were a lot more people in town because of the gold, I never remember anyone by the name of Hudson, man or woman. Can't say I ever remember anyone coming all the way from Los Angeles, either. Although, when the mine operated, people came from all over the country, even from foreign places."

Something struck Tucker. "So, the mine is closed now?"

"Has been for some time now."

Tucker didn't want to appear too curious about the mine. She knew it closed in 1870. So obviously, in Olivia Justice's world, it must be sometime after that.

She decided to take another chance and ask her about the Leah look-alike. "I saw a woman get off the stage this morning. She has blonde hair." The woman she saw looked like Leah except for the length and curl of her hair. The woman from the stage wore hair much longer than Leah's, and she sported an abundance of curls—banana curls they used to call them—elongated ringlets in thick bunches all around her head. The Leah she knew wore some curl in her hair, but it came slightly above her shoulders, and the way she wore it looked nothing like the frilly-attired lady she spied through the window earlier.

Olivia waited.

"She got off the stage this morning, dressed in a fancy blue dress with lots of lace and a big hat to match."

Olivia's look changed to recognition.

"Must have been Lily."

"Lily?"

"Yes, Lily Hart. She was off to visit someone in Hatchet, I heard."

If Hatchet was anywhere near Elder Creek, Tucker wasn't aware of it.

"I'm not familiar with Hatchet, Miss Olivia. Where is it?"

Olivia's eyebrows shifted downward, shading her eyes. "Hatchet? It's about two hours or so by stage." She stared at Tucker before she added, "You're not from anywhere near here, are you?"

Tucker chuckled at her observation. "Not even close."

After another brief moment, Olivia looked down at Tucker's empty cup and said, "You want some more coffee?"

Tucker's stomach threatened to revolt at the question. No. Never again, she thought. She never wanted to drink the rot-gut Olivia Justice tried to pass as coffee. She looked into her remaining half cup, grounds floated amid an oily slick of black liquid. "No, thank you." She hoped the pathetic smile she gave Olivia didn't betray her real feelings about the drink. She still felt the gritty grounds between her teeth and the bitterness on the back of her tongue. "I think I've drunk enough, but I appreciate the offer."

She'd wasted enough time. She needed to figure out what was going on in Elder Creek. She wondered if Olivia knew where Lily Hart might be found, but her instincts told her not to try. She'd have to figure it out on her own.

"I'd best be going, but I thank you for the tasty breakfast." Except for the coffee, she added in her head. She pushed her seat back from the table, legs scraping across the wooden floor. Since she noticed previous diners only left their ten-cent pieces in payment for their breakfasts, she didn't leave an additional tip before walking out the door.

Out on the boardwalk in front of Olivia's place, Tucker looked up and down the street and wondered where she should begin her hunt for Lily Hart. She decided to continue down the walkway in the direction she watched Lily go after leaving the stagecoach.

PEOPLE WENT ABOUT their business, coming and going up and down the street. Horse-drawn wagons pulled up near various business establishments. One man loaded large sacks of something in the back of a wagon already filled with small kegs and wooden crates. Two women walked arm-in-arm across the street, gingham drawstring bags swinging from their elbows as they walked. Tucker again realized she saw no one in modern dress since she left the hotel. Was she a victim of time travel, deposited here soon after 1870? She looked down at her own flannel shirt and jeans. She supposed she fit right in. With her attire, including her cowboy hat, and her lanky body, she looked like almost any other male inhabitant of this town today.

She squinted up at the leaves on the trees along the street. They showed off their orange and yellow, helping Tucker identify the season. At least that was unchanged. The sun warmed the fall air enough for her to remove her cowboy hat and fan herself a few times before placing it back on her head.

Under her flannel shirt, Tucker wore a silky tank top. Normally, on a warm day like today, she would open her flannel shirt to let the breeze circulate around her torso. However, she thought better of it because doing so would clearly show the outline of her small breasts, and she risked exposing herself as a woman. Since Olivia mistook her for a man during breakfast, she thought it wise not to reveal her true gender. She might need the advantage.

Her boots clapped the boards beneath her feet as she headed down the street, passing the mercantile. She acknowledged the man loading up the wagon, relieved he didn't look familiar to her. At this point, strangers comforted her, offering less confusion, less chance of getting into trouble by mistaking them for someone else.

She continued down the street until she saw another familiar building. The large sign over the door read The Saint Charles Saloon. The script appeared different from The Charlie sign she knew, this one embellished with scrolls and flourishes all around the letters. Her Charlie's sign, which also read The Saint Charles Saloon, was smaller with plain, bold lettering.

Curiosity got the better of her and she crossed the street toward the building. One of the heavy metal double doors stood open and she peeked in. The place lacked the larger windows adorning the well-lit Charlie she knew. She waited for her eyes to adjust as she stared into the dimness. Several oil lamps hung from the ceiling, giving barely enough light to illumine the place. She saw no one inside.

Tucker couldn't help herself. Curious about the place she knew so well, she stepped over the threshold to get a better look.

It looked different, yet the same. The rich wood molding

around the bar was identical. The upright piano on the far wall looked a little different, but not by much. The chairs at the round tables were cane-backed and rounded instead of the ladder back chairs so familiar to her. As she glanced along the length of the room to the far wall, she realized something was missing. A wooden balcony and the stairs she knew, added some time after 1900 to accommodate musicians and entertainers as a stage, according to local history, didn't exist in this Charlie. The clues to the time floated all around her she now realized. She deduced it to be sometime after the mine closure in 1870 but before the early 1900s. Tucker felt a lump form in her throat as she confirmed she'd been thrust back in time.

AS TUCKER CONTINUED to take in The Charlie's differences and similarities, someone entered the bar from the back room. She wondered if she should ask about Lily Hart, but when she met the man's eyes, she shivered. Nigel Dunbar.

He glowered at her but didn't say a word as he took his place behind the bar and began mopping the surface with a stained rag. She stepped toward him, her heart pumping wildly. She didn't understand why the stranger evoked such a reaction.

He held her gaze as she approached and finally snarled at her. "What do you want?" He added, "Get you somethin' to drink?"

"Bakers, neat."

"Don't know what Bakers is. And this isn't the neatest place in Elder Creek as you can see." He cackled at his own joke as he waved the cloth around. "You best take your city slicker ways elsewhere. We don't need your kind in Elder Creek."

He looked mean. He felt meaner—menacing, actually. She didn't think of herself as a coward, yet her instincts told her to be very careful around him. Maybe she should turn around and walk out the door. Maybe she made a big mistake in coming into The Charlie. She'd have to try to find Lily Hart another way. But, before she could leave, she saw movement from the corner of her eye and heard a familiar voice say, "Why Nigel, you didn't tell me we're graced with patrons already. Why didn't you call me? I was primping out back to look my best."

Tucker watched Lily saunter toward her. She wore a different dress from the one she wore on the stagecoach. She now wore something a little less fancy. This dress was a deep red wine color with an off-white lace trim around the neckline and sleeves. The neckline—plunged—revealed cleavage, making Tucker's tongue stick to the roof of her mouth. She licked her lips trying to lubricate them in an attempt to speak.

"Good morning, Miss Lily." She removed her hat.

Lily stared at her. "Do I know you, Mister..."

Tucker's mind raced as she tried to figure out what she would say next. She wanted to get Lily away from the intimidating bartender, but how? Then a thought struck her.

"No, ma'am. You don't, but we have a mutual friend. And she asked me to give you a message if I saw you."

Lily looked skeptical. "What friend might you be referring to, Mister—"

"Tucker. The name's Tucker, ma'am." She needed a name— some name—any name. No, not merely any name. Because if it proved to be a name Lily didn't know, Dunbar would probably come around the bar and pummel her until only her head stuck out from the floor boards. She eyed him surreptitiously. Her heart beat faster. She wondered if fear of Dunbar or a reaction to Leah—no, Lily's beauty—caused it.

And there it was. The name—Leah. Would it work? Maybe if all the stars and planets lined up right, Lily might have a friend named Leah and it might be the means to get her alone. She could say she was in possession of a confidential message from her and at least get Lily into a corner out of earshot of Dunbar. The man looked as if he would pull out a gun and shoot her right there if she misspoke one word. She stifled a shiver.

Tucker decided to hedge her bets by opening with, "If I have the right person, you may know our mutual friend. Her name is Leah." She saw Lily's eyes widen ever so slightly. She continued, "and she asked me—"

Lily squealed, "Leah? Oh my goodness, gracious, Leah sent me a message?"

Tucker tried not to show too much surprise at her success. "Uh, yes ma'am."

"Oh, wonderful." Lily clapped her hands together, expressing her delight. "Let's go sit down and you tell me all about her message."

She tugged Tucker by the arm, pulling her toward the far end of the saloon, far away from Dunbar. Tucker glanced back at him while Leah dragged her away. She registered his displeasure. They only made it halfway across the room before he spoke.

"Lily," Dunbar snapped. "You need to tend to customers."

Lily stopped and gave an exaggerated sweep of the empty

saloon, looked at Dunbar and said, "Nigel, this," she pointed at Tucker, "is our only customer and he's here to see me, so calm yourself and bring us a couple of whiskeys, then leave us alone." Lily's face reddened as she spoke. She looked angry.

Dunbar turned his back on them and fiddled with a bottle he pulled from under the counter, grumbling something under his breath. Tucker raised an eyebrow at Lily for her brazenness, thinking Lily and Leah endowed with some similarities of personality. Lily gestured toward a table at the far corner of the room and they continued toward it.

Before she sat down, Tucker remembered her manners and pulled out Lily's chair for her, helping her get settled. Lily smiled up at her and Tucker felt a thrill run through her body. It finally stopped at her nether regions. She tried to ignore it as she took a seat opposite Lily and squeezed her legs together.

Dunbar approached the table with two glasses, each containing two fingers of brown liquid. Fortunately, the contents didn't splash out on Tucker when he slammed the glass in front of her. Lily gave him a challenging look. He squinted back at her then disappeared into the room at the back of the saloon without saying a word.

Lily's facial expression changed from irritated to excited as she said, "I must say, I never thought I'd hear from Leah Washington again. Please, Mister Tucker, tell me what she said."

Uh-oh. Leah's name was Washington? Now what should she do? Tucker sat staring at Lily. Think, Tucker, think. A person capable of making Lily's face light up in such a way probably would say something very personal to her. Then it dawned on her. Lily must have feelings for this woman. She cleared her throat and started in with a little bit of apprehension.

"She said to tell you she sends her love." Lily placed her hand over her bosom. Tucker tried to ignore the gesture. She plunged on. "She said to tell you she misses you." Lily let out a small gasp. Where was she supposed to go with this? She regretted not having a plan. Keep it safe. Don't say anything you'll find coming back and biting you on the butt. "She says she wishes it were possible to come and see you—" Lily let out a whimper this time. Tucker felt guilty for lying. She needed to bring this to an end. "—but it's not."

Lily's expression changed to utter devastation. Tucker wracked her brain to come up with something else to say to console Lily. She found nothing. Anything she might say to give Lily false hope would only hurt her more since it was never going to happen, and Tucker found the thought of inflicting pain on this beautiful woman who reminded her so much of Leah—her Leah—difficult. It might also put her in jeopardy. She couldn't risk it. "I'm sorry, Miss Lily. I wish I brought better news for you."

Lily smiled through glistening eyes. "I know. It doesn't surprise me. I entertained a moment of hope, though. It's fine. I know this is how it has to be. I resigned myself to it a long time ago." She took a deep breath and wiped at a tear escaping from the corner of her eye.

Tucker searched for something to comfort Lily. Finally, she said, "If nothing else, bringing Miss Leah's message to you let me meet you. I would be pleased if we could be friends, Miss Lily." Why was she talking like a cowpoke, she wondered? Another effect of this whole experience of another time? Perhaps.

Lily whispered, "I'd like that. I'd like it very much, Mister Tucker."

"Please," Tucker said, "Call me Tucker. All my friends do."

Lily broke into a wide smile. "Why thank you, Tucker. I'll do that." She lifted her glass to her lips and took a sip of the whiskey.

Tucker did the same and almost choked on the foul, burning taste, far worse than the coffee she drank earlier. When she recovered, she looked down at the glass and cringed. Suddenly the small quantity of the awful liquor left in the glass looked like an impossible amount for her to finish. She'd have to drink it or Lily would wonder what was wrong with her. As she debated between dispensing with it in small amounts or taking one large swig and be done, another man walked into the saloon, another stranger, she noted.

Dunbar emerged from the back room and hailed the man. As he walked over to the bar, he scowled at Tucker and Lily in the corner. "I'd better get back to work," Lily said. She chugged the rest of her whiskey and stood up. Panic surged through Tucker as Lily turned to go. Inexplicably, she knew Lily was key to helping her figure out this riddle. Maybe Olivia was, too, but one thing she knew for sure, she wouldn't allow this to be the last time she saw Lily. She needed to do something to ensure they'd meet again.

"Say, Lily."

Lily faced her, beaming.

"How about you and me get some supper tonight at Miss Olivia's?"

Lily's face saddened. "Can't tonight. I'll be working until

late. Maybe tomorrow night, though. Francesca will be back from San Francisco later today and I'll be able to take some time off for dinner while she's working tomorrow."

"Oh, all right. Good. I'll look forward to it. Tomorrow then. Shall I meet you here?"

"No." She glanced back at Dunbar, who still stared at them. "I'll meet you at Olivia's. Let's say around five o'clock"

"Yes. Five o'clock. I'll see you then."

Before Lily started toward the bar, she said, "Tucker, this is dinner with a friend, right? Nothing else?"

Tucker smiled. "Yep. Dinner with a friend. That's all, Miss Lily."

Lily's face brightened. "Good. I'll see you then, Tucker."

She took a few steps and stopped again. "Don't worry about the drink, Tucker." She plunged her hand into her bodice and pulled something out. Tucker's eyes widened at the gesture. Lily held up the coin, pulled from between her breasts. "It's on me."

The gesture made Tucker's heart flutter for a few beats. The sight of Lily's hand plunged into the region of her bosom kept repeating in her mind's eye like an echo. However, it wasn't actually Lily performing the gesture, it was Leah.

The beads of sweat on her forehead returned. She lifted the glass and saluted Lily in thanks, hoping against hope she looked more casual than she felt. Then she chugged the god-awful drink in one big swig, wiped her mouth with the back of her hand, got up and left The St. Charles Saloon.

Chapter Three

TUCKER WOKE WITH the morning light shining through the window. The problem was she found the window on the opposite side of the wall from when she fell asleep. She groaned. Where would she find herself today? Would she end up on some distant planet in a different solar system? She chuckled in response to her own bizarre thought, but she didn't feel amused. Instead, fear coursed through her veins, riding on her life's blood like a surfer in treacherous, shark-infested waters. She took in a deep breath. She'd have to get up to find the answer and she'd have to face the day, even if she didn't know if today would be the day she'd confirm her own insanity.

She sat up and rubbed her eyes then opened them and looked around again. On her bedside table, she found the phone with the usual instructions about which buttons to push for services and what charges would be incurred by making particular types of calls. When she looked over at the credenza across from the foot of her bed, it held a flat-screen TV and an ice bucket with two glasses on a small tray. A ball of pressure built up in her chest, stopping below her throat. She felt like she might cry in relief at her familiar, modern surroundings, but no tears came. She swallowed the emotion down until it disappeared, then she threw off the bedcovers.

When her feet touched the floor, they met the sheaf of papers she discarded as she settled in for the night. She failed to make any progress on her notes from the previous day's meeting, so she would have to finish going through them before she did anything else today.

One thing she knew she needed to do—find Joe Dawson and figure out why he opposed the opening of the mine. Maybe she'd even get him to divulge what he told people as he walked around the room after the meeting. She still felt pretty certain he was up to no good.

When she talked to him, she knew she must make him understand the tours alone would bring in considerable income to the town, which in turn would help the revitalization project flourish and the businesses thrive. The future success of Elder Creek depended on it.

Before she walked into the bathroom to shower, she switched

on the television. Maybe some distracting noise would help orient her and keep her grounded in the present.

When the picture materialized, the face of a middle-aged, distraught woman filled the TV screen. A local news reporter held a microphone up to the woman's face. Tucker stood, riveted to the woman's image. She looked fragile, as if she might shatter into tiny pieces if someone touched her. The interviewer asked about the missing young woman, apparently the older woman's daughter.

She hesitated before speaking but finally straightened as if coming to a decision, saying she felt her daughter may have fallen under misguided influences, adding she'd always been impressionable. The reporter pressed her for more on the subject, but she declined to say anything more.

The reporter asked, "Do you have anything else you'd like to add for our viewers?"

She looked directly into the camera, a resolute expression on her face, and added, "I would like to plead for the safe return of my daughter. Please let her come back to us. She's very precious to her father and me and we want her to come home to us." She paused, composing herself and added, "My husband was admitted to the hospital in Portero last evening with an angina attack. He was so distraught over Amy's disappearance that it has affected his health. He's stable now, thank goodness, but needs to rest and be monitored. He wanted me to send his love to Amy and add his appeal for her release by her captors." Emotion overtook her then, her eyes filled with tears and her voice caught. She wasn't able to continue.

The reporter's face filled the screen and he said, "We wish Mr. Hammersmith a speedy recovery. Today marks two weeks since the disappearance of Amy Hammersmith and as you just heard from her mother, her parents are pleading for her return." He summarized the missing girl's description and reminded his viewers if they had any information, they should call the Portero police at the number flashing on the screen. Then he signed off and the anchors back in the studio came on screen, switching to another story. Tucker blew out her breath. So much tragedy these days, she thought as she headed for the bathroom. Maybe her present reality wasn't as attractive as she thought.

A shower and clean clothes did Tucker a world of good. The hotel room coffee helped a little. She hoped to finish up her meeting notes and then get some breakfast. With some *real* coffee, she thought.

TWO HOURS LATER, Tucker sat at the desk in her small hotel room, pleased with the notes she'd made for herself, as her expanded plans congealed in her mind.

While she re-read and annotated, something about her dream during the night pushed its way to the front of her mind. She kept trying to push it back to the recesses for later scrutiny. She needed to get this work done, but the thoughts were insistent, demanding to be heard. When she finally let them flow, she found they weren't related to her own experiences back in the Elder Creek of the post-gold rush days, but instead they were a suggestion for the here and now—a good suggestion.

Why not propose each person who met the public take on the persona of a real-life personality from Elder Creek or the surrounding area? They might dress in the clothing of the era and speak within character, regaling tourists with stories of their character's lives. The shopkeepers would become docents of sorts. Maybe others in the town would like to become guides, too, giving tours of the main street of Elder Creek, telling colorful stories to visitors, giving them a real flavor of life around the time when the mine was in its heyday.

Leah, as a historian, possessed resources and knowledge to research potential characters the citizenry of Elder Creek might be willing to adopt as their own. Asking Leah about this project went on her list of things to do. After entering this new task on her list, Tucker grinned. She'd have another excuse—no, an opportunity—to talk to Leah again soon.

When Tucker finally looked at all the information, questions, and things to do written on the page, she felt a little overwhelmed by it all. She'd have to figure out a way to delegate some of this. Otherwise, she'd never get anything done. Jackie offered to talk to Doris and Phil Ackerman. They weren't at the meeting yesterday afternoon. She'd have to confirm with Jackie to make sure she'd be the one to talk to them. Joe, she knew, might be tricky. She wanted to talk to him herself, but it looked like he was trying to avoid her. As she thought more about it, she realized he might be avoiding everyone, except for his brief appearance at the meeting.

With the list completed, she felt better about the direction of the project. Now, the thoughts about the dream crowded in on her, filling the empty space left by putting the task details aside. She found herself a little disturbed Jackie and Leah were a part of the dream. But their roles were very different. As a matter of fact, they weren't Jackie and Leah at all. Instead, they were Olivia and

Lily. Then the face of the bartender loomed in her mind's eye. Dunbar. He didn't look like anyone in Elder Creek she knew. She felt his animosity toward her, even though they never met until she walked into The St. Charles Saloon. She wondered why.

His hostility niggled at the back of her mind where her fear resided. She pushed it down, not wanting to feel it, not wanting to know what it all meant. Maybe he would be the one to open a doorway, finally confirming she did, indeed, lose her mind. She wasn't ready to face that possibility yet.

"HAVE YOU SEEN the news about the missing woman from Portero?" Jackie asked.

"Yes, I saw it this morning. They were interviewing the woman's mother. Terrible," Tucker said.

They sat in Jackie's living room. Tucker hoped to talk to her about two things: the project and her most recent experience of a very different Elder Creek. Jackie, however, needed to talk about this missing woman. The look of concern on Jackie's face made Tucker realize she should allow her the opportunity to vent.

"Sad about the father," Jackie said. "Although he's supposed to be okay, it must be so stressful. People around here are getting jumpy about it. It's too close to home."

"So, does the missing girl live in Portero?"

"On and off, I guess. From what I've gleaned from the news reports, she lived with her parents until recently. They're from Monterey. According to the reporters she met the boyfriend at some kind of spiritualist's conference there a while back. Evidently, she comes to Portero quite a bit. I'm not sure if she stays with him or someplace else. Apparently she was pretty taken with this guy. They interviewed him on the news a few days ago. He cried—big crocodile tears, if you ask me—and said how tragic it was, but he looks kind of oily to me. It's a feeling I got while watching him. I guess he's pretty controversial in Portero. A lot of people don't care too much for him. Others from out of the area think he's god's gift. He's supposed to have psychic powers or something, but you know how I feel about that."

"Yes, I do know how you feel." Jackie thought all spiritualists and psychic gifts were a load of hogwash. Tucker didn't believe in it either, but she tried to keep an open mind.

"I didn't see him—you know, the guy—on TV. I saw something last night on the missing woman, and this morning I saw her mother's plea for her return, but that's about it. You know I'm not a big television person."

Jackie laughed, but the smile didn't reach her eyes as it normally would have. Now Tucker understood how upsetting she found this whole thing. When she said it affected people in Elder Creek, she meant it included Jackie herself.

"Have they looked at Mr. Oily as a suspect?"

"The Portero police called him a person of interest early on, but I haven't heard any more about him being a concern. Apparently, they questioned him at length but didn't see any need to hold him for anything. When they released him, he cried his big tears on TV and we haven't heard anything from him since."

Tucker added her "hmm" to the conversation while she tried to figure out how to ease Jackie's worry. "Well, I guess if the police haven't seen any reason for him to be a suspect, he's probably in the clear."

"I know, but there's something about him. I find him a little bit creepy. I don't know why. I've got nothing to base it on but a gut feeling. I've never even met the guy. It's strange."

Tucker believed strongly in gut feelings. They were usually right, in her experience, but she knew if she voiced such a thing, it would merely feed Jackie's concern, so she commented with another "hmm" and decided it was time to change the subject to get Jackie's mind off the whole situation.

"Actually, Jackie, I stopped by to talk about the project. Do you mind?"

Jackie shook her head as if pushing away unpleasant thoughts. "No, not at all. Let's do it. It might be good to focus on something else."

Tucker plunged ahead. "Well, I've come up with this idea. I want to run it by you and see what you think of it. What if we got Leah to sign on to do some research for us about townsfolk at the time when the mine was open? We might find some colorful personalities people might want to adopt, and they could use those personas while they're at their places of business or if they volunteered as docents doing tours of the town. What do you think?"

Jackie smiled her first real smile since Tucker walked into her home. "It's a great idea. And if Leah can do the research, maybe write up bios for the people she finds, then people might be inclined to take on the personality more readily because they won't have to do the work."

"And if they want to know more than Leah comes up with,

she can give them an extended bibliography, so they can read up more on the person," Tucker added. "They can get into it as much or as little as they want. Hopefully, they will want to get into it more. It might actually enhance the experience for visitors."

"So have you settled on the exact time period?"

"I think so. Since we don't want to go anywhere near the bad stuff around the mine, we should probably concentrate on when it first opened, say 1850 or so. The town was booming then. There'll be lots of interesting characters around."

"Really? I would have thought you'd want to concentrate on a later period. After all, they sealed up the mine because of rumors of ghosts and strange happenings there."

"Yes, but do we want to bring up the story about a young girl being killed? I know ghosts are a very popular attraction, but that little girl's death was supposed to be pretty gruesome, according to the stories. I don't think we want to go there."

"You're probably right. Maybe interjecting information about someone being killed later in the mine's period, in passing, might work. So we don't have to go into too much detail. But if there's any interest, maybe later we'd do a ghost walk or something and make clear it's after the period we're implementing. After all, we wouldn't want to say no to a good thing if it brought in visitors, now would we?"

Tucker broke out in a big grin. "Great idea, Jackie. This is exactly the kind of thinking we need from the chairperson for the Elder Creek Living History project.

Concern returned to Jackie's face. "What? What are you talking about?"

Tucker pulled a piece of paper from her shirt pocket, unfolded it and smoothed it out flat against her thigh. "Well, it says here Ms. Jacqueline O'Malley has signed up for this gig. *And I recall a certain friend of mine informed me only recently she actually acquired more time since she has one Tracey, the beneficent, newly hired and properly trained bartender, in her employ.*"

"No, Tucker. Not happening," Jackie said. She pushed her lips out in a pout.

Tucker ignored her, continuing, "Also, if I recall, someone recently told me I should delegate responsibilities to people who signed up to work on this project—"

"Now, hang on, Tuck. I don't have that much time—"

"Oh, don't worry. If it's too much for you, you, too, can *del-e-gate.*" She thrust the flattened paper toward Jackie. "I hereby appoint you committee Chairperson for the Elder Creek Living History Project."

Jackie snapped her mouth closed. When she opened it again, she asked, "Well, what the heck are you going to do, Miss High-and-Mighty?"

Tucker continued to hold out the piece of paper, her smile widening again. "I, madam, am the High-and-Mighty Executive Director."

"Tuck, no. You can't—"

"I can. I did. And I will." She pointed at the wrinkled sheet of paper with her other hand. "This is an outline of the things to be done. You'd better get the committee together again and schedule out some meetings. We've got a lot of work to do."

Jackie snatched the paper from Tucker and scowled. "This isn't fair, you know."

"I know. But nobody said life and living history was fair. Now get cracking, girl. Let me know when you've got a calendar for the meetings. I'm wide open."

Jackie stuck her tongue out at Tucker. Tucker glanced around as if the room were filled with people. "Jackie, not in front of the children," she chided. Then they both laughed.

"All right, you," Jackie said. "Uncle. I should have known you'd rope me into doing your dirty work for you."

Tucker raised her eyebrows. "Jackie, you wound me. You think I've given you the dirty work? You're quite mistaken. I've given you the easy part. I've put you in charge of rounding up the posse—the people who have already volunteered for service, I might add. I've kept the proverbial dirty work for myself. Don't you have a list for me?"

Jackie's face softened. "Oh," she said. She grabbed a small notepad, scribbled something and tore off the page, handing it to Tucker. "You're going to take on the naysayers. I didn't want to do it, anyway."

Tucker saluted. Maybe it would be better if she talked to the Ackermans herself, anyway. She'd have a clearer picture then of what the people who opposed the mine opening thought. "Yes, I'll talk to them," she said.

Jackie put her hands together and bowed before Tucker. "Thank you for your cooperation, your High-and-Mighty-ness. May abundant blessings be upon your endeavors."

"Yeah, well, we'll see about that."

She lifted the paper Jackie handed her into her field of vision. Mr. and Mrs. Ackerman weren't a surprise. Everyone in town called them Mr. and Mrs. Curmudgeon. Everyone knew them to be old and cantankerous. It was already Elder Creek lore, even when Tucker was a kid. They were vehemently opposed to anything different in the town. They threw a fit when the city decided an old bus shelter needed to be torn down on the main road outside of town. She figured they were only still alive because of their innate stubbornness.

Joe Dawson's name came next. She didn't have any idea what his issues were, but she intended to find out. The most difficult part would be pinning him down. He was clever at avoiding people when he wanted to, and he mostly kept his opinions to himself. She wondered how he ventured to verbalize anything at all to get him on this list. Well, she'd find out one way or another.

"I notice you've assigned me the unpleasant jobs. It also hasn't escaped my notice you've decided to re-assign me one of the jobs I assigned to you. The Curmudgeons. Joe. Are you kidding?"

"I'm sure you'll enjoy talking to the last person on that list."

Tucker looked at the list again. Her eyes widened when she saw Leah Hudson's name.

"Leah?"

"That's right."

"Why?"

"I have no idea," Jackie said. "She called me and asked how to get on the list. She didn't say why. Looks like it's your job to find out, oh, delegated one. Not only that but if you're serious about opening the mine, you'd also better be prepared to use all your charm on every one of those people to change their minds."

Leah's name on this list proved to be a strange turn of events. Didn't she come across as supportive when they talked last? Why would Leah be opposed to opening the mine and not say something to her? She didn't even have a history in this town. Or did she?

"I'll make a deal with you," Jackie said.

Tucker gave her a wary look. "What deal?"

"I'll take the Curmudgeons. I have an idea of how to win them, or at least him, over. You have to take Joe, though."

Tucker brightened. "And Leah?"

"Yes, Tucker, you take Leah. Of course." She smirked.

"Stop it," Tucker said.

"What?"

"Stop your grinning."

"I didn't grin.

"Yeah, right," Tucker said with a note of disgust. "You were so grinning."

"Fine, I was grinning. So, when are you going to see her?"

Tucker took out her phone. "Do you know what time she gets home from work?"

"I think she's usually home by four o'clock."

"I have an hour, then. I think I'll go see if Joe's around."

As Tucker headed toward Jackie's front door, her back to her friend, she said, "And stop smirking, Jackie O'Malley."

"DEVIL'S ADVOCATE," LEAH said. "I'm not opposed to it, per se, I'm concerned about everybody in town. That's why I told Jackie if there was a campaign to change the mind of the opposition, I wanted to be first on the list. People were affected by what happened back in the late 1870s and there's still some lingering unsettling miasma floating around about it."

"The little girl's family relocated to the East Coast after she died," Tucker said. "This town consisted mostly of miners and merchants, tough birds who'd seen a lot of tragedies. Once it was over, they continued on with their lives. The rumors of ghosts and strange occurrences didn't start until later, probably by a bunch of frustrated parents trying to make their children behave and stay away from the mine so they wouldn't get hurt. They didn't even put those reinforced wooden doors and padlock on the mine entrance until around the 1900s. Until then, its doors were made of flimsy wood and there wasn't even a lock."

Tucker ran her hand across the back of her neck in irritation. Devil's Advocate, indeed. Why was she forced to come back to see Leah and defend her position about the mine when there were other people she needed to talk to? She didn't mind seeing Leah again, but she didn't understand how someone who only lived in Elder Creek for a few years, and who gave the impression she understood the concept of what they were trying to do, would have any deeply embedded opposition to opening the mine for escorted tours.

"I know all that, Leah, but we need the mine if we're going to succeed."

The discussion continued with Tucker defending the opening of the mine until Leah finally smiled and said, "Good. I'm glad to see you've thought this through, Tucker."

Tucker pulled her eyebrows down into a frown. "So, I'm confused. Are you for it or against it?"

Leah let out a little chuckle. "Oh, I'm for it. I always have been."

"Then why—"

"Tucker, when I heard a small faction in town opposed opening the mine—in spite of the fact that it's a terrific idea to bring in both revenue and curious people who will spend money on food, lodging, souvenirs and mine tours—I researched the whole history of the mine and what happened to the little girl so I'd have all the facts. Then I researched the later information on rumors and concerns and knew those were mostly invented by people with concerns and fears about mine access until 1905. You're right. They probably were afraid for their kids who loved to explore the area around the mine. Their fear and some overheard half-conversations transformed into ghosts and other eerie things that probably never happened to try to scare their children off. When it didn't work, the citizenry demanded the mayor do something to keep kids out of the mine. The doors went up then, and the padlock went on. Of course, it only fueled the gossip fire more and the story became bigger.

"Did you know an article in the *Portero News* in 1906 said there was another cave in and this time three kids, all brothers, died while exploring the cave the same day as the San Francisco earthquake? The paper said they never concluded if it was coincidence or if it was related to the quake."

"No. I didn't. But that was after the mine was locked up. There have always been rumors of another entrance, though—a 'secret entrance.' Did someone actually go to the mine and get inside?"

"Nope. A follow-up story says someone from some town called Hatchet came to Portero. They met the reporter in an eating establishment, quite by accident, and told him the story someone related to him. It was all rumor, not founded in any facts."

"You're kidding. Portero is less than an hour away on horseback and they didn't come and check it out themselves before publishing the story?"

"Exactly right. Apparently, the Reddman Mine has always fueled a great story so whenever anybody said anything about it, the old ghost would appear, literally and figuratively, and people took notice. In the second story the paper published, they admitted it was all unconfirmed rumor, but they never actually published a retraction and they didn't put the information out about the 'mistake' until weeks later."

"I just have one question. Why? Why take on the Devil's Advocate role?"

"I knew you'd have to face them, the naysayers. I wanted to

make sure you got the story straight and possessed all the ammunition you needed to change your real opponents' minds. I put my name on the list because I wanted you to be able to talk it through, bringing out all the facts and the fiction, before facing the firebrands in town who might not be so quick to listen. I knew you knew all the positives of the commercial enterprise. I wanted to make sure you knew the truth, historically, in case any of it got thrown in your face as part of the arguments you might hear."

Tuckers said, "It wasn't necessary to give me a heart attack."

Leah tilted her head. "What do you mean?"

"When I saw your name on my list, my heart nearly stopped. Why you would be so opposed and not have said something before this?"

Leah laughed.

Tucker reeled. Leah's laugh always made her feel a little faint for some reason.

"There's something else you said. You said the rumor came from Hatchet. I've only recently heard of the place." She didn't want to reveal how she'd heard about it. "Did the article indicate Hatchet's location?"

"No. The article implied a place everyone in the area would know, though. I guess it didn't matter where the rumor started. It would have stirred up the gossip mill no matter where it came from."

"I guess you're right. Still, it's kind of strange to hear Hatchet is related to the mine, even if only through the gossip mill."

"Where did you hear about Hatchet, anyway?"

Tucker didn't know how to answer. If she told her, Leah would, indeed, think she'd lost her mind. The silence dragged on as Tucker looked down at her boots.

"Tucker?"

Tucker looked up. "Have dinner with me." The statement startled Tucker. Where did that come from? She pushed on. "This time, let's go to a nice restaurant, maybe over in Portero. Let's make a night of it. I mean—if you want to. Maybe you don't. It's okay if you don't."

"Tucker."

"I don't' want to push you, Leah."

"Tucker."

"There's a lot you don't know about me. If you did, you might not want—"

"Tucker," Leah said, louder this time. When Tucker finally made eye contact with her, she added, her tone softer now, "I'd love to have dinner with you."

Tucker breathed a sigh of relief. "Good. Because I have something else to ask you, and after I do, you might not want to spend time with me, but remember, you already accepted."

Leah wrapped her arms around her torso. "Okay."

As Tucker told her about the character idea, Leah exchanged the look of caution for one of excitement.

"Tucker, what a great idea. Of course I'll do it. It'll be fun. I already have a lot of resources from the research I've done on the mine. It'll be a piece of cake." Then she added, "For an *old* librarian, that is."

"Oh, not that again. Will you ever stop throwing my embarrassing remark in my face?"

"Only if it suits me, Ms. Stevens."

Leah laughed again.

The butterflies took a lap around Tucker's stomach. She felt as though she were carried far up into the clouds on their wings. She fidgeted while trying to get some control of her soaring spirit before she spoke. "Well, I can't take all the credit. Actually Jackie came up with part of the idea."

"And it's a great one. Sign me up. I'll work on character studies. Exactly what time period are we doing? Have you decided?"

Tucker told her.

"Sounds like a good time. The mine operated full bore. The town was growing. And tragedy was still off in the future. It has a lot of potential."

Leah quieted for a few seconds before adding, "One thing. About dinner."

Uh-oh, here it comes. Second thoughts. Excuses to wiggle out of it. Tucker put up her guard, trying to keep the disappointment from her expression. "Yes? What about it?"

"When we go, no talking about the project."

Tucker frowned. Not what she thought, then. "Why's that, Leah?"

"I want to leave everything behind and let us get to know each other. It'll be the two of us, learning where we've come from and what we like, what we don't like, what our dreams are."

Dreams? Maybe Tucker wished Leah would have canceled. Tell this woman about her dreams? Not *those* dreams. Dreams or hallucinations, whatever they were, she suspected if she did tell Leah about them, she would run as far away as possible into the night—away from Tucker. She didn't want to take a chance on that happening.

THE CHARLIE DIDN'T open for another hour, but Tucker knew Jackie never kept the door locked once she started getting ready to open for business. Tucker stood at the saloon door with her hand extended, hesitating before she pushed it open. She hoped she'd find Jackie behind the bar and not some stringy-haired, stubble-bearded miscreant.

Instead of striding in confidently, as she usually did, she felt a reticence foreign to her, holding her back. When she finally mustered up the courage to push on the door, it felt as if it were too heavy, unyielding. She tried again, putting her whole body into it, and the door gave, opening enough for her to poke her head inside.

Through a thick, viscous swirling fog, Tucker peered into the bar, empty of patrons. From behind the bar, not Jackie, but Tracey looked up from stacking glasses. Tucker breathed a sigh of relief and the fog lifted.

Tracey brightened and said, "Hi Tucker. Jackie's in back." She tilted her head. "Want me to get her or are you coming in?"

"Oh. Yeah. Um. I'll come in." Tucker stepped from behind the door and squeezed through the opening. One residual cloud hovered in the center of the room. It wasn't real, Tucker told herself. As she stared, the miasma imploded and disappeared in a curl of smoke-like wisps onto itself.

"You okay, Tucker?" Tracey asked.

Tucker gave her a nervous smile.

She took another step into the bar as Jackie came out of the back room, several bottles of liquor cradled in her arms like precious children.

"Hi, Tucker." She set the bottles on the counter but didn't take her eyes off Tucker. "Something wrong, sweetie?"

"No, nothing really," she lied. The pressure on her chest told her she should be truthful. "Well, it's no big deal, anyway." Her breathing rate increased. Who was she trying to convince? Man, she hated it when she felt so out of control, and why did she feel this way now? Bewildered, she said, "I...I um..."

Jackie came around from behind the bar and approached Tucker as she might a feral animal. When she reached her, she took her gently by the elbow, guiding her to a table at the far corner of the room, out of Tracey's earshot. "Don't lie to me, Tucker Stevens, something's going on. Spill."

Sweat beaded on Tucker's upper lip. She wiped her hand across her mouth. "That's just it, Jackie. I have no idea what's going on."

"Well, the Tucker Stevens I know usually doesn't look like she's seen a ghost and she's usually not afraid to walk into my establishment like she owns the place."

"It's the flashes I'm getting. I thought it was a dream, but now I'm getting them during the day when I'm awake." She leaned forward. Her eyes glistened with tears as she whispered, "Jackie, I really think I'm losing my mind."

Jackie's countenance changed. The look of concern vanished. She now looked angry. Her lips pursed tightly before she said, "No. You are not, Tucker."

The saloon door pushed open and a group of five jostled each other for entrance. A young woman among them said, "Can we get some coffee? I know it's early and you aren't open yet, but we'd appreciate it."

Tucker raised her eyebrows at Jackie. Opening and closing times at The Charlie were sacred—no one in before opening, everybody out at closing time.

Jackie sighed and said to Tracey. "Can you get this?"

Tracey quickly controlled her look of surprise and said, "Sure, no problem. I've got the coffee brewing now." She gestured the group of men and women toward a table close to the front door and said, "Have a seat, coffee will be ready in a minute."

They all shuffled obediently to the table, settled in and started talking among themselves in quiet tones.

Jackie turned her attention back to Tucker. "Tuck, what's going on?"

Tucker wasn't ready to talk about it. The recently settled group proved to be a good distraction. "I might ask the same of you. How come you let those people in? It's a good forty-five minutes 'til opening."

"It's the press. Remember the other night when you and Leah were here for dinner and we were so busy Tracey called me in?"

"Yeah, the two of you ran around like crazy to keep up with demand."

"The press has overrun Portero. It's about the missing woman. There's not a hotel room available there, so now Elder Creek has the overflow. It's going to be busy until this blows over."

"Wow. Maybe you should hire a couple more people."

"Denise Miller-Sanchez is starting later today. She's got experience. She's worked in restaurants over in Portero and she even worked here filling in a few summers ago, so she should be able to hit the ground running after a quick orientation. But let's get back to you. What's going on?"

She told Jackie about her dream. How when she went to bed it was today, and when she woke up, she found herself in yesteryear. She told her about the bartender at The St. Charles Saloon and how he projected an innate hatred of her. She told her about Leah—or Lily, rather—about how she looked like Leah, but wasn't her.

Then she told her about Olivia. "...she ran a sort of restaurant, a little place with a stove at the back. I think it's where the bookstore is now. There's no menu, just whatever Olivia's serving that day, take it or leave it. And if you take it, it costs ten cents for breakfast and fifteen for lunch or dinner. And Olivia has green eyes, red hair, and a no-nonsense personality when it comes to running her business."

Recognition dawned on Jackie's face. "She sounds just like...me?"

"Yep. Looks exactly like you. Acts like you. Talks like you, although I did detect a slight bit of a brogue when she spoke. However, she claims she's not you. Said Jackie was a boy's name." Tucker smiled for the first time since entering The Charlie.

Jackie chuckled at the tease.

Tucker felt the mirth quickly replaced with a feeling of desperation again. She tried to keep it from her voice as she spoke. "Why do you suppose you and Leah are a part of this dream or vision or hallucination—whatever this is, but you're not yourselves? And why is this guy, Nigel Dunbar, so hateful. I swear, if he'd gotten the chance and only half a good excuse, he'd have pulled out a gun and shot me right there in the saloon. And you wonder why I think I'm losing my mind?"

Jackie stretched her arm across the table and placed her hand over Tucker's. "Tucker, look at me." When Tucker met her eyes, she saw compassion and concern again. Jackie said, "You are not your mother. She may have suffered with bouts of depression. You may have endured a tough childhood when she did, but you are not her. This is some crazy subconscious thing going on. You experienced a bad dream. I've encountered a few weird dreams myself. Some have stayed with me for days, I'm sure you know the kind I'm talking about. This might be the same thing. If it continues, let's see if we can get you some help. Okay?"

"You mean, like a shrink? No thanks."

"Tucker, seeing a psychologist or even a psychiatrist doesn't mean you're crazy, okay? You know it as well as I do."

Tucker looked down at Jackie's hand on hers and shook her head.

Jackie reiterated, "Right, Tucker?"

In a barely audible voice, she said, "I guess."

She met Jackie's gaze again and flipped her own hand over, palm up grasping Jackie's. When she spoke this time, she sounded more confident. "Maybe you're right. Maybe it's only some crazy dream haunting me. I'll give it a few more days, then if it's still bothering me, maybe I'll see if I can find someone to help."

"Good," Jackie pronounced. "Now, maybe you haven't realized it, but while we've been talking about fifteen more people have come in here, so I'd better get over there and help Tracey."

Jackie's chair scraped against the floor as she rose. She hesitated before walking away. "Are you going to be okay?"

She needed to reassure Jackie so she could get back to work without worrying about her.

Tucker gave her a tentative smile. "Yeah. I'll be fine."

Chapter Four

TUCKER FELT ANXIOUS to find herself back in the Elder Creek of the past. Her background and her livelihood should have made her excited to have this experience, but all she could think of was the menacing look on Nigel Dunbar's face. Maybe she should avoid The St. Charles Saloon altogether. But that might prove impossible since Lily worked there. She found herself on a cart path behind Main Street and spent some time exploring it until her stomach rumbled, helping her decide her next destination. She'd go to Olivia's, have some breakfast and see what information she might gather there.

As Tucker sat in a quiet corner of Olivia's place eating a plate of scrambled eggs and sourdough bread, she glanced through the newspaper someone left behind. The single printed sheet smelled of the ink running across the page to form words a little difficult to read at times because of the typeface used. The masthead clearly read *The Elder Creek Weekly Star* and the date at the top said October 15, 1873. If the date was correct, it certainly would clear up one mystery.

The first article she read said a relief effort was under way to help the people of Kansas after what the piece called "the Locust Plague," swarms of insects darkening the skies, wreaking havoc as they went. It proclaimed they ate everything in their path as they passed through an area, leaving crops—and people—devastated.

An announcement caught her interest next. "Mister William Frederick Cody announces his show, Buffalo Bill's Wild West, coming to California in the spring of 1874, and the public is notified to prepare for the greatest entertainment ever to be witnessed in this land." She furrowed her brow, trying to remember something slightly beyond her grasp. When nothing came to her, she stabbed another piece of her fluffy egg and brought it to her mouth as she continued to read.

A sprinkling of local news listed a Mr. Jackson's need for help on his ranch and indicated anyone looking for work should report to his foreman.

The local volunteer brigade of the Elder Creek firemen would discuss whether or not to buy the new helmets available at a cost of ten dollars each at their next meeting. Each man would be responsible for the cost of his own headgear, it said.

According to the paper, a certain Mrs. White searched for two of her prized laying hens known to escape their pen last week. If anyone sees them, the article stated, please capture them and bring them home. Their names, the article said, were Henrietta and Harriet, "...but neither one answers to her name. Mrs. White misses them and has suffered from the sale of her eggs since they went astray."

Tucker chuckled to herself as she shoveled in another mouthful of eggs and wondered if Olivia bought them from Mrs. White. Probably not the case, since the hens went missing a while ago.

The final story began, "After a harrowing five months, the First Cavalry Regiment under Captain Jack has successfully returned a band of Modoc Indians to the Klamath Reservation in southern Oregon." Some fifty Modoc warriors in northern California held off hundreds of soldiers until the military finally prevailed.

She folded the paper and laid it at the edge of the table, feeling a wave of sorrow rush over her at the details of the last story she'd read. Like so many stories of the native peoples of the time, this Modoc tribe experienced brutality at the hands of the military. She pushed the sadness away and scraped up the bits of food remaining on her plate.

Olivia wasn't around when she finished her breakfast, so she left her dime on the table as she saw others do. Because she finished reading everything the *Weekly Star* offered, she decided to leave it for another patron. She spent the rest of the day going in and out of the shops and businesses, browsing, exchanging pleasantries with people, and finding it odd she never met another person she recognized from her own time. What was all this about, she wondered? What was her psyche trying to tell her?

As soon as she thought it, she knew. It all contained a message and, if she could puzzle it out, it might contain the answer to what was going on. A little thrill ran through her chest. Hope, she recognized. Maybe she wasn't losing her mind after all. Maybe her subconscious was trying to get her to listen, to hear the message, to figure it out.

What's the "it" I need to know? What's the message? How can I decipher it when I don't even know what the puzzle picture is, she wondered?

More questions didn't help her cause. Instead, they only added to her frustration.

She'd be seeing Leah soon—no, not Leah, Lily. She reached

into her pocket looking for her phone to check the time. She found nothing. Of course. It would be absurd to find a cell phone in her pocket in this time. She looked up at the sky to note the position of the sun.

Now she knew there was something wrong with her mind. It was absurd that she try to tell time by the sun. She wasn't capable of it any more than she could build a clock from scratch. As she walked along the boardwalk on Main Street, she noticed a man dressed in a suit hurrying toward her from the direction of the bank. As he drew closer, she spotted the chain of a watch looped from his waist to the pocket of his tailored trousers.

She spoke when they met on the walk. "Excuse me."

He looked up at her. "Yes," he said, wariness resonating through his voice.

"Can you tell me the time?" she asked.

He hesitated and she wondered whether or not he would provide the information, but he finally pulled out his gold pocket watch. He cradled it in his right palm, brought his left hand up to the case and pressed the tiny knob at the top. She heard the *tick* sound as the cover snapped open.

He glanced at the face of the instrument. "Five minutes before five o'clock." His mustache rose at the corners of his mouth as he gave her a tentative smile.

She tipped her hat and thanked him. He stepped around her down the street, resuming his quick pace. Tucker headed back toward Olivia's. She didn't see any sign of Lily as she walked down the street. She hoped Lily remembered. Hoped she'd get away from the saloon. She also hoped she might give her some answers. As she headed toward the restaurant, uncertainty blossomed. How would she get answers if she didn't know the right questions to ask?

TUCKER STOOD UP as Lily approached her table. She held out Lily's chair and when they were both seated, Olivia approached with glasses of lemonade and slammed them down in front of them. Some of the liquid in Lily's glass sloshed over onto the table, but Olivia ignored it and walked off. Tucker raised an eyebrow at Lily in surprise. Lily leaned across the table and whispered, "I guess I should have told you. She doesn't like me much."

"Why's that?"

"I have no earthly idea. You'd think I was one of Madam T's

girls the way she treats me."

"Madam T?"

Lily sighed. "You don't know who Madam T is?"

Tucker shook her head.

"Her place is on the outskirts of town—her brothel." She whispered the last word. "Soiled doves, women of ill repute, as some folks like to call them. Although I've always found them to have better morals than some other people in this town." She glanced in Olivia's direction, and saw Olivia's back toward them. Lily folded her arms across her chest and snorted.

Tucker thought this an opportune time to find out about Lily's own job description at The St. Charles Saloon. "Then you don't..."

Lily's expression changed. She looked annoyed, embarrassed, as she said, "Don't what? Are you insinuating you think I'm—*that* sort of woman? I assure you I am not!"

Tucker held up her hands. "I—I didn't mean anything. I—I didn't mean to insult you, Lily. I don't know what your actual job is at the saloon. I'm sorry."

Lily spun her drink in her hand, letting the glass glide around in the puddle on the table.

"Forgive me?" Tucker said, trying to catch her eye.

Lily lifted her glass and took a sip, holding Tucker's gaze. A drop of liquid fell into the pool of lemonade on the table. When she put the glass down, she said, "You're forgiven."

Tucker wondered whether she should let this conversation go. Change the subject. Forge ahead. Against her better judgment, she asked, "So—what is it you do at The Charlie?"

Lily eyes went wide. "The Charlie? What a strange thing to call it. And for your information, my job is to be pleasant to the customers, give them their drinks, and encourage them to drink more. No extra benefits. Fellows want that sort of thing, most know exactly where Madam T's is. They can go visit her for those. They will not get them from me and they know it."

Tucker held up her hands again, palms toward Lily. "Okay, Miss Lily, message received. I'm sorry if I offended you. I didn't mean to."

They sat quietly as Olivia approached and banged their dinner plates on the table. Food rose off the dishes and fell back down into place.

As Olivia walked away Lily said, "This is probably a mistake—coming here, I mean. Let's eat and get out of here."

Tucker and Lily ate with haste. Tucker left three dimes on the table and they got up to leave. When Olivia heard their chairs scrape across the floor, she shouted to their backs, "You get dessert with dinner, you know. Don't you want it? It's apple pie. Fresh made."

Tucker halted and said, "Thanks, Olivia, but we found your dinner so filling—so delicious, too, by the way—I don't think we have room. Maybe next time."

As they walked out the door, Tucker heard Olivia mutter, "Suit yourself."

Tucker ran to catch up with Lily to escort her back to the saloon. As they headed to The St. Charles, Lily asked Tucker how she spent her day.

"I explored the town up by the school and followed the cart path behind the hotel. When the town grows and that cart path becomes a real street—"

She realized her error as soon as the words slipped past her lips. Lily stopped in her tracks.

"What do you mean?"

Tucker felt the panic rise in her chest. "Well, er, I just meant you can't stop progress, Miss Lily. And with the gold mine going at full tilt the town should prosper. It looks as if it already has. Who knows, in a few years that old cart path behind the main street could become an official road. Hey, maybe they'll even call it Gold Street." She felt pretty smug at her save. She wondered if Lily would accept her explanation and change the subject.

"Those are pretty wild ideas." She smacked Tucker lightly on the forearm. "I can't imagine us needing more streets in Elder Creek. Why, we're doing just fine the way we are."

Tucker said, "I saw what looked like an old jail up on the cart path opposite the school. Is that just some old abandoned building?"

Lily laughed. "No. That's what we refer to as our no-frills hotel. The sheriff runs the place with an iron fist. Best to stay out of trouble while you're with us, Mr. Tucker. You don't want to become one of the patrons of that place."

Lily's remark made Tucker shiver, though she couldn't say why. Needing a change of subject, Tucker decided to risk another question. "Lily, why do you think Dunbar is so hostile toward me? I've never met him before, yet he dislikes me a great deal. Do you know why?"

"Haven't a clue. Why does Olivia hate me, do you think? I've never done anything to her. This is the worst it's been, though, I have to say."

Tucker registered her surprise when Lily added, "Maybe she's taken a liking toward you, Mr. Tucker."

Tucker pondered it as they strolled on. "Why would Olivia be jealous?"

"Maybe because you've taken up with me and she doesn't care for you doing that, although I don't understand why she would care."

"Well, you are pretty, Miss Lily," Tucker said. She felt her neck redden and the heat worked its way around to her cheeks.

Lily looked away from Tucker as if she were casually glancing into the shops, but they were no longer open. Finally, she said, "You flatter me, Tucker, but Olivia is a beautiful woman in her own right. Those green eyes would make anyone's heart go all a-flutter."

Would they? Tucker never thought of Olivia, or Jackie, that way. She and Jackie were friends—close friends—but she never felt a physical attraction to her, certainly not the way she felt attracted to Lily—or Leah. Especially Leah. The thought gave her pause, sending her back to thoughts of her previous relationship.

She met her last girlfriend in Phoenix. They quickly settled into companionship once the initial hot sex attraction cooled. Of course, Tucker realized afterward, her girlfriend already found someone else and pushed ahead with a new relationship. The only problem was, she did it without bothering to tell her, hastening the cooling even more. Still, that relationship felt different, a little off from the start, and they never developed a real friendship. No wonder it didn't last.

At least she could boast some kind of growing friendship with Leah, even if she wouldn't allow it to blossom into something more right now. She couldn't put someone like Leah in a position of having to decide to end a relationship because of her mental instability. She cared too much for Leah to subject her to that possibility.

Lily and Tucker walked on in silence. When they reached the saloon door, Tucker held it open for Lily, who asked, "Don't you want to come in and have a drink?"

Tucker glanced at the bar and saw Dunbar behind the counter with his back toward them. "Maybe I'd better not."

"Oh, don't let him keep you from coming in. Come on. Have one drink. It's still early."

She tried to decipher whether the invitation stemmed from not wanting them to part company, or because her job to encourage people to come in and have a drink motivated her.

Tucker probed Lily's face, looking for an answer she knew she wouldn't find.

"All right," Tucker said. "Maybe one drink."

Lily smiled and Tucker felt her stomach flutter a little at the gesture. She stepped in front of Tucker and entered the saloon. As she approached the bar, she said to Dunbar's back, "Nigel, my friend here will have a whiskey."

Dunbar whirled around and leered at Tucker. For the second time in an hour, Tucker experienced a glass slammed down on a wooden surface. This time, though, she saw an empty glass. Dunbar only poured the liquor after he smashed the glass down. *Good. If I have to pay for that, I don't want him to spill any of it—even if it is the most god-awful stuff I've ever drunk.*

Chapter Five

EACH MORNING WHEN Tucker opened her eyes, she never knew where she would find herself. This particular morning, she realized she'd awoken in her own time. She picked up her phone to check the date. She and Leah last spoke two days ago. Tonight they would be going to dinner together. She tried to quell her excitement. After all, she didn't think she should be involving herself with Leah right now. Not the way Leah apparently wanted, anyway. Then the voice in her head asked the question. Why not?

She gave the same answer since her first encounter with the beautiful and charming Leah Hudson—because she questioned her own mental state. "Well, it's only dinner."

Leah said she wanted to spend the time getting acquainted. She didn't want to talk about the revitalization project. She wanted to talk about them. She wanted to know who Tucker was. And there was the problem, looping back around on itself. Well, she'd have to see how the evening went to know whether or not Leah would ever want anything else to do with her, other than when the plumbing broke.

Tucker pushed the thoughts away as she drank hotel room coffee and ate instant oatmeal out of a disposable cup. She booted up her laptop, opened her manuscript file and focused on her story. The present day soon faded around her and she tapped out chapter after chapter of her tale of the Colorado territory.

When the alarm on her phone sounded, it astounded her to find she spent the whole day engrossed in her story. She saved the file, pleased with her accomplishment, and shut down her laptop to get ready for her date with Leah.

When Tucker arrived at Leah's house to pick her up for dinner in Portero, Leah announced a change of plans.

"Why's that?" Tucker asked as she helped Leah put on her coat.

"Portero is a madhouse. I think we want to stay as far away from there as we can. Reporters have overrun the place, making getting a reservation impossible, anyway."

"Still nothing on the missing girl, then?"

"The police are baffled. They've questioned the boyfriend again. You know, he's actually kind of a strange character. He doesn't have any sensible answers, but he can certainly lead those reporters in circles until even the most tenacious of them gives up."

"Hmm. Kind of a snake oil salesman, would you say?" Flashes of Dunbar darted through her mind but she quickly blocked out the image. Tonight, she wanted to enjoy Leah's company and not think about her experiences somewhere in the past, whether real or imagined.

"Yes, an apt description I'd say. Have you seen him? He's been all over the news."

"No. I've been so busy with the town project and my manuscript, I haven't watched much TV." In reality, Tucker couldn't account for some of her time, but she wasn't about to tell Leah she spent it somewhere other than in the here-and-now.

They continued down the walkway from Leah's house to Tucker's truck. Tucker opened the passenger door for Leah, and before climbing in, Leah said, "Apparently, he tried to keep under the radar, but since they've got him talking, he can't shut up. Says he's devastated at the loss of the love of his life, making pleas for her return. Funny, though. When they asked the girl's parents about him, they merely said they kept no contact with him and preferred not to comment on any of his statements."

"Sounds like they don't care for him too much."

"No, I don't think they do."

When Tucker settled herself behind the wheel, she said, "So, if not Portero, where are we headed for dinner tonight?"

"I made us a reservation in Pine Grove. I know it's a longer drive, but I didn't want to try to find a place to eat with the crowds I'm sure we'll find in Portero. I hope you don't mind the longer trek."

Tucker smiled. "Not at all. It'll be more time for us to get to know each other, wouldn't you say?" Once it rolled off her tongue, she felt a pang of regret.

"Exactly what I thought." Leah giggled.

Her laughter tickled Tucker as it always did—right down to her core—and in other tantalizing places.

WHEN TUCKER PULLED into the parking lot of Mitchell's Steakhouse, she found an empty space next to the side of the building. As she and Leah walked around to the front entrance, Tucker informed her she'd never been there before.

"The steakhouse?" Leah asked.

"The steakhouse or to Pine Grove," Tucker said. "There wasn't anything here but a bunch of campgrounds when I was a kid. Nothing to bring us all the way out here when we enjoyed the same scenery and camped all we wanted to right around Elder Creek."

"Well, I guess it's grown up a little since then. This place," Leah gestured toward the doorway they were about to walk through, "has a reputation for great food. I've been dying to try it."

Tucker held the door open for her and made a sweeping gesture. "Then, let's get to it, shall we?"

When Leah laughed at Tucker's grand wave, Tucker knew she'd done the right thing.

The restaurant bustled with activity, but there were a few empty tables. Once seated, they perused their menus. Tucker decided on what she wanted and flipped her menu over to the back cover to read a brief history of the Pine Grove area. Its current population of a few thousand inhabitants grew up around several popular campgrounds and mountain hideaway communities. In the summer, vacationers doubled the size of Pine Grove as they came to soak up the serenity and the clean air, "getting back to nature," so the information said. Fishing, hiking, swimming and biking drew people to Pine Grove. The town started as a settlement for loggers in the early 1800s. It continued to grow as it provided lumber for the mining industry during the gold rush. The men who came here logged farther up the road, but because of their occupation, they dubbed the area Hatchet—.

Tucker gasped. She met Leah's eyes. "Wow, look at this," Tucker said.

"Look at what?"

"The back of the menu." She pointed. "It has the history of this area. This place was once the settlement called Hatchet. It's the place you mentioned when you told me about the rumors about kids being killed in the mine. You know, the ones which proved not to be true."

"And I remember you said you'd heard of Hatchet before, but you didn't tell me why it was familiar to you. So, how did you know about it?"

"Well, actually, it's kind of hard to explain. Like I told you the other day, I'd never heard of it. Well, I did hear of it, but—" She chomped down on her words, exasperated.

"Well, talk about confusing, Tucker Stevens. What am I supposed to make of what you're saying? You never heard of

Hatchet, but you have, but you — what? Haven't?" She grinned at Tucker, the teasing tone apparent in her voice.

Tucker's cheeks blushed a dark rose. "It — it's a long story, Leah. Let's leave it for another time and enjoy our dinner. Okay?"

"Is it about you?"

"What?"

"The long story. Is it about you?"

"Yes. It's about me and a little about my mom."

"Wonderful. Let's order dinner. Then you tell me your story."

Tucker grimaced. It wasn't what she planned for the evening.

The waiter approached. They listened to the specials, ordered, then Leah said, "Okay. Let's have it. I love a good story."

"Really, Leah, it's old history. Well, most of it is."

"Remember me, Tucker? I'm the librarian — and a historian — I love old history. This dinner was for us to get to know each other. I'm all ears." She raised her hands to the sides of her head and flicked the ears Tucker knew were under her mop of pale limoncello-colored hair.

As they ate, Tucker slowly overcame her embarrassment about her history.

"My mom was a single parent who loved me deeply. Sometimes, though, she found it difficult to cope and functioning in the world day-to-day was sometimes impossible. When I was little, all we lived on were peanut butter sandwiches when mom was having her 'bad days,' as she called them. Once I got a little older, I learned how to cook. Mom was a great cook, so I figured out if I got her to show me how to make some of her recipes on her good days, we'd eat better on her bad ones — at least I would, sometimes it was difficult to get her to eat."

Leah said, "That must have been very difficult for you."

"Oh, the cooking wasn't too bad, but when I'd come home from school, I never knew how I'd find her. Some days she'd be fine. She'd wrap her arms around me and tell me she loved me and have me tell her all about my day. I loved those times. On the weekends, we'd go for long walks and pick daisies from a nearby field, stringing them into garlands and wearing them in our hair, laughing and generally being silly, having a good time.

"The really worrisome times were those days when I'd come home and find her curled up in her bed unable to function because of debilitating depression.

"In the last twenty years of mom's life, she finally went on medication. It made all the difference. She evened out. She told me even though there was a bit of a fog around her head all the time, at least she didn't plunge into the black depression she experienced before the treatment. I was happy for her. I only wished it possible to go back to my early childhood, so she didn't have to go through such an awful time, and life could have been one long string of good days and no bad ones."

They grew quiet, cleaning up the last bits of their meals from their plates. Finally, Leah said, "Thank you for sharing your story with me, Tucker. I appreciate it. It must have been challenging for you growing up and having to be your mom's caregiver at times." She held up her hand to stop Tucker's protest. "I know there were good times, and I'm glad you experienced those. But no kid should have to be a parent's caretaker when they're a child."

"I loved my mom, Leah. She wasn't much of a burden. I'm glad she found some help in her later years and didn't have to struggle so much. It's too bad her weak heart took her in the end."

Leah reached across the table and placed her hand over Tucker's resting there. "I'm sorry your mom's gone. I would have liked to have met her."

Tucker's mouth twitched as she tried to suppress a smile. "But if she was still alive, where would you live?"

When Leah laughed, enjoying the teasing, Tucker felt a now-familiar thrill run down her spine and the heavy burden of her story lifted.

The waiter returned and they decided to share a dessert. When he left, Tucker said, "All we've done is talk about me. I want to hear about you, too. What was your life like before you came to Elder Creek?"

"Chaos. Turmoil. Always running in several different directions at the same time."

Tucker smiled. "I think that's physically impossible."

"Maybe, but it's what my life felt like. I thought it would be an adventure, living in LA. Living in a big city didn't generate the kind of excitement I hoped for. I longed for the country, the quiet of the mountains. Being in Elder Creek, in the foothills, is like a dream come true. The pace is so much slower. I have time to think and be. It's wonderful. In southern California, especially my last few years in LA, I thought I was going to lose my mind."

Tucker played with her fork, not wanting to look at Leah. Maybe it was time to be honest. Her breathing increased as she thought about telling Leah she feared she was the one losing her mental grip. If she did tell her, she risked the loss of the budding friendship with Leah, and she wasn't sure she wanted to take such a risk. If she didn't, though, they'd be starting their friendship surrounded by an unspoken lie, and any possibility of their relationship evolving into something else would evaporate in a mist of betrayal if the deceit ever came to light.

"Did I say something wrong? Oh my goodness, I'm sorry Tucker—your mom. I didn't mean anything by it. It's just a figure of speech."

Tucker looked into an ocean of blue staring at her across the table and found nothing but concern. Taking a deep breath, she made the decision to tell Leah about her own recent experiences. Leah could decide if she didn't want anything to do with her afterward. If that's what happened after she heard her story, Tucker would just learn to get beyond these feelings building for Leah and get on with her life. It was better than prolonging it into some unknown future.

"It's nothing to do with my mom. Like I said, that's all in the past. But what it has to do with is me and—well, I guess it does have to do with my mother, too, but not directly. You see I have always been concerned I would end up like my mom. Battling depression. Not being able to function. Plunging off the edge of a cliff into some unknown darkness over and over again. I haven't experienced that. Oh, sure, I get down in the dumps sometimes, but I don't experience the deep, dark hole or feeling like it's impossible to climb out of it like my mom did."

She took a deep breath and told her the rest, "However, I have been having some strange experiences of late and I'm trying to figure out if they mean something or if my mind is playing tricks on me."

"What kind of experiences?"

"Strange ones. Things difficult to explain." Tucker looked around the restaurant. She didn't want to tell Leah the rest sitting here surrounded by strangers. "Let's get out of here and I'll tell you about it."

TUCKER UNLOCKED HER truck and held the passenger door open for Leah. By the time they were halfway back to Portero, the silence surrounding them filled Tucker with dread.

Leah said, "So, are you going to tell me the rest of your story?"

"You may not really want to hear it."

"Or is it that you don't want to tell it?"

Tucker hesitated.

"Maybe."

"Tucker—"

"I know, I know. It's just, well, I'm warning you this is going to sound pretty strange."

"Stranger than you finding yourself at the door of The Charlie and not knowing what happened."

"Afraid so."

Tucker could feel Leah staring at her. She finally said, "Then you'd better start from the beginning and get it all out. I'm ready."

"But am I sure I'm ready to tell you?"

Leah's voice softened as she said, "Just tell me. I promise I won't pass any judgments."

Tucker felt a little of the weight lift from her chest.

"Okay." She took in a deep breath. "Here it is. All of it."

She saw Leah shift a little under her seat belt, giving her full attention to Tucker.

"I've been having these...episodes...visions...something. I don't know how to explain it. It feels like I've gone back in time or something. Back to Elder Creek during the post-Gold Rush days."

"Fascinating," Leah said.

"Please, Leah, if you want me to tell you, just let me get it out. Don't comment, don't say anything until I'm done. This is difficult enough."

Out of the corner of her eye, she saw Leah nod.

"Okay, in this...experience...whatever it is, you're there. Well, not you, but someone who looks like you. Her name is Lily Hart and she works at The Charlie—only they don't call it that yet."

She glanced over at Leah and saw her eyes wide and her lips pulled together, taut and thin, as if she were trying to keep the questions from exiting her mouth.

"Jackie's in this—whatever it is I'm experiencing, too. Only her name is Olivia and she runs a kind of restaurant, serving people meals, out of what's now the bookstore. It's all kind of crazy."

She glanced Leah's way again. She still held her lips firmly shut.

"And for some reason, Lily and Olivia don't like each other, but I don't know why."

When Leah remained silent, Tucker said, "Okay, you can say

what's on your mind now."

The weight of worry in Tucker's chest threatened to make her heart stop beating and the voice within taunted her, telling her she made a crucial error telling Leah about her terrors and her confusing excursions back in time. Most of all, the growing fear of a grave miscalculation in telling Leah about her part in her whole twisted experience into the past made it difficult to breathe. With these details, she would truly think Tucker was experiencing a mental breakdown.

Finally, Leah broke the silence. "So, am I pretty — back in time?"

The weight lifted and Tucker took in her first full breath since leaving the restaurant. She gave Leah a sideways glance and smiled. "You're as beautiful there as you are here."

She thought Leah's cheeks darkened in the nighttime grayness of the truck cab and barely made out Leah's shy smile.

"There's something else, too," Tucker said. "There's this bartender. He's mean and surly and he seems to have it out for me. I can't figure that one out either."

Leah asked, "So, this saloon-keeper. Is he a familiar face, too?"

"No," Tucker said. "I don't know who he is and I can't place him in this time either. I don't know anyone who looks like him. As a matter of fact, it's only you and Jackie that look like someone I know back there — back then."

"Interesting," Leah said.

Tucker thought about the whole chain of events, exposing herself to Leah. She realized she no longer felt the dread. The weight on her chest didn't return.

"Are you okay with all this? I'll be the first to admit, it's kind of weird."

Leah said, "I think there must be a reason for these kinds of experiences. Even if you don't know the purpose now, I'm willing to bet it will be revealed in time. We'll figure it out."

Was Leah actually offering to help? Tucker breathed a sigh of relief.

As they drove back through Portero to Elder Creek, they counted five satellite vans from various television stations, including one from Sacramento and one all the way from San Francisco. Their dishes were tucked in close to the vehicle roofs, not a soul around, everything locked up tight for the night. It made sense. No doubt nothing new materialized to report at this late hour. Most of the TV personnel probably frequented the restaurants and bars in town, crowding out the tourists and the locals. Tucker smiled to herself. Leah chose well to opt for a different place for dinner.

Leah's questions floated up in the consciousness of Tucker's mind and she thought about her last encounter with Lily at Olivia's during dinner. Her wandering thoughts then pulled her back into breakfast the same morning, and she mulled over the newspaper articles in *The Elder Creek Weekly Star*. Something didn't ring true, but identifying the problem proved impossible. Nothing in the folksy local news back in time indicated something might be off, but an uneasy feeling about something in the newspaper niggled at the back of her mind. What was it?

Then, it hit her.

"I've got it," Tucker shouted.

Out of the corner of her eye, she saw Leah jerk and knew her outburst caused it.

"Sorry," she added. "I just realized something."

She told her about breakfast at Olivia's and reading the local weekly. Then she asked, "Do you know when Buffalo Bill's Wild West show started?"

"The early 1880s, I think. I can't recall the exact year."

"I do know the exact year, 1883. The paper I read was dated 1873. How did it contain an advertisement for the Wild West show when it didn't even start until ten years later?"

"Are you sure about the date of the paper?"

"I'm positive. Ever since my first encounter, I wondered about the year. When I finally saw the date on that paper, it surprised me, but I also felt relieved at finding an answer to one of my questions. I wouldn't forget it. The date clearly read October 15, 1873. As I read it, though, some things didn't sit right. I thought it threw me because one of the stories told about a Native American massacre, which upset me, but now I'm not so sure that was the only reason I felt like something was off. I think some of the information was just plain wrong and I might have been reacting to the errors subconsciously."

"I should be able to get a copy."

Tucker looked over in surprise then fixed her attention back to the road.

"Yes, silly. It's what I do, remember. I'm a librarian. I subscribe to *newspapers.com*. If the *Star* actually did exist, I should be able to pull up the exact paper you saw and we can verify what's in it."

"Wow. How great, Leah."

They pulled into Elder Creek and took Yankee Hill Road to Leah's house. Tucker switched off the ignition and they sat in silence, parked under a sweeping elm tree with golden leaves visible in the moonlight. A gust blew and leaves fluttered onto the hood of the vehicle.

Tucker said, "I hope I didn't freak you out with all this, Leah. I know it must sound very strange."

Leah looked into Tucker's eyes. "It must mean something, Tucker. Maybe your subconscious is trying to give you information. You merely have to figure out what it is."

Tucker huffed. "The problem is I have no idea how I'm going to do that."

"Well, looking at the newspaper might be a start. Since tomorrow's Saturday, why don't you come over for breakfast? It will pale in comparison to the meal at Mitchell's, but I consider myself a decent cook. We can look up the paper online afterward and see what we find."

Tucker smiled. "I'd like that Leah. But I have one request for breakfast."

"Okay. I said I was a decent cook." Leah emphasized the word decent. "I didn't say I did anything terribly fancy or gourmet."

"I didn't mean what you'd cook. I meant what we'd talk about during breakfast. No more about me. I want to hear about your life. Deal?"

Leah sighed. "Deal. I guess. Oh, and I should tell you about the character research I've done. I've found about a dozen interesting Elder Creek personalities with the potential to be entertaining. I've only done a little on each of them but if you think it's what you imagined, I'm willing to do more."

"Great. We'll talk about it *after* we talk about you."

"If we must."

"What time shall I come?"

"How about around nine o'clock? I'll make something easy so we have plenty of time to search through the newspaper site and I can show you what I've got on character studies."

"Sounds good," Tucker said.

Leah surprised Tucker by leaning over and giving her a quick kiss on the cheek. "See you in the morning," she said as she opened the door of the truck. "Thank you for dinner. I enjoyed our evening."

Tucker watched Leah ascend the porch steps and unlock her front door. She waved, then stepped across the threshold into the light of a small table lamp. She closed the door and Tucker saw the living room light go on for a few minutes. When it went off again, she knew Leah probably made her way to the back of the house.

She cranked the truck to life and headed for the hotel. Tucker smiled at the thought of seeing Leah in the morning again. At least she hoped she would see her in the morning instead of finding herself back in the Elder Creek of old, with Lily Hart.

Chapter Six

TUCKER REALIZED HER worst fear of not making it to Leah's for breakfast was coming true. Instead, she found herself sitting in The St. Charles Saloon drinking whiskey with an odor akin to sewer gas. The only redeeming quality of it was the fierce burn, which quickly wiped out the awful taste even before she swallowed it.

A few patrons sat scattered around the dimly lit room. Two older men with long hair and beards, one graying and frizzy, the other black and stringy, sat opposite each other playing some type of dice game and drinking what looked like the same foul excuse for an alcoholic beverage sitting in front of her. When she ordered, Dunbar offered her the whole bottle, for the going price, of course.

Lily appeared at her elbow and whispered, "If you take the bottle, I'll be able to join you for the duration."

Tucker felt a pleasant tingle wash over her at the suggestion.

"In that case, I'd be pleased to have your company for the whole night." She knew she'd never be able to consume the entire contents of the disgusting alcohol. Apparently, The St. Charles Saloon didn't serve anything but the worst booze in the country.

As they sat with drinks in their chipped, scratched glasses, Tucker said, "By the way, Lily, have you heard about the coming of the Wild West show?"

"No, I've never heard of it."

Her answer made Tucker even more suspicious of the advertisement she'd seen in the *Star*.

"How about the Locust Plague out on the plains? Have you heard of it? It's been in the newspaper." Lily said she never heard of that either, but then she admitted something that stunned Tucker completely.

Staring into her glass, Lily spoke softly, "I don't know how to read."

Wow. How could two people be so alike, and yet, be so different? Leah was an avid reader, a researcher, a person who made her living dealing with books and other documents, both paper and electronic, and Lily wasn't even able to read. Amazing.

Thinking of Leah brought up her concern about breakfast with her. What would Leah think if she didn't show up? She didn't know the answer, but it didn't matter because it was apparent she didn't have any control over the situation.

The sound of Lily's voice drew Tucker back to the saloon, to the table where she sat with her. As Lily recounted a little of her trip to Hatchet, Tucker felt as if she were standing at the opposite end of a long tunnel, hearing Lily's lilt transform into a drone, echoing off the shaft walls.

She'd consumed too much of this loathsome liquor. She should stop drinking. She watched Lily's mouth moving, but she only registered a buzzing sound. Someone approached their table. He loomed over them, sneering at Tucker. Words traveled from his mouth as if moving through thick, dark goo in slow motion. The letters formed sounds as they slogged through the molasses-like substance. "You need to leave. I don't want you to ever come back here. If you do, I'll have you thrown in jail. Do you understand me? Forget about this place. Forget. Forget."

She opened her mouth to ask Dunbar what his problem was, but the words stuck in her throat. Her eyelids felt heavy. So heavy.

She kept hearing his words over and over, surrounded by the buzzing sound.

Dunbar pushed his face into her personal space. She watched little bits of food, stuck to his mustache, quiver as he spoke. His breath smelled as bad as his liquor. She looked into his eyes, so dark they were almost black, and tasted fear on the back of her tongue.

"Leave. *Forget.*"

The last word echoed for several seconds as if they were standing in a tunnel with a high ceiling looming overhead.

The buzzing grew louder until it was impossible to ignore. She opened one eye. The sound came from her alarm clock—her digital alarm clock. The one plugged into the electrical outlet. The one she set so she wouldn't be late for breakfast at Leah's. She reached over and pounded the thing into silence. Peace and quiet finally surrounded her, but the word *forget* still ricocheted off the inside surfaces of her mind.

TUCKER STOPPED BY Jackie's house before heading to Leah's. Jackie always got up early, so she knew she'd be out of bed, even on Saturday morning. She found her in her kitchen. "Hey Jackie, thought I'd stop by to see if you've found a chance to talk the Curmudg—I mean—the Ackermans?"

"As a matter of fact, I did talk to Phil and Doris Ackerman. But after we talked for a while, it was apparent they were being recalcitrant because they just don't like change. They took whatever rumor is floating around town and used it as fodder to dig their heels in because that's what they do if left to their own devices, but I took care of the situation."

"How'd you manage that?"

"Oh, Phil Ackerman is a pretty easy mark. All you have to do to talk him over to your way of thinking is use a little logic and a healthy dose of sweet talk."

"And Mrs. Ackerman?"

"I don't think we have to worry about her. I'm not so sure she was set against what we're doing in the first place, but she just lets Phil carry on because there's little she can do to change him. When we walked out to get the Twigs out of my car, she just sauntered into the kitchen mumbling about the old coot being so easily influenced by a pretty young thing." Her grin widened. "I took it as a compliment."

"Wait. Twigs? What did root beer have to do with it?"

Jackie sighed. "You have absolutely no political acumen at all, do you?"

"Okay, I'll accept that, but I still need an explanation."

"The freshly brewed quart of Twigs was my ace in the hole. I offered it to him free when I saw him start to falter, and he took the bait. He followed me out to the car like a little puppy and held out his meaty hands to eagerly receive the prize. You'd think I was offering him a bag of money. He's my best buddy now that I've given him craft brewed root beer at no charge. I've got him wrapped around my little finger." She held up her pinky and twirled it in a small circle.

Tucker burst out laughing. "Heard anything about Joe Dawson?" Tucker asked.

"He's disappeared. No one knows where he went or when he might be back. I checked his house a couple of times. His truck is gone and everything is buttoned up tight, so I guess he's gone for a while. If we're lucky, he'll stay away long enough not to pose a problem. With him out of the way, the Ackermans on our side, and Leah having clarified she's not against the mine opening, we can go forward with the plans, and if we've made enough progress before he gets back, he won't be able to do anything to stop us. Not that he could in the first place, incidentally. He doesn't have any influence in this town, not really."

"I know he doesn't wield any influence, but it's always nice to get people on the same side before doing this type of thing. So, do you think we should be concerned about him disappearing? After all, they have that missing woman over in Portero. What if something happened to him?"

"Nah, I wouldn't worry. He does this sometimes. He gets a whiff of some great bargains at a flea market or a second-hand store closing and he's gone for a while. I wouldn't be too concerned. I think Joe can take care of himself. He'll probably be back with a truckload of junk he'll turn around and sell to the antique shops in Portero. He'll probably be in a great mood if that happens, actually, and it'll be easier to pull him over to our side then. He's usually grinning from ear-to-ear for at least a week if he's made a big haul, especially if he gets paid well for it.

"Three or four years ago, he left for weeks. When he got back, he told me he'd been all over the state, buying and selling. Said he made enough money to pay his property taxes for the year. It made him a happy man."

Tucker latched on to Jackie's reassurance. She didn't need something else to worry about. "I haven't talked to the mayor about the recycling idea yet. I planned to try to see him Monday. Maybe I'll hold off for a bit, wait until we see Joe's face and his old beat-up truck back in town before I suggest anything to the mayor. Fortunately, we have time.

"Right now, we need to focus on what we need to get the mine open. It might take some time to figure out and complete whatever work needs to be done to it before we can add it to the town activities. We also need to get a list of people together who might be interested in leading tours."

Tucker stopped, staring at Jackie, waiting. After some seconds passed while they continued to stare at each other, Jackie finally said, "What?"

"When the executive director speaks, it's customary for the appointed chairperson to write down the ideas so said chairperson can execute them."

Jackie's expression changed from scowl to glare. "Chairperson?" Jackie blew out her breath and ran her hand through her thick cinnamon colored hair. "Chair-*flunky*, you mean."

Tucker raised an eyebrow. "Ah, but you're *my* chair-flunky."

They both laughed.

Tucker added, "Don't worry about it. We'll take care of it at the meeting on Monday night. Right now, I need to get going."

Jackie glanced at the clock. "Where are you headed so early

in the morning, Miss I-Am-Not-A-Morning-Person?"

Tucker put her hand on the doorknob. "Breakfast." She gave Jackie a wink. "With Leah."

She opened the door and stepped over the threshold, letting it slam behind her.

TUCKER SAT SHOVELING Leah's home cooked breakfast into her mouth. Leah watched her, her chin resting in her palm. Tucker stopped, a fork full of bacon and spinach omelet halfway to her lips. She lowered the fork slowly to her plate.

"I'm being rude, aren't I?"

"No, not at all. I'm glad you're enjoying my cooking." Leah laughed.

The sound tickled her insides, her new go-to reaction. She pushed the egg mixture around in her plate.

"I'm sorry," Tucker said, not looking up. "Living at the hotel, well, I haven't eaten a home-cooked meal since I got here. No, wait, I'm lying. Jackie and I did have dinner at her place not too long ago, but she made a salad. Not really what you'd call a home cooked meal. At least not in my opinion."

She met Leah's eyes. They were sparkling, mirthful. "And wine," Tucker continued. "We drank lots of wine." Then Tucker laughed, too. She glanced at Leah's plate. It didn't look like she was eating. Tucker said so.

Leah smirked and said, "Well, somebody's kept me busy talking about myself—one of the conditions of you sharing this meal with me, as I recall."

"Oh, yeah, you were telling me about your first day at the Portero school. I'm enjoying your story. Please, go on."

"I think you were enjoying your food a little bit more, though."

Tucker picked up her fork again and shoveled in a pile of the egg concoction, followed by some potatoes and onions, caramelized to perfection. As she chewed, she waved her fork in a little circle, motioning Leah to continue.

"Well, the library is well stocked for such a small place. It's one of the reasons I decided to take the job. I was prepared to do something other than library science if I was forced to, at least for a while, as a way to get out of LA."

"It's that bad down there? I know there's a lot of traffic, but don't people kind of Zen out and go with it, accept it as part of life?"

"The traffic isn't what made me so desperate to leave."

As Tucker scooped another forkful of food, she realized a prickly silence developed. She put her fork down and met Leah's eyes again. A cold, blue iridescence rippled through a gray color in Leah's irises, the bright blue replaced with dullness, the color of tempered steel.

"I was desperate to get away from—"

Tucker knew from Leah's tone it was bad. "You don't have to tell me if you don't want to, Leah. It's okay."

"No, I want to. You should know."

Tucker waited. Leah would talk in her own time.

The tick of an electric clock reverberated around them as Leah looked down at her lap, wringing her hands. Tucker got up from her seat and walked around the table to Leah's side. She stooped down beside her and took her hands.

"We can do this another time, if you need to, Leah."

"No. I'll do it now. It's better if you know."

"Okay," Tucker said slowly. "Do you want to go into the living room? Get more comfortable?"

"No, Tucker, this is fine. Please, go sit down."

Tucker did as Leah asked. Leah pulled herself together and looked into Tucker's chestnut eyes.

"I met Kaz shortly after I relocated to LA. I was with friends at one of the lesbian bars in West Hollywood one night—"

When Tucker raised an eyebrow, Leah shrugged, adding, "I was young."

"Anyway, I was there with friends, having a good time, celebrating somebody's birthday, as I recall. Kaz came over and started talking to me. It was a bit rude because we were obviously there as a group, celebrating, but she started sweet talking me. She was older, in her forties, but she was very beautiful and very sexy. We danced a couple of times. After that, someone invited her to join our group for the evening. I found out later—much later—no one wanted her to stay. They, too, thought she was rude and much too domineering. Anyway, one thing led to another and by the end of the evening, she charmed me out of my phone number.

"After one date, I knew it was a mistake. She was into some "bad shit" as she termed it and I agreed with her. I don't know why she thought a sweet, mid-Western girl like me would be attracted to S&M and rough sex, but I told her on our first date I wasn't interested in any of it. She kept pushing, trying to get me to agree to meet her at this place called *The Crypt*. The whole thing started to feel extremely creepy.

"I don't know how I managed to extricate myself from our date with my dignity intact and without being manipulated into something I wanted no part of, but I did. Fortunately, we met at the restaurant and I brought my own car. I literally shook all the way home.

"The harassment started soon after. First it was phone calls. Begging. Pleading. Then the tone changed. She became abusive. Threatening."

"Oh God," Tucker said. "I hope you called the police."

"I did. They suggested I change my phone number. I did. To an unlisted number. Then, one night, she broke into my apartment. I don't even know how she learned where I lived. I never gave her my address. No doubt she'd followed me around and I didn't even know it."

Tucker wanted to offer something supportive, but she sensed Leah was on a roll and she shouldn't stop her. If she did, she might never get the whole story out, and she knew she needed to talk about it.

"Fortunately, I wasn't there when she broke in. I knew it was her when I found the handcuffs on my bed with a note saying, 'You'll be my prisoner of love soon.'

"It became difficult to leave my apartment after the break-in. I didn't know if she would pop out from behind a car one day and kidnap me, take me to some deserted location and keep me there as a hostage or something. You hear about those things happening, you know?"

One tear escaped from Leah's eye now. She brushed it away as if annoyed.

"I barely functioned. The fear ruled my life. It took everything in me to go out to work every day. Otherwise, I stayed home, with everything locked up tight and a chair jammed under the doorknob."

Tucker got up and went back to Leah and took her hands again. She felt her trembling.

"I tried to pull myself together to be able to get out of LA. It took a while. I found a good psychologist. My friends were supportive. I found a new apartment and settled in. Things calmed down. I calmed down, but by then, LA no longer held the excitement it once did for me. It took me a couple of years, but while I worked on getting beyond the trauma of it, I also worked toward finding a more peaceful, slower-paced place to live." Leah looked up at Tucker and gave her a nervous smile. "Safe," she murmured.

Tucker didn't know what to say. She held Leah's hands

wanting to do more, wishing she could scoop her up in her arms in a comforting embrace, but in light of Leah's revelation, she thought better of it. Finally, she whispered, "I'm so sorry you were involved in such a terrible experience, Leah. I hope you do feel safe here."

Leah freed one hand from Tucker's hold and wiped more wetness from her cheek. "I do. I knew right from the start I would. This house," she gestured around the room, "it's filled with love from you and your mom. It makes me feel so good to live here. It's been healing. And you've been good for me, too."

Tucker cocked her head. "Me? What have I done?"

"You've made me feel...possibilities...again."

They stared into each other's eyes for a moment. Tucker wondered if she wanted to know what those possibilities were. For now, she judged it the wrong time to ask.

"I hope you haven't felt like you were all alone here, though," Tucker said. "I mean, moving away from your friends, your psychologist. I hope the distance hasn't been too hard."

"No. It's been okay. I talk and text with many of my friends down there. But over the past couple of years, it's been less and less. Their lives are so different. It's been good to make friends here. Although, I must admit, you and Jackie are the only people in town my own age. I'm friends with teachers at school in Portero, but they're all married and have families, so we don't have too much in common except school. There's one woman I talk to a bit, but she has her own family and interests. She's more of a friendly colleague than anything, I guess. Jackie's been good for me, but she's so busy with The Charlie." She hesitated, then added, "It's been nice...having you around, Tucker."

Tucker saw the sparkle returning to Leah's eyes. The steely blue-gray melted away to reveal the azure reminiscent of the clear waters surrounding distant Pacific Islands Tucker only saw in magazine pictures. She felt a wave of protectiveness for Leah wash over her. She was falling for this woman—but letting her know it would be too dangerous—for Leah.

LATER THAT MORNING, with Leah recovered from the recounting of her harrowing experience in LA and the breakfast dishes done, Leah and Tucker sat close, heads together, at Leah's computer in the converted bedroom she used as an office. Tucker stared at the October 15, 1873, edition of *The Elder Creek Weekly Star*.

"This looks nothing like the paper I saw," she pronounced.

"It's completely different, and all it contains is local news, no national reporting at all. It doesn't even have any advertisements. No Buffalo Bill's Wild West coming soon, no Modoc Indian troubles, no Locust Plague. The newspaper I saw mustn't even have been real."

Leah grunted. "I don't know what it means, Tucker. Maybe nothing, but maybe something."

An idea struck Tucker. "Instead of looking up a paper by date, can you look up events reported by any paper?"

"Yes. We can." She checked a box on the online search form to indicate a search by keyword rather than by newspaper title. "What would you like to search for?"

"Let's start with 'locust plague.' Is it enough, do you think?"

"Let's try it and see."

Leah typed the words into the search field. A paper out of St. Louis called *The Republican* reported the details of the terrible plague. The locusts ate the clothes right off people's bodies. Crops were decimated in a matter of minutes. Children and their parents went hungry. Nothing stopped the devastation. However, the report clearly indicated this so-called Locust Plague of the Great Plains didn't start until 1874, not 1873 as Tucker read in the Elder Creek newspaper.

They tried the Indian incident and found the story of the First Cavalry Regiment under Captain Jack and the battle of Lost River. The Modoc War took place in 1872. It, too, incorrectly reported in her Elder Creek of old. Why did some incidents happen long before the date in the newspaper when others had not even happened yet, like the locust plague and Buffalo Bill Cody putting together his Wild West show?

Frustration bubbled in Tucker's chest like water reaching a rolling boil. "What does it all mean? I feel like I should understand, but I don't."

She sprang up from her seat and started pacing. Leah got up and met her head on as she came around the small room again, forcing her to stop moving.

"Tucker, if there's something to figure out, I'm sure you'll do it, but it'll probably be easier if you're able to calm down, relax. Don't let it get to you. Now, close your eyes and take in a deep breath."

Tucker did as instructed.

"Now let it out slowly."

She did.

"Now, breathe normally. Keep your eyes closed."

At first, Tucker didn't understand the sensation. The soft touch on her lips felt so good. Then, the pressure increased and she automatically parted her lips a little as Leah continued to kiss her.

She opened her eyes wide. Oh God. Then she closed her eyes again and gave in completely. Leah's kiss felt like heaven. Leah felt—

No! They must stop. She pulled away with a whimper and a sucking sound, reminding her they barreled toward full throttle engagement. She grasped Leah by the shoulders and held her at arm's length.

"Leah, we shouldn't."

She watched Leah's eyes cloud over again and hated herself for pushing her away.

"Why, Tucker? Why shouldn't we?"

"Because...you're vulnerable and I'm—"

"What Tucker? Say it. You're what? What's preventing you from letting yourself go with what's between us? Go ahead. Say it, Tucker."

Tucker's breathing increased as if they'd engaged in sex. Was it the kiss? Or was it Leah's pushing her to speak her worst fear? Maybe it was both, but clearly her mental state prevented her from allowing this to happen.

The tension between them crackled. Tucker felt pressure exerted on her chest, pressing in on her from all around the room. She tried to pull in a full breath but found it impossible. Desperation filled her. Finally, she took in enough air to get the words out. "Because—" Tucker shouted. Then softer, "I told you. I might be crazy."

The room pressure deflated. Tucker took in a deep breath, feeling like she emerged from deep water, submerged for way too long and now, blessed relief came with the intake of air. It felt so good. But it wasn't good. It was bad. Now Leah would understand how loony she actually was. With the words spoken, they would be real, true. She waited for Leah to run. Instead, she stood there, staring at Tucker.

Probably in shock, mused Tucker. But instead of running, Leah grasped Tucker by her upper arms and pulled Tucker toward her until they were bosom to bosom. She kissed Tucker firmly on the lips again. When she thrust her tongue through Tucker's lips, Tucker's own tongue, now with a mind of its own, pushed into Leah's mouth and Leah took it in, sucking gently, caressing it, fondling it with her lips. Tucker's knees went weak.

She thought she might not be able to stay upright. She started to tremble.

Leah pushed against her, pulling away. The blue of the Mediterranean looked opaque, like a hard turquoise stone. Her tone, when she spoke next was adamant, "No, Tucker Stevens. You are not crazy. I know crazy, remember?"

Tucker knew she referred to Kaz.

"And I am not vulnerable, except to you right now—and I want to be."

She pulled Tucker back in and engaged her in another passionate kiss. Fear and worry dissolved. Tucker kissed her back. This time, neither of them wanted to stop.

Chapter Seven

TUCKER SAT HUNCHED over the bar at The St. Charles Saloon nursing the awful whiskey. Lily sat beside her. Every time Tucker took a sip, Lily tipped the bottle and refilled the marred glass with a few more drops of amber liquid. Tucker knew Lily did it to look like she engaged her, encouraging her to finish off the bottle, or Dunbar would make her go pay attention to one of the other patrons who might not be drinking enough.

Out of the corner of her eye, Tucker saw a man approach from Lily's exposed side. He leaned on the bar and put his face close to Lily's cheek. Tucker saw Lily flinch as she stared straight ahead.

The man ignored her and pushed his short, round body against Lily's, breathing hard through his mouth. His rancid breath, mixed with bad alcohol, wafted past Lily. He cocked his head then tipped his hat back to get a better view. His voice sounded like gravel and glass rubbing together as he said, "Miss Lily, why do you want to hang on to this no-account drifter when I have need of your ministrations at this time?"

Tucker kept her head in the forward position while shifting her eyes to get a clearer look at him.

Lily answered through clenched teeth, "As you can see, Mr. Cutter, I'm engaged. I am not available. You know the rules. I attend to one customer at a time."

"Miss Lily, now, how many times have I asked you to call me by my given name? It's Axl, Miss Lily. Call me Axl. And I think you'll agree I deserve a little rule bending, now don't I?"

Lily pinned him with her gaze. She still kept her voice low, but her tone said she wanted no argument. "Look, *Axl*. If you'll have a seat, I'll be with you in a little while. For now, my friend and I are finishing off this bottle and until then, I won't be available to serve you."

The man glared and said, "You'd better watch your step, Missy." He stomped off, retreating to the far side of the room. Lily and Tucker swiveled around on their stools and looked at the men scattered throughout the bar. They all found something else to look at.

"Who is that guy?" Tucker asked.

"You don't want to know," Lily snapped. "He's nobody. A

nobody who thinks he's somebody."

"Do I need to do something about him?" Tucker puzzled over what she would do, but she felt compelled to defend Lily somehow.

"It's best if you leave him alone, Tucker, believe me. He's a little confused, that's all. He thinks I'm one of Madam T's girls."

She knew how Lily felt about being taken for one of Madam T's girls.

Tucker contemplated how she might try to lighten the conversation a little. "You know, the first time you mentioned Madam T, I thought maybe she worked as a fortune teller. It's kind of funny, don't you think?"

Lily didn't look amused.

"Madam T runs the bawdy house at the end of town."

"I know. So you said. I was only trying to make you laugh. I'm sorry."

Lily mouth twitched a little at one corner. "Actually, it is funny," she said. "I can see her in traveling gypsy clothes, flipping over cards, telling people their future. Maybe she'd have her girls sitting around her, fanning her with big feather fans as she told people's fortunes." Lily laughed at the prospect.

The sound tickled Tucker.

"How many ladies work at Madam T's anyway?"

"Three or four of them—and I assure you I am not one of them!"

Tucker raised her hands in surrender. This was definitely a sore subject with Lily. Her cheeks colored red as she spoke her protest. It might be from anger or embarrassment at being lumped in with these women. Either probably would be justified.

Lily continued, raising her voice as she spoke without facing the other patrons, she said, "I am a saloon girl. Granted, it's not the noblest profession in this world, but it's respectable, and I don't allow anyone to take any liberties not required of me. I believe I told you this before." By the end of her statement, her voice reached a crescendo.

From out of the back room of The St. Charles Saloon, Dunbar emerged, lumbering forward like a wraith filled with rage. The man who vied for Lily's attention followed behind him. One word popped into Tucker's head—tattletale.

When Dunbar reached Lily, he grabbed a fistful of her bodice and wrenched her up from her stool. Tucker saw Lily wince as her head pivoted away from Dunbar and she wrinkled up her nose. Dunbar leaned in toward her and spoke in a controlled voice, his obsidian eyes dark and menacing. "If Mr. Cutter wants you to be one of Madam T's ladies, you damn well will be. You understand me? You'll do anything he wants or you can go find yourself other employment."

An angry ember burst into a raging inferno within Tucker. This man's bullying must stop. Now. Lily needed someone to stand up for her. She rose to face Dunbar.

He faced Tucker and growled, "What the hell do you want?"

Then she pulled back her fist and hit him in the jaw with all her might. Cutter scurried away to a dark corner as Dunbar crumbled to the floor in a heap.

TUCKER SAT ON the dirt floor of the thick walled wooden structure nursing her injured hand. She peered out into the sunlit day around the bars in the jail window. When her hand met Dunbar's face, she registered her surprise at the rock hard impact. She watched in amazement as he dropped to the floor, unconscious. A surge of adrenalin must have given her more power than she knew she possessed.

Her hand hurt like hell, but she didn't think anything was broken since she wiggled her fingers with only slight discomfort. When she tried to get up from her seated position, she found her shoulder hurt, too, probably from the shock wave, which traveled up her arm when she made contact with Dunbar's stony face.

She tried to remember the details of what happened after she hit him, but the word *forget* overpowered any memories of what followed. Why would that word be so firmly implanted, reverberating in her mind over and over again?

It occurred more often now. She thought it curious before. Now she questioned the word's significance and wondered if she was supposed to forget more than punching Dunbar.

Lily came to mind. Oh God, she thought, what have I done to poor Lily? Worry and dread filled her whole body. She put her head in her hands. Tears threatened to emerge and she scrubbed them away with her palms, but the gesture made her hand hurt more, so she willed herself to stop. It wouldn't help either of them for her to plunge into the mire of regret and self-pity.

When she took her hands down from her face, she found a young man—boy was a more accurate description—staring at her through the bars of the window. The full impact of her situation hit her. She was a prisoner. The realization filled her with dread. The boy tilted his head, watching her as if she were an exotic animal in a cage.

She pulled herself together, tried to sound casual as she said, "Hi, what's your name?" She didn't know what else to say to open up the lines of communication in an attempt to get information.

The boy looked down at his feet. "Name's Joey—Joseph—but I prefer Joey."

"Well, Joey, would it be possible to get some water? I'm very thirsty." Bad liquor and stress will do that to you.

Joey said nothing. He pulled away and disappeared from view. A few minutes later he reappeared with a squat, dented tin cup. He passed it through the wide slot below the bars, probably a meal slot, she realized.

She took the cup. The water in it looked clear enough. As thirsty as she felt, she didn't care. She downed the contents in three gulps and wiped her mouth with the sleeve of her shirt. "Can I have some more?" She thrust the cup back through the opening toward the boy.

Joey took the cup and glanced to one side, then the other. "Best not," he said. "I'll bring more later."

Tucker didn't want him to leave. She needed to determine what the future held for her. Maybe he'd be able to provide some answers. She decided to start with the basics.

"Who are you?" she asked.

"I'm the sheriff's helper."

"His deputy?" He looked too young.

"No, not his deputy. Maybe someday, though." His eyes brightened when he said it. "I take care of people when they're in the jail. Bring 'em water. Sometimes food if they tell me to. Otherwise, I'm not supposed to. If they behave, they let me bring 'em to the outhouse."

He punched the air over his shoulder with his thumb. In the distance, Tucker saw a tiny building under a dead-looking tree, the outhouse. The path to it bisected a larger trail. She recognized the area now. The outhouse was probably the same one she visited the first morning she woke up in this time. She walked the path in front of it the day she explored the town. The front entrance of the National Hotel on Main Street ran behind her. The gravity of the situation struck her again. She was locked up in the run-down town jail she passed on her recent walk.

A thought struck her. "Joey, if I promise not to give you any trouble, can I use the outhouse?"

He didn't answer. She pressed him, "I really need to go. Please?"

He thought for a few more seconds. Without a word, he disappeared from sight again. She thought he'd gone for good, but he came back eventually. This time, he held a large key in one hand, and a gun in the other.

He held them both up to her line of sight. His face hardened. He no longer looked like a child as he said, "I'm going to use this." He waved the large, worn skeleton key back and forth. "We're going to walk directly over there." He pointed the key toward the outhouse. "You're going to go in and do your business. When you come out, we come directly back here. If you do anything else or give me any kind of trouble, I use this." He brandished the gun. "Understand?"

She accepted his terms, her face solemn.

He shoved the gun into the waistband of his baggy, ragged pants and told her to step away from the door and stand still until he told her to move. He conducted himself as if he'd done all this before.

She heard him put the key in the lock and metal scraped against metal. When the door opened, he held the gun pointed directly at her. He stepped back a few paces and told her to come out slowly. She did as instructed, keeping her hands up, level with her shoulders.

THE WALK TO the outhouse gave her a chance to stretch her sore muscles and clear her head a little. As they approached the small structure, the putrid smell wafted under her nose. The unpleasantness of this experience to relieve herself didn't strike her until this moment. You'd think she would have remembered from her previous encounter at the hotel, still, what choice did she have?

Joey waved the gun at her, indicating she should go into the outhouse. She held her breath as she put her hand on the wood handle to open it, but knew she'd never survive her entire stay inside that way. She'd have to breathe eventually or she'd pass out. She pulled open the door and tried to beat the increased fetid smell by taking another breath, but she took the full brunt of it, choking as she stepped inside. It took all her willpower not to upchuck, though she did gag a couple of times.

She did what she needed to quickly and realized for a second time during her stay in this time that toilet paper didn't exist. "Damn!" No doubt she should have picked up a leaf or something from outside. Too late, she realized.

She heard Joey's muffled voice from outside. "Everything all right in there?"

She dreaded opening her mouth again, but knew she'd better respond or he might come in after her since she'd found no lock on the door.

"Yes, everything's just great." The irony of the situation made her stifle a laugh. Laughing meant breathing in with more than the shallow breaths she took now. Not a very good idea.

She wiggled around before standing and pulling up her jeans and tried not to feel too much disgust. When she opened the door, the sun blinded her after the darkness of the tiny place, but fresh air and a normal breath felt good. When her eyes focused, she found Joey standing a few feet from her, gun trained on her gut, a determined look on his young face.

As they trudged back to the jail, Tucker wondered how easily she might overcome the skinny kid walking behind her. She looked around trying to figure out an escape route, but this empty section of town spanned open, barren grassland. A tree shielded the outhouse behind her, probably in an attempt to keep the smell down in the blistering heat, but it didn't have many leaves on it. The noxious contents of the outhouse must have seeped to the roots of the tree, killing it, making it ineffective.

She took in more of her surroundings as they trekked. Rocks, strewn here and there, didn't offer anything big enough to hide behind. The only plant life, some scruffy looking shrubs and dry grass, wouldn't provide any cover if Joey decided to shoot at her. By the time they approached the jail, Tucker concluded if she decided to run, even if she escaped past the gun-toting would-be deputy, there would be no place for her to hide from his bullets.

TUCKER WATCHED AS night fell outside the barred window of the jail. Joey disappeared after the trip to the outhouse. She wondered if she would be one of the lucky ones and the boy would be allowed to bring her some food. Her stomach growled as she realized her breakfast was the last meal she ate.

She considered the events bringing her to this point. Dunbar was her undoing. As soon as she thought about him, she heard the word again.

Forget.

She heard it over and over until she held her palms to her ears in an attempt to block it out. It did her no good. The gesture only served to make her injured hand throb. She felt sorry for herself now, wondering how long she'd be trapped in this cell. Maybe she'd never get out. Her incarceration plunged her into despair.

When she heard scraping outside, she wondered if she'd now be attacked by some wild animal. Then, she heard whispering, someone calling her name. She struggled to stand up and look through the bars of the jail window.

Olivia stood in the moonlight wrapped tightly in a shawl, with a basket draped over her arm. When Tucker appeared at the bars, she stepped closer. She looked solemn, frightened.

"I brought you some food," she whispered.

Beautiful words to Tucker's ears. She smiled and thanked Olivia.

While Tucker chewed on the slab of meat wrapped in the heel of a sourdough loaf, Olivia pushed a small canteen of water through the food slot. Then she looked around in the darkness and said, "Lily put a gun in the outhouse."

Tucker looked up. "What? What the heck am I supposed to do with a gun?"

"I don't know. I told her it wasn't a very good idea, but she said it was the only one she could come up with. Next time you go to the outhouse, take it and use it at the best opportunity you can find. You've got to get out of here. Dunbar, the crazy beast of a barman, is telling everyone you need to be hanged and Cutter is riling up the sheriff, telling him you're a dangerous outlaw who should be drawn and quartered."

"I can't use a gun, especially on Joey. He's a little kid."

Olivia frowned at her. "Don't discount the danger Joey poses. He's not as innocent as he looks."

"He's got a gun, too, so what advantage does a gun give me? Am I supposed to have a gunfight with him? Anyway, I've never even fired a gun, but I'll bet he has." Desperation swirled around her as she spoke. "And I'll guarantee you he's a much better shot than I am."

"I don't know what else to say. It's the best we came up with. You'll have to figure something out. All I know is, if you stay here, you're dead."

Tucker stopped chewing. When she swallowed, it felt as if the bread stuck in her throat. "You're right. I don't have much choice, do I?"

Realizing Olivia and Lily plotted for her to escape, Tucker added, "So, have you and Lily made up? You feel different about her now?"

Olivia gave her a serious look. She didn't answer. Then she glanced around, her nervousness apparent. "Look, I've got to get out of here. They can't know I brought you food or I'll be joining you in there. Keep the canteen for now. Keep it out of sight. Joey won't come inside there. It's too dangerous. So chances are he won't know you have it."

Tucker put her hand out the food slot. "Thank you, Olivia."

Olivia grasped it for a second then said, "Don't thank me. Lily's the one who put me up to it. I told her this sounded like a crazy idea," she motioned toward the basket, now empty of food, "and the gun idea is even more foolish, but she wouldn't listen. She said we shouldn't let you waste away in here until they decided to do away with you." She licked her lips as she looked around again. "I've got to go."

"Wait," Tucker said. "You didn't answer me. It sounds like you and Lily came to a reconciliation of sorts. Is that true?"

Olivia gave her a weak smile. "You might say we've called a truce. After all, if we didn't put our heads together to help you, who would?"

Who would indeed? Tucker watched Olivia disappear into the darkness. She took another long draw from the canteen, then she peered around her holding cell, looking for a place to hide the flask, wondering if she'd be able to get out of this predicament without harming someone else—or getting herself hurt—or worse.

TUCKER CONTORTED HER long body onto a munchkin-sized bench to try to get some sleep. She dozed for a while, but the pain in her shoulder woke her. She knew from her experience earlier in the evening, if she tried to change positions without standing up first, she'd find herself face down on the ground, spitting dirt out from between her teeth.

She sat up on the edge of the bench, feeling groggy, irritable. She smelled the pungent, earthy scent of dirt and wondered if some got up her nose when she hit the ground earlier. She pulled at her nose and blew out. Nothing. She took a deep breath in and smelled—what was that smell—musty oak? Fireplace smoke? There was no heat source in the jail.

Then she saw it. The glow beyond the bars outside, orange, flickering—fire!

She sprang to the window. Below it she saw the pile of debris, flames jumping from leaf to branch and other rubble piled up into a small cone shape. Maybe the smell of smoke woke her, not her aches and pains. Tucker put her hand on the wall beside her. The jail was built a long time ago. The wood felt rough and very dry. It wouldn't take long to catch and start to burn. She knelt and felt along the bottom of the wall where she estimated the burning debris to be. She didn't feel any heat yet. Time might be on her side. But she needed to figure out how to get out of the locked cell. Panic set in, her breathing rate increased. She felt claustrophobic.

She wondered if Joey lurked close by. She shouted his name through the bars. In response, she heard the echo of her own voice and the incessant crackle of the fire. She screamed again, louder, "Jo-ey!"

Nothing.

Calm down, Tucker. This is no time to panic. There's a solution here. You simply need to find it. She took in a deep breath to try to calm herself, but when she smelled the smoke from the fire again, terror sprung up in her anew.

She tamped the panic back down, trying to get control over it, not allowing it to overwhelm her. She'd never be able to think if she did. Emotion propelled her back, away from the source of the smoke and fire. When her legs met the bench, she plopped down on it. Her foot hit something as she went down. Metal. The canteen. Water.

She popped up again and grabbed it from its hiding place. In her frightened state, the cork stopper resisted, refusing to yield to her fingers. No, fear didn't prevent her from opening the canteen, she realized. Her hand did. The hand she hit Dunbar with. Stiffness and swelling made it unyielding, unable to do her brain's bidding. She switched hands, holding the canteen in the crook of her arm. This time, she pulled the plug out with ease.

Swirling the container around, she estimated there to be a little more than a cup of water left in it. She tried to aim the spout through the bars, but they were too closely spaced together. She'd have to use the food slot below the window, but she'd have a narrower view of where she aimed and less directional control. The orange flames glowed brighter. The heat indicated the wall may have ignited. She forced the canteen halfway through the slot, but couldn't get enough of an angle on it to spill out the contents. While she tried to manipulate it, she screamed Joey's name several more times into the black night.

She managed to thrust some of the water through the slot and heard it sizzle as it hit the flames, but it didn't do much good. She looked out to the horizon and saw the first light of dawn and watched as an animal crested the top of Tenderfoot Hill. She concentrated on the outline—no, not an animal, a person. The specter stopped for a minute then took off running in her direction. As the form sped toward her, she recognized it. Joey. She hoped to God he held the key in his pocket. As she saw him coming toward her, she yelled his name again and grabbed one of the bars on the window.

The delay between her brain registering the searing heat and screaming at her to let go made her curse as she pulled away. When she glanced down at her palm, she watched several blisters form.

Much to Tucker's dismay, when Joey reached the jail, he kept going, running around the side of the building out of sight again. Panic overwhelmed her brief relief, but in seconds he materialized again with an old burlap sack and started beating at the fire with it. It did little to beat back the flames and forced him to retreat, giving up when the bag caught. To Tucker's horror, he threw it into the fire where it flared up even more, giving the flames more fuel.

"Joey, the key. Let me out. Please."

He stopped for a second and looked at her then tried to stomp out the edge of the flames. These attempts were even less effective than the sack.

"Joey, listen to me, the fire isn't near the door yet, but it will be. Soon. You've got to unlock the door and let me out before it gets there. Please, Joey."

The anguish in her voice may have caught his attention. Uncertainty filled her. She did know this would be her last chance. She tried again. "Joey, please. I don't want to die."

He stopped again, considering. "I can't." Smoke from the fire swirled all around him. The bright orange flames reflected off his skin and clothes.

Anger flared up in Tucker, fueled by desperation, matching the flames outside. Beyond begging now, she shouted, "Yes, you can and you will. Open. The damn. Door. Now!"

Joey jumped back, his eyes wide. He reached into his pants pocket, hesitated, looking at her again. Finally, he pulled out the key and Tucker breathed out a sigh of relief.

He fumbled the key in the lock. Tucker heard him groping, the metal scratching and scraping as he tried over and over to put the key in the keyhole. She waited and felt her anxiety crawling over her skin, like so many insects moving over her. She heard one final grinding noise and the door swung open with a grating squeal of its rusty hinges.

Tucker lunged for the opening in case Joey changed his mind and slammed it shut again. She knew she'd never get another chance. She pushed the door the rest of the way, harder than she'd planned. Adrenalin, she thought, as the door hit the boy in the shoulder and knocked him into the dirt. Tucker jumped over him like a gazelle.

As she landed, part of her thought she should stop, pick him up, dust him off, and make sure he wasn't hurt. But part of her, the part engaged in survival mode, kept running, faster than she ever knew herself capable.

With her first few steps, she heard him yell for her to stop. By then, she lost control over her feet. The rush coursing through her veins and muscles propelled her forward and she sped away from the fire and the jail—away from Tenderfoot Hill in the distance, away from Elder Creek.

By the time she reached the forested area of the foothills, tears flowed freely. She thought she might be crying in relief because she knew she could hide among the trees, find protection, and rest from her ordeal.

Then she realized the real reason for her tears. By escaping, she knew she'd never return to this Elder Creek. She would never see Lily Hart and Olivia Justice again. She escaped more than the jail, though. She escaped something deep within her psyche.

She kept running. A new sense of freedom washed over her.

Chapter Eight

TUCKER AWOKE TO the smell of pine forest. Her body hurt. Her hand hurt. When she tried to open her eyes, she found her eyelids unyielding, stuck together by dried tears. She needed to open them. Her mind insisted she run, get out of the forest, away from Elder Creek, make sure she held on to this new freedom she felt inside and out.

The specter of young Joey, lying on the ground, haunted her. Her last image of him as the fire raged nearby, of him flat on his back with the large skeleton key still firmly in his grip, loomed before her. She didn't know if he was dead or alive. Then she thought she remembered seeing him stir when she glanced over her shoulder as she ran.

A small pinpoint of light formed in the darkness of her psyche. Hope. Perhaps she only knocked the wind out of him when she escaped. She'd have to believe he'd escaped the fire, too. She didn't need to add another worry to her already overflowing bag of them. She tried to open her eyes again, desperate to be able to move away from this place. This time, she succeeded. When everything came into focus, confusion burned in her chest and her mind. She didn't see the forest as she expected. Instead, she saw her hotel room, but which hotel? Then? Or now?

She forced herself into a sitting position in her bed and concentrated on the nightstand. The digital clock read six forty-five. Morning, she thought, realizing the early morning sun streamed through an opening in the window curtain—on the window whose position also confirmed her presence in the here and now.

She blew out a breath of relief. Her hand trembled as she reached for her cell phone. She needed help. Her grip on reality felt so tentative. She made a phone call, exchanged a few words. Then, she blacked out.

WHEN SHE CAME to, she felt a little more in control—just a little. She no longer thought she'd find herself in the forest. When she concentrated on the clock on the nightstand again, she realized she'd only been out for about ten minutes. Her attempt at getting dressed proved to be awkward because her hand hurt so much, but she managed.

After dressing, she sat on the bed and stared at her palm. A bright red slash mark crossed it, but the skin appeared undamaged. But damn, it hurt as if it were blistered.

She remembered grabbing the bar on the jail window. Realized seconds later it burned too hot. Her muscles refused to obey her brain as it screamed at her to let go. She jerked her hand in pantomime, repeating the memory of pulling away from the searing heat of the jail bar. She fought to gain control again, panting, then slowly, with each breath, calm returned. Her breathing became more normal. The terror receded.

BY THE TIME Tucker stumbled out the front door of the hotel, she found Jackie sitting in her Mini Cooper, waiting for her. A thought crossed Tucker's mind as she folded herself into the car. After they implemented the living history plan for the town, motorized vehicles should no longer be allowed on Main Street to add to the authenticity. She didn't have the energy to voice the idea.

Once she settled herself inside the car and closed the door, Jackie took off like a bullet without waiting for Tucker to put on her seatbelt, something she usually insisted on. She looked over at Tucker as she drove and said, "You look like hell."

"Thanks. I love you, too." Tucker gripped her seat with her good hand. "Seriously, thanks for picking me up, Jackie. I'm not sure I'm fit to drive right now and I'm too sore to walk."

The car slowed and Jackie glanced over toward her. "Are you okay?"

"Not really."

Jackie picked up speed again and Tucker realized she was heading away from her house.

"Where are we going?"

"I called Leah. She's making us breakfast."

Tucker decided she shouldn't argue. She remained quiet for the remainder of the short trip.

LEAH OPENED THE front door when Tucker came toward her up the walkway. Her concern registered on her face. When Tucker stepped into the living room, the aroma wafting from the kitchen reminded her of her childhood and good days with her mom, and she felt comforted.

"Come into the kitchen." Leah motioned them to the back of the house. "Breakfast is almost ready. I have a vegetable frittata in the oven and the muffins are already cooling. I thought I'd make it an easy breakfast, so we can talk without interruption."

She walked over to the tiny TV sitting on the corner of the kitchen counter and turned the volume off. Tucker recognized the morning news program by the Portero local newscaster. A timer sounded, drawing Tucker's interest from the images on the screen.

Leah said, "The timer's for the frittata. Please, sit anywhere you two. I'll serve it up."

Tucker saw there were already three glasses of orange juice on the table along with coffee cups and silverware. Leah instructed them to pour their own coffee from the carafe in the middle of the table. When Tucker didn't act, Jackie grabbed her cup from in front of her and poured, doing the same with her own cup afterward.

Jackie sat fingering the cup in front of her, giving Tucker a look of grave concern. Tucker smiled, but she didn't telegraph much happiness. Jackie got up to help Leah and returned with a basket of muffins and a plate of the egg concoction. Leah followed with two more plates in hand.

They shoveled a few bites into their mouths in silence. Out of the corner of her eye, Tucker registered the picture on the television flickering as it changed from announcer to on-the-scene reporter. Lack of sound made it impossible to discern the topic of the news segment.

Jackie said, "Tucker, you need to get something in your stomach. Eat."

Tucker concentrated on her plate and lifted her fork to her mouth.

After she ate a few more bites, Jackie spoke again. "Okay, Tucker. Give. What's going on?"

She spoke haltingly at first. It took every ounce of determination she could muster to keep the tears from falling. She told them about Lily being harassed, the fight with Dunbar, and the jail. When she told them about Lily and Olivia's plot to rescue her, they both muttered appreciation for the women's ingenuity but voiced concern about using a gun. Tucker told them it didn't matter and added the details about the fire.

When Tucker showed them the red mark across her palm, Leah jumped up from her seat and disappeared into the next room. She returned with the thick, sappy leaf of an aloe plant, cradled Tucker's hand in hers, and slathered the clear juice over the mark. Tucker felt the cooling effect instantly. The sensitivity dissolved as Leah rubbed the fleshy side of the leaf over the mark a second time. Tucker relaxed.

Her eyes went to the TV again. The scene changed. On the screen, Tucker registered recognition of the familiar, ominous face. She jumped up from her seat so quickly, the aloe went flying. Leah grabbed at it, trying to catch it, but missed. Jackie sprang up and whisked a roll of paper towels from the counter, tearing off a few to wipe up the slippery mess on the floor.

Leah asked, urgency in her tone, "Tucker, what is it? What's going on?"

Tucker tore her attention away from the screen and pointed to it. Tightness squeezed at her throat as she asked, "Who is that guy?"

Now Leah and Jackie gave their full attention to the TV. A female reporter, a talking head, held a news sheet in front of her, her lips moving as she read. Behind her, a large, flat image of a man's face loomed on the screen over her shoulder.

Leah looked at Tucker, her brow furrowed in confusion. "He's the missing woman's boyfriend. The guy from Portero. Noll, maybe? North? No, Notch. I forget his first name."

"No," Tucker growled. The dread filled and surrounded her and made her voice shake. She took in a deep breath before she added, "His name is Dunbar—Nigel Dunbar. And he wants to kill me." As she said it, she heard the now familiar whisper rattle in her mind...*Forget*.

LEAH AND JACKIE stared at Tucker as she watched the silent images on the television change to a commercial. Leah switched the set off.

"Let's sit down," Jackie suggested.

Once they were seated, Leah spoke first, "Tucker, you've never seen Notch before?"

"I hardly ever watch TV and with all the extra work I've been doing for the town project, my writing, and my other distractions, I haven't caught much news. I have seen a couple of reports, but they never said anything about the boyfriend, and they never showed his picture. I've only heard from you two about him."

"Well, I never liked him from the first time I saw him on TV," Jackie said.

"My impression of him is he's sort of a strange bird," Leah added.

"And the only encounters I've experienced were with Dunbar, the bartender at The St. Charles Saloon in 1873. But Dunbar holds some extreme animosity against me. I've felt it from the first time I encountered him back there and I have no idea why.

"And something else has been happening to me. I keep hearing one word over and over again and it's bothering me a lot. I keep hearing the word 'forget' and I have no idea what it means, although now I'm realizing it's connected to this whole thing, whatever this is." She waved into the air, suggesting nothing—and everything—at the same time.

"Okay," Leah said, "let's take a deep breath and calm ourselves. Then, let's try to figure out how Tucker's Old West encounters, the missing girl, and the connection to this guy are related."

Jackie looked down at her half-empty coffee cup and pulled the carafe toward her. "I think I need more coffee."

Tucker said, "I think I need something stronger than coffee."

Leah walked over to the cupboard and pulled out a bottle of whiskey. She brought it to the table and dumped an unmeasured amount into the coffee in Tucker's cup. "This is all you get. You need to be clear-headed to figure this thing out."

Tucker picked up the cup and smelled it. It didn't smell unpleasant like the stuff she got from Dunbar. A fleeting thought wafted through her mind and she wondered if he tried to poison her, but she dismissed it quickly. As Leah stretched to put the bottle away, Tucker touched her arm and took the bottle from her. The label read Bushmills 16.

Impressive, she thought. How does a librarian afford such expensive and excellent whiskey? She handed the bottle back to Leah without remarking, picked up her cup and took a huge gulp.

The smooth, spiked coffee calmed Tucker. She felt the gears engage and questions popped into her consciousness like so many helium balloons rising into her line of sight. If she didn't commit them to memory, they might float away. "I need something to write with. Quick." She looked at Leah, pleading in her eyes.

Leah scrambled to the counter and pulled a lined pad and a mechanical pencil from a drawer. As soon as she handed it to Tucker, she started to scribble:

```
    Nigel Dunbar / Notch
    Leah is Lily
    Jackie is Olivia
    Why does Dunbar want to kill me?
    What does the missing girl have to do with
this?
    Start of it all: in front of Charlie - beat up
and confused - WHY?
    1873 - why incorrect articles in the
newspaper?
    Forget - What? Why?
```

Leah watched over Tucker's shoulder as she wrote, unable to offer any help.

Jackie took her phone out and looked at the time. "I'm afraid I've got to go. I'm opening The Charlie today. It's Tracey's day off. I wish I didn't have to go, but I must." She met Tucker's eyes. "I hope you understand."

Tucker stopped writing and said, "It's okay, Jackie, go."

Leah said, "No school for me today. It's a teacher's work day. I have some research to do. I thought I might go into the school later, but I can do what I need to do from home. I think I should stay with Tucker. I'm not sure how much help I can be, but I can offer moral support."

Tucker looked up from the list. "I scheduled a meeting with the mayor today for two o'clock. I'm going to call him and cancel. I think I'm coming down with something." She fake-coughed a few times and added, "I'd be grateful for your help, Leah, but if you need to take care of business, I'll understand. You go on, Jackie. We'll catch up later." She felt as if things were becoming more stable around her, although more and more questions filled her mind and no answers materialized.

Jackie gave each one of them a hug and let herself out.

Once Jackie left, Leah said, "I'm going to put a call in at school in case anyone looks for me." She left to use the phone in the living room.

Tucker called the mayor's office from her cell phone and made her excuses. When she hung up, she sat staring at the list she'd made, a scowl painted across her face. Leah found her still gazing down at it when she came into the kitchen.

"Having any luck?"

"None whatsoever," Tucker said. "It's so frustrating. I keep thinking I should understand all this. It's got to be related somehow, but I can't make any sense of it. I have this feeling there's something just out of reach, and I can't find it to grab onto it."

Leah gave her a sympathetic look.

Tucker drank the last of her augmented coffee. When she put the cup down, she said, "I don't suppose I can convince you to pour me some more of your Bushmills, can I?" She poked a thumb in the direction of the cupboard. "Maybe without the coffee this time?"

Leah blew out a breath. "You're incorrigible, you know? It's ten o'clock in the morning, for crying out loud."

She walked to the cabinet and removed the bottle and brought it to the table. Tucker noted the level of liquid in the bottle. By her estimation, only the small amount Leah put in her coffee earlier appeared to be missing.

Tucker looked up at Leah and said, "What's a nice librarian like you doing with such an expensive—and exquisite, I might add—bottle of whiskey like this?"

She thought she saw a shadow of something like sorrow pass across Leah's eyes. It disappeared as fast as it came.

"A gift," Leah said.

When Tucker realized she wouldn't say any more, she said, "Well, it helped calm my anxiety over all this. Thanks for being willing to share it."

"Wait," Leah said. She picked up the bottle and stared at it as if she might divine its secrets. When she looked back at Tucker, she said, "How much does this stuff cost, anyway?"

The grin on Tucker's face appeared slowly. "Promise me when I tell you, you won't take it away?"

"Depends."

"On what?"

"Tell me how much." Leah's voice carried an insistent tone now.

"About seventy-five bucks a bottle."

Leah stared at the flagon in her hand for a few seconds. Then she placed it carefully on the table and smiled. "I guess you're worth it, Tucker Stevens."

Tucker stretched her hand out toward the bottle, but Leah reacted faster and grabbed it back. "But only one small glass, do you hear me? You need to be clear-headed."

Tucker knew she was right. "Yes, ma'am," she said.

Leah deposited the bottle on the table again and walked to the cupboard. Standing on tiptoe, she removed two cut crystal glasses and brought them back to the table. As she put them down, she said, "Seventy-five-dollar whiskey should be served in glasses deserving of it, wouldn't you say?"

Tucker smiled.

"Only give me a mouthful. Unlike you, this stuff is *not* going to clear my head."

Tucker poured half a glass for herself and a finger-full for Leah. They lifted the glasses, toasted without words, and drank.

Leah took a tentative sip and proclaimed, "God, this is good."

"Indeed it is." Their eyes met and Tucker felt a tingle not entirely brought on by the superb quality of the alcohol. "Thanks for sticking with me on this weird journey, Leah. I appreciate it."

"What can I say, I'm a sucker for an adventure, and this promises to be a doozy." They each tipped their glasses to their mouths, making sure they got the last drops from them, then Leah added, "Okay, let's take a look at this list and see what we can figure out."

"HOW CLOSELY HAVE you been following the story of the missing girl? Do you know much about it?" Tucker asked.

"Only what I've seen on television," Leah replied. "Apparently, her parents reported she went silent several weeks ago. She called them regularly, according to the news reports, but then, the calls stopped and her parents got worried."

"So, she lived with this guy? Notch? In Portero?"

"Well, news reports have been confusing. The first claims said she did, but later they said she didn't. Then reports said she attended college in Monterey and she only knew Notch as a professional associate, interested in some New Age theories of his. But the last report I heard returned to them possibly being involved in a relationship again. The details have been so muddled, with most of the confusion coming from him, contradicting what the police have to say. But no matter how you look at it, this Notch guy is certainly questionable."

Tucker watched as Leah's eyes widened in surprise or astonishment.

"Demetrius," Leah shouted.

Tucker stared, puzzled.

Leah added, "His first name. Demetrius Notch. He bills himself as a hypnotist and New Age guru over in Portero. Conducts sessions to cure people of all kinds of things: smoking, weight issues, mental illness."

Tucker raised an eyebrow. "Mental illness? I would think a claim like that would get him into trouble with the medical establishment."

"He says he's some kind of doctor. If he is, there's something fishy about his bedside manner. Anyway, I'm glad I finally remembered his name. It would have driven me crazy until I did."

"Speaking of being driven nuts: hearing the word 'forget' every time I think about certain things, repeating over and over again, is driving me to the point of thinking I might lose my mind. It's one of the reasons I thought—"

"Tucker, you are not losing your mind. Something's going on in your subconscious and we've got to figure out what it is. This guy—this Demetrius Notch—is somehow related to it."

Tucker looked down at the list. She picked up the pencil and added the name Demetrius after Notch's last name.

She stared at the list, repeating the names over and over to herself.

Nigel Dunbar / Notch - Demetrius

At last, she looked up at Leah and said, "It's the same initials. Nigel Dunbar, ND. Demetrius Notch, DN, ND." She looked at the list again. Leah Hudson, Lily Hart. Jackie O'Malley, Olivia Justice.

"They're all the same initials. Some are reversed, but they're all the same," Leah said. "Maybe your brain put us into the wrong context and gave us different names while giving clues to our own names as a means to get your attention."

"But what about the newspaper? Why would the newspaper contain information about things from the previous year as if they were happening right then, and report on other things from far into the future, another year or more?"

"I don't know. Another attention-getting device?"

"Maybe, but it might be too easy an explanation. There's got to be more to all this. The only problem is, how the heck am I going to decipher it all? And what does it have to do with the missing girl?"

"We should call the police," Leah said.

"And tell them what? I've been having these strange experiences, these incidents of something in my head, where people I know are in the wrong time and place with names containing the same initials, only different and backwards, and this guy I've never seen before is in these visions and I have no idea what it all means?" Sarcasm filled her voice as she added, "But it means something, officer, I'm sure of it."

They stared at each other. Then, Leah said, "I guess it's a bad idea, huh?"

"At least until we figure out something substantial—until we have something to tell them where I don't sound like an escapee from a mental institution."

Leah opened her mouth to protest.

Tucker stopped her before she objected. "I know. Yes, I now realize I'm not losing my mind. Unfortunately, until we can figure this out a little more, I'll still sound crazy to the police."

Leah said, "Well, one thing is for sure, Tucker. It's obvious this has something to do with the missing girl. So let's start working on this problem so we'll have something concrete to tell the police soon."

"Fine with me, but where do you suggest we start?"

"Let's start by looking at all the news reports about the girl we can find online. It'll help refresh my memory about what I've heard and we can both learn anything new to help us."

They spent the morning looking at news clips. *Portero News* reported conflicting information at first. They finally settled on the girl being from Monterey, a college student with an interest in metaphysics. She met Notch at a conference in the nearby town of Seaside, where she went to school. They became friends, the reports said. She often came to Portero to spend time with him, possibly studying with him.

With a hint of sarcasm in her voice, Leah remarked, "Yeah, I'll bet he studied her instead of the other way around."

They continued their review of online information. One of the reports they found said Notch and the young woman were in a relationship, but her parents said she told them she wanted to break it off. Shortly after, Notch appeared on TV, crying big crocodile tears, as Jackie described it. He did put on quite a show, pleading for the young woman's return, saying he cared about her and wanted her back in his life. Shortly after his appearance, another report reiterated the police were still looking at Notch as a person of interest, but a follow-up report, soon after, said the police cleared him.

As they already knew, news spread of the missing girl's story. They found news reports from Sacramento, San Francisco, Fresno, and Los Angeles, but no new information. The girl disappeared without a trace, and the authorities started speculating she was a run-away, in spite of the fact that there was nothing to support the theory. True, she gave the impression of being a little flighty at times, in her parents' estimation, but she always behaved responsibly in the end. She'd never exhibited any desire to run away. They didn't like her taking up with an older man, but they tried to be supportive because they didn't want to alienate her. They didn't want to do anything to put her in danger because of their actions. Tucker and Leah remarked about the evident remorse and pain on the parents' faces as they spoke, wracked with guilt over what they may have done differently.

"Man, what a rotten situation," Leah said as she closed the last report on the computer screen.

They sat in silence, letting the information soak in. Leah said, "I keep wondering if we're missing something—if there's some kernel of information we aren't paying attention to. Something might be key and we're not recognizing it."

Tucker stood up and started pacing around the small bedroom office. "All this information is good to know, I'm sure, but I don't see how it can help me. Let's think about what I know from back in 1873, see if I can get a bead on something from back then in light of everything we now know."

"Okay, but let's do it in the kitchen or the living room."

Tucker stopped pacing. "Okay, but, out of curiosity, why do we have to go to another room?"

"Because you're making me dizzy." Leah laughed and pushed Tucker out of the tiny office.

Tucker plopped down on a seat at the kitchen table and stared at the list again. "How do you suppose Demetrius Notch ended up in my head as Dunbar when I never saw the guy before today?"

"Are you sure you've never met him? Seen him on the street in Portero, maybe?"

"I guess it's possible I may have passed him on the street, but I've never met him. And why would he be haunting me like this?"

Forget.

There it was again, the word. "Why do I keep hearing the word 'forget'? It's driving me crazy."

"What does it sound like? Is it the voice of anyone you know?"

"I don't think so. It's another voice, not the voices I usually hear in my head." Tucker chuckled at her own joke.

Leah cocked her head, a curious look on her face.

Tucker added, "You know, when I'm writing, I hear the character's voices in my head."

Leah cocked her head to the other side and scrunched up her brow.

"Never mind. It's a writer thing."

"You'll have to explain it to me one day," Leah said. "But what do you mean by 'another voice'?"

"It's like someone else is whispering the word in my ear, over and over again. It happens every time I think about Dunbar or something associated with him, like Lily. And why does Dunbar want to kill me? I'm sure he made the sheriff throw me in jail to keep me from snooping around and taking up Lily's time. I'm almost as certain he's the one who started the fire outside the jail. I thought maybe jealousy drove him because he thought I got too close to Lily, but now, I'm not so sure. Maybe there's another reason. Maybe it's something I've *for-got-ten*." Her elongation of her last word made it reverberate in her mind again.

That voice. She was convinced she'd heard it before, but where?

Leah shook her from the question with one of her own. "The other day you told me this all started when you staggered from The Charlie, banged up and confused. Right?"

"That's correct."

"Do you remember actually being inside The Charlie before any of this happened?"

"No. And actually, it was closed when it happened."

Forget.

"What about the year 1873? When we looked through the newspapers, nothing stuck out as significant news that year. Do you think the year itself means anything?"

The numbers materialized in her mind's eye like numbers on a page. One-eight-seven-three. They appeared bold and dark, surrounded by a halo of light.

Forget.

How bizarre. "I have no idea why it would be that particular year," she said. She ran her hand through her long, mahogany hair, frustration washing over her.

Chapter Nine

A WEEK LATER, Tucker sat at a table at the front of the small Elder Creek Elementary School auditorium at a community meeting.

"The next item on the agenda is our plan to open the mine."

Someone from the crowd said, "I'm not so sure that's a good idea, Tucker."

Her brow furrowed as she scanned the audience for the speaker. Before she figured it out, someone else spoke. This time, he stood to identify himself.

"We've heard opening the mine would be too dangerous. We think you should forget—"

She heard nothing more. The word "forget" echoed in her brain. Her skin went pale. She plopped into her chair. In the background she heard the crowd roar in protest. She'd lost all control. As she struggled to refocus on the meeting, she saw the mayor, who sat beside her, raise his eyebrows as chaos erupted around them.

She pushed the reverberating word from her mind and wished she'd brought something to use as a gavel to rap on the table in front of her, but she'd only taken a pen and a few sheets of paper with her.

As the chaos continued, the mayor leaned over and said, "I think you better do something, Tucker."

She returned a look of panic and gazed around in the midst of the hubbub. When she spotted a huge hunk of worn wood by the door to the stage behind them, apparently used for a doorstop, she jumped up and hurried over to it and watched her hands shake as she clamped onto it. It took all her effort not to lose her grip. When she returned to the table, she took a deep breath, trying to calm herself as the bedlam continued all around her. She lifted the block above her head. It felt so heavy, more like an anvil than a block of wood. Rather than lose control of it, she let the weight of it carry her arms down as it slammed on the surface with a loud bang. She didn't know where she found the strength to lift it two more times. Each time, she felt a little calmer, strength returning to her limbs, and she heard the room noise quiet a little with each loud explosion on the table surface. When she lifted it again, she saw three large dents in the tabletop.

She regretted the damage, but it did the job. The people in the room froze. The commotion stopped. Everyone turned their attention to Tucker.

She took in a deep breath, hoping to convey her thoughts forcefully enough to get people beyond the figurative blockades they tried to erect.

"Look," Tucker said. "This idea has been on the table for weeks now and none of you have come forward with one good reason about why we shouldn't do this or suggest what we should put in its place to have a decent draw to keep this town alive. There have only been a couple of vocal dissenters, and most of those questions and concerns have been addressed." She exaggerated, she knew, but desperation drove her to get a handle on the situation.

The man who stood up before all hell broke loose stepped forward to speak. "We've been concerned, but we weren't sure if the rumors we heard were true. Then Joe Dawson said—"

"Joe Dawson is a gossip and a rumor monger and you shouldn't be listening to him. He's just trying to stir up trouble and make sure nothing changes in this town. If you want to listen to him, you'll all end up with a ghost town with worthless property values."

The man's eyes widened. He held up his hands in surrender and melted back into the crowd.

She glanced over at Leah, who sat in the front row. She wore a smirk, leading Tucker to believe she tried to control a bigger grin from erupting. Although Tucker wanted to stay focused on those luscious lips, she knew she'd lose her train of thought if she did.

The Curmudgeons remained silent tonight. They both sat in the audience without uttering a peep, and now Tucker sent up a prayer of gratitude to the Universe for small favors and a quart of root beer.

The attendees shuffled and took their seats again. The rumbling of quiet conversation dissipated until only a cough and some rustling of people settling back into place broke the silence.

Tucker inhaled deeply and said, "Mine tours will be a real shot in the arm to the town's coffers. It will mean infrastructure improvements everyone here wants to see, and the people who will come for these tours will spend time in our hotel, they'll buy meals in our restaurants and saloons, and they'll purchase goods and souvenirs from our shops."

A low murmur rolled through the crowd like a wave at a

football game. Then everything went silent again.

"And when these people come into town, they'll gain something in return. They'll be able to get a sense of the history here, and they'll leave with an appreciation for the people who founded this place and the hard work we've done to preserve it. We can't let myths and tall tales used to keep children from misbehaving stop the momentum we've started. Elder Creek has unlimited potential to become a great town again, like back in the Gold Rush days and in the years following. Maybe it can be even better. We can't merely throw this opportunity away. If we do, Elder Creek may head the way of other abandoned towns in the state—boarded up, empty has-beens, drawing people to walk dusty streets and gawk in windows at the leavings of our existence. I don't think anyone wants to be a party to turning Elder Creek into a ghost town."

A few mutters came from the crowd. Tucker continued before they died away, trying to prevent another uproar.

"We need the mine as our centerpiece. We need to have this draw. If we make it entertaining, interesting and throw in a little bit of history, everything else will flow from it. People will come to Elder Creek and spend their time and their money here, and who here wants to stand in the way of something so productive?"

She called off the names of some of the people who surprised her with objections a few minutes before. Most were merchants who owned small businesses in the town. She knew singling them out would call them to accountability for their unfounded reservations. When she finished the list, she added, "If you don't want an increase in business, if you don't want this town to thrive, then you'd better say so, right here, right now. Go on record right in front of your friends and neighbors, otherwise, we proceed as planned."

A deafening silence followed. She said nothing. People shuffled uncomfortably in their seats. Someone at the back of the room coughed again. No one spoke until Tucker finally continued, "I don't hear any objections. This is your last chance." Again, she waited. "Then we'll open the mine. I'll arrange to have someone come in to do a safety inspection, and we'll see what needs to be done to make sure our guests and our guides are safe, first and foremost. We'll also ask for local volunteers to do a thorough inventory of what's inside the mine to make sure we don't have any surprises." She refrained from a sarcastic remark about finding rumored ancient dead bodies inside.

"Jackie, would you send a sign-up sheet around so people

can volunteer to do the walk-through with us. Anyone who volunteers will have to be able-bodied because we may need to crawl around a bit. We have no idea what it will be like in there.

"After we get those two inspections finished, we'll do what needs to be done to get the mine opened for anyone to tour and you merchants can get ready for an increase in revenue."

The murmuring from the crowd sounded more upbeat this time.

"The rest of you townsfolk can get ready to see improvements we'll all be happy with, I'm sure. I can't see any reason anyone will have a problem with positive changes, things like improved roads and city services, can any of you?"

Heads shook back and forth. She saw a few faces brighten, saw some smiles. The buzz in the room took on a much more positive feel. She knew she succeeded. They'd open the mine and get things moving. Elder Creek would get the shot in the arm it needed. For the first time since they opened the topic for discussion, Tucker smiled.

Then she said, "I have one more proposal regarding the mine."

The noise in the room ebbed.

"Since a lot of people in this town voiced some negative reactions at the mention of the Reddman Mine, and since it's been abandoned for a lot of years now, not belonging to anyone in particular and actually claimed by the town itself anyway, I propose we change the name to the Elder Creek Mine or something similar. A new name will give it a fresh start with a new purpose and great possibilities. The Elder Creek Mine will give us nothing but positive returns. What do you say?"

She looked at the mayor to see if he approved. She never thought to discuss a name change with him ahead of time. When she saw him grinning from ear-to-ear, she knew he accepted the proposal. The hum in the room grew to a crescendo. Finally, one of the merchants shouted above the noise. "I think it's a great idea, Tucker. I think we should put it to a vote right now."

"Thank you, Mr. Jenkins," Tucker yelled.

She didn't want to do any more damage to the table than she'd already done, so she held up both arms, waiting for quiet. When the crowd settled down, she lowered them and said, "Okay, folks, you heard the man. All those in favor of renaming the Reddman Mine to now be called The Elder Creek Mining Company, signify by saying 'aye.'" She made up the new name on the fly, smiling wider at the sound of it.

The crowd's assent reverberated off the walls. Tucker eyed everyone in the room, then added, caution and a bit of warning in her voice, "Opposed?"

No one spoke. More shoe scuffs and a cough or two followed. She picked up the block of wood in both hands and slammed it down on the table again. She'd apologize to the school for the damage later.

"So moved. The Elder Creek Mining Company is now the centerpiece of the Elder Creek revitalization project. Thank you, everyone. This meeting is adjourned."

The noise pitch rose again as people got up from their seats and started moving around, engaging friends and neighbors in conversation. Tucker walked over to the mayor as he rose from his seat.

He shook her hand with enthusiasm and said, "Quite a speech you gave tonight, Tucker. It certainly made *me* want to jump up and shout my support. I knew we picked the right person for this job. Thanks for all the hard work you're doing."

Tucker's cheeks colored at the compliment. "No problem, Mr. Mayor. I signed on to see this to completion and I'm determined to do it."

"Renaming the mine was quite a master stroke. You know we didn't need a vote, though, don't you? The core revitalization committee has the authority to make such changes. It's part of the charter."

"Yes, I know, Mayor, but since everyone appeared to be swept up into the spirit of it, I thought it best to let everyone have their say. Now, they own their decision. I don't think we'll have much trouble going forward. Anyone who objects after this will find themselves standing alone. And most people in town will put any naysayers in their places quickly."

The mayor agreed.

When several people approached them, wanting to shake Tucker's hand, she obliged until they wandered toward the mayor to engage him in conversation. Tucker took the first opportunity to look for Jackie and Leah.

She found them pouring a red-colored liquid, punch no doubt, into small paper cups from a huge punch bowl. When she approached Leah, she handed Tucker the cup, then poured another for herself.

"I'll bet the meeting went better than you thought it would," Leah said with a smile.

Jackie joined them and chimed in, "Yeah, for a while there, I thought they might string you up when you started on the mine, but I've got to hand it to you, you pulled it off without a hitch. It looks like they love the idea now. Look around, everyone's smiling. We might have to start calling you The Magician after the rabbit you pulled out of your hat tonight."

They all laughed. The people in the room, including Jackie, faded. Leah's eyes danced as she held Tucker's gaze. Tucker's heart raced. Then, Jackie called Tucker's name. Asked her where she was, since she obviously wasn't listening to her. Leah laughed at the question. The sound of her mirth took Tucker's breath away. The other people in the room came back into Tucker's view. She cleared her throat and directed her attention to Jackie. "I'm sorry. What did you say?"

Jackie looked from Leah to Tucker. "Never mind," she said. "It's not important."

They continued watching the crowd. The energy in the room reflected the good mood of the gathering. People stood in small groups, laughing, talking, all with smiles on their faces.

One section of the crowd opened up as people shifted about. Some headed for the door to leave, some changed their positions in the room to talk to a new group. Was that familiar figure Joe Dawson's that appeared in the newly created opening?

"Is that Joe Dawson?" Tucker asked. She glanced back at Jackie. "I didn't know he'd returned."

"Neither did I," Jackie said.

Jackie inched closer to Tucker, and they both craned their necks as the group reorganized again and the gap closed.

"Where is he?"

"I don't know," Tucker said. "It looks like he's disappeared again."

SEVERAL HOURS AFTER the meeting, Tucker and Leah sat in the empty Charlie, drinking a local draft Jackie served them. Jackie was busy training Denise Miller-Sanchez in the process of closing up the bar at night. Jackie and Denise chatted quietly while Denise stacked glasses into a large rack to take to the dishwasher in the back room. Jackie wiped down the bar surface with a bar towel.

Leah said, "Jackie told me you saw Joe Dawson at the meeting."

"I think I did, anyway, but he left before I got a chance to talk to him."

"Are you still thinking about him for the recycling project?"

"I'm not sure. If he's going to disappear the way he did, then it means we can't depend on him. I might have to find another way to do it. Maybe you, Jackie and I can put our heads together to see if we can figure out something else. I'd hate to have to hire a recycling contractor from Portero. It'll cost a lot more than if we let Joe take a cut, but we've got to do something so we're prepared for the influx of people once we get up and running."

"Well, we still have time to work all those details out, don't we?"

"Yeah, a bit. Anyway—" Tucker broke out in a sly grin,"—I'll put it on Jackie's list to worry over. I've got other things to think about. With the town's buy-in to proceed with the mine, there will be a lot to do."

"By the way," Leah said, "What a stroke of genius that was to rename the mine."

Tucker's smile widened. "I'm a regular Albert Einstein, aren't I?"

"Yeah, Einstein, now what are you going to do about that list of questions you're carrying around in your pocket? The ones about what's going on with you and your other experiences of late?"

Tucker's smile changed to a grimace.

"By the way," Leah continued, "I did some snooping around the internet. Apparently, Notch is big in some strange fringe circles. He bills himself as *Professor* Notch, but I found nothing on any actual degrees he may have earned from a reputable university. His biography is very vague about his education, too.

"He dabbles in a lot of different areas. He's given workshops and spoken at conferences—mostly, of the New Age variety. His theories have gotten stranger and stranger over the years. He gained popularity on the circuit about ten years ago, but lately, he's not been so much of a star."

"So what types of things is he into?" Tucker asked.

"At first there were workshops on the use of hypnotism. Pretty common stuff. Hypnotism to get positive results in life's little problems like smoking cessation, weight loss, insomnia, all kinds of problems like that. Later on, the information says he gives talks on numerology, reincarnation, psychic ability. The most recent information I found said he held private gatherings in small groups consisting of sessions in iridology and psytrance, nystagmus—"

Tucker held up her hands. "Whoa! You lost me on those last

ones. What the heck are iridology and psy-whatever — and that last one?"

As Tucker waited for Leah to respond, she felt a tickle in places she didn't want to think about.

"I needed to look them up, myself. Weird stuff. Maybe even bordering on the occult. Iridology's been around for a long time, but it's certainly not popular anymore. It's the study of people's eyes, the irises more specifically, to diagnose ailments. It's basically been debunked as not founded in science. But he took a different tack with it, claiming he could predict what people should be doing with their lives and their livelihoods by looking at their eyes."

Tucker raised an eyebrow.

Leah continued, "Yes, I know, strange stuff."

"Who would believe in such a thing?" Tucker asked.

"I have no idea, but apparently people are paying him to attend his sessions."

"And this psy-whatever. What is it?"

"Psytrance. It's using music to put people into a religious-type trance. The music oscillates at certain frequencies, causing people to go into a dazed state."

"Like Sufism? The guys who twirl?"

"Dervishes," Leah said. "I didn't find anything to associate the two, I'm not sure Sufism wants to be associated with Psytrance. Besides, the Sufi religion is thousands of years old. Psytrance is much newer."

"New Age?"

"Yes, like New Age, but believe me, even most New Agers don't want to be involved with it. It's considered a little too fringe-y. Then there's the whole nystagmus thing."

"Oh, do tell. I can't wait to hear this one." Tucker's voice dripped with sarcasm.

"Nystagmus is actually a medical issue, where people have involuntary rapid eye movement from side to side. But, like psytrance, some people swear it will send you to nirvana if you do it right — and no music is required." Leah smiled at her own joke. "But it's clear Notch was well on his way into the land of weirdness with all this, and some people were actually packing their bags to make the journey with him. Apparently, Amy Hammersmith, the missing girl, joined them. She appeared to be gaga over the guy. It's why she spent so much time in Portero."

"Sitting at the feet of the guru?" Tucker asked.

"Evidently."

Tucker absorbed the information.

"Do you think she disappeared off to some cabin in the woods staring at her irises in a mirror and practicing her psycho-whatever? Maybe nothing's happened to her at all and she's somewhere without a television and doesn't even know there's this big to-do over her being gone."

Leah sat quietly, staring down at her hands.

"Leah?"

She didn't look up.

"What's wrong, Leah?"

She looked up. Tucker recognized sadness in her eyes. "They found her car this morning. Someone set it on fire on some abandoned property several miles north of Pine Grove. Her purse and phone were in the car."

"Did they find her in the car?" Tucker asked.

"No. The police say they didn't find any trace of her, but the whole 'to-do,' as you call it, has started up all over again. Portero is in turmoil. The New Age community is up in arms, too. They interviewed a couple of their people on the news this morning. They are denouncing Notch and his beliefs and practices. None of them want to be associated with him. He's becoming an outcast."

"Sounds like he already achieved pariah status, but if they're decrying him on TV, they're probably making it official. I guess a place like Portero, which tends to attract people and businesses from the New Age movement, can also attract weirdos. So, is Notch a suspect again?"

"The police aren't saying. Apparently, they've tightened up on information. They've circled the wagons, so to speak. You know something's up when the police spokesperson answers every reporter's question with the same procedural citation over and over about not wanting to compromise the investigation by commenting on whatever a particular reporter asked. Before I left for the meeting tonight, all the TV interviews were like that."

Tucker and Leah drank the rest of their beers in silence. The information Leah gave Tucker about Notch's practices proved interesting and supported the theory that Notch was a strange goose. Most likely he wasn't to be trusted, but what his connection with Dunbar was and why she encountered him back in 1873 still qualified as a mystery to her. Something about all this should make sense to her, but it remained out of her grasp, just out of reach. If she grabbed for it, it would disappear—but what was it?

Forget.

Frustration boiled up inside of Tucker's chest. Right now, that word, more than anything, was driving her nuts.

Forget.

She couldn't take it anymore.

Forget.

She felt as if fire ants were running all over her body, compelling her to get up and run.

Tucker jumped up and shifted from one foot to another. "Are you okay with getting home on your own? I need to get out of here."

Leah gave her a curious look. "I'll be fine. Don't worry about me."

Before the words were out of Leah's mouth, Tucker darted out The Charlie's front door. The look of concern on Leah's face brought Jackie over to the table in a rush.

JACKIE LOOKED TOWARD the door and said, "Is something wrong with Tucker?"

"I'm not sure," Leah replied. "We were talking about Notch and some information I found on him on the internet. He's an extremely strange bird, by the way. Then I told her about the latest report on the missing girl—how they found her abandoned car burned. Did you hear about it?"

Jackie said, "Someone at the meeting told me."

"She got very quiet by the end of our conversation. Then she started squirming and jumped up from her seat, like it was on fire, and asked if I was okay to go home by myself. When I told her I'd be fine, she practically ran out of here."

"Do we need to go after her?"

"I don't know. Maybe we'd better let her be for now."

"Okay," Jackie said. "But tomorrow morning, I'm going to drag whatever's going on inside her head out in the open."

Leah smiled for the first time since Tucker bolted. "Sounds like breakfast at my house again."

Jackie gave Leah a wide grin. "Your breakfasts are the best."

Leah looked apprehensive. Jackie stared toward the door, worry lines appearing across her brow.

After a few moments, Leah said, "I hope she's okay. I'm concerned. I'm not so sure about giving her some space. If I knew where she went, I think I'd go after her."

"I think I might know," Jackie said.

"Should we go look for her, then?"

Jackie hesitated. "Maybe I'd better go alone."

Leah grew quiet. "Are you afraid we might spook her if we go together?"

"Yes."

"Then go. I can get home fine. I have my car."

"Okay, but let me close up. I'll follow you in my car. Tucker will kill me if I let you go by yourself."

Leah didn't protest.

TUCKER SAT STARING up at the stars, wondering if the sky looked any different in 1873. She may have been a history buff, especially about the Old West, but she knew almost nothing about astronomy. However, she certainly appreciated the sky on a night like tonight.

On this moonless night, with no reflected light in the sky to dull the spectacular sight above her, Tucker stared as stars shimmered against an indigo background. In some areas of the heavens, it looked as if someone dipped a wide paintbrush in a bucket of stars and swiped the brush across the night sky.

She breathed deeply and thought of Leah. Leah should be here, sitting beside her, taking in this breathtaking sight above her head. Yet it always looked as if Tucker was pulling away from her, fear and confusion getting in the way of what promised to be a very rewarding relationship. Tucker sighed.

Leah's beauty, like the sky above her, stunned her. Her intelligence fascinated her. Her sexiness amazed her—and she must stop thinking about Leah. Her feelings for Leah added one more layer of distraction to the one big frustration swirling around her. She needed to make sense of it.

Deep down inside, she knew she should be able to sort through all the clues. All she required was the ability to fit them together. She touched her shirt pocket, the one holding the list she wrote days ago. She hoped touching it might trigger something. She didn't take it out. The darkness wouldn't allow her to read it, anyway. It didn't matter. She knew the list by heart.

The clues spread out before her were like a ten-thousand-piece puzzle begging to be put together. She needed to make sense of them and hardly knew where to start. Worse than having a missing piece or two, there might be some extra pieces, useless bits, which might cause her some problems, sending her scurrying in the wrong direction looking for answers that didn't even matter. She sighed. Where should she start? She looked at the black expanse of sky again, watching the twinkling lights, and quieted, waiting for inspiration.

As a kid, during the good times, she and her mom worked puzzles on cold winter nights. They would sit in quiet comfort, drinking hot chocolate, sometimes with miniature marshmallows floating in the cocoa colored liquid if there were any in the house. Time passed slowly, comfortably, as they patiently fitted piece after piece together until the picture in front of them bloomed like a flower to match the one on the puzzle box cover. Her problem at present was the missing cover.

They always started with the edges. Tucker stopped, the thought striking her. You can always identify an edge, her mom used to say. If you start with the edges, you have someplace to build from. They never looked at the picture once they started with these pieces. They didn't need to. The edges give you information without the picture.

A potential answer? She needed to look at all the peripheral information. Maybe along the way, she'd figure out if there were any extra pieces, not matching the picture when it began to form from the border. Eventually, she might be able to put those extras aside and not be distracted by them.

Now, what did she know about this whole situation? She began by recalling her stumbling out of The Charlie weeks ago.

THE MEMORY WASHED over her in waves. She hunched over beside the door of The Charlie, holding herself up against the wall so she wouldn't slide down to the boardwalk and end up sitting down. She felt her body tremble. If she ended up on her butt, she knew she would never be able to get back up. Darkness surrounded her as she tried to catch her breath and work through an unknown fear. She heard a vehicle rumble to life and drive down the street, but her eyes wouldn't open to allow her to see it. The noise made her head hurt. Relief filled her when the racket faded away and the acrid smell of exhaust dissipated. A dog bark pierced the air from several streets over, then everything went quiet again. She willed herself to open her eyes, but her eyelids felt so heavy she couldn't make them obey. Finally, she managed to pry open one eye. When she looked around, a pain stabbed her through her forehead, but she was able to see The Charlie's windows were dark, except for a small nightlight behind the bar.

"No," Tucker said into the night. "I was never in the saloon.

I'm positive now. I was only on the outside. The Charlie was closed." She felt a wave of nausea, reliving the sensation of her body being dragged from a vehicle and hurled onto the boardwalk in front of the saloon. Several puzzle pieces clicked together. "I was dropped off in front by someone." This single memory gave her a small section of the puzzle and, in an instant, she knew the truth. She wasn't losing her mind. It happened. She didn't know who dropped her off or what part the mystery person played in it, but something actually happened to her.

Forget.

She spoke into the darkness. "I was somewhere else before The Charlie. But where?"

Forget.

Tucker blew out her breath, feeling the fear accompanying the word until a different emotion began to emerge.

Anger rose up inside her. She let the rage bubble up. She wouldn't allow this to beat her. She already knew more now than a few minutes ago. An edge of the puzzle formed. As she suspected, nothing happened inside The Charlie to make her stagger from it. Something happened in front of the saloon. Whatever else went on, where it happened, it occurred in the here and now, not back in 1873.

She tried to allow the experience to flow over her again. In her subconscious, she heard the rattle and rumble of a vehicle. She'd been dumped in front of The Charlie.

Think, Tucker, think. Where were you before being dumped? What were you doing?

Forget.

It was like looking into a smoke-filled room. Nothing came to her.

Well, she acknowledged the new information. It was a start. An edge, a very small piece of an edge allowed her some insight. She'd have to take the tiny fragment of information and build on it. She gazed up at the beauty of the sky again, breathed deeply, and knew with certainty she was on the right track.

Tucker felt drained, but she knew she wasn't ready to go back to the hotel and sleep. Besides, the opportunity to be out here like this, sitting on Tenderfoot Hill in the dark, felt good. The last time she'd sat up here she made the decision to leave Elder Creek, strike out into the world on her own by accepting the scholarship to college she'd been offered.

When she heard footsteps crunching on the loose stones, her heart jumped and she wondered if she should get up and run, but when she turned toward the sound, she barely made out the outline of Jackie's silhouette in the dark.

Jackie came closer. She spoke in a gentle tone as if she were afraid to scare Tucker off.

"What are you doing up here, Tucker?"

"I needed some time to think."

Jackie chuckled. "You always did do your best thinking up here. No wonder you want to live on this hill."

Tucker smiled at Jackie's insight, but she doubted her friend saw her face in the darkness.

"What made you look for me up here?"

"I know you, Tucker. When we were kids and something bothered you, you'd always come up here. You've got a lot on your mind lately, so I figured this was the most logical place to look when you took off from The Charlie the way you did."

Tucker waited a few beats before asking, "Did Leah get home okay?"

"You'll be happy to know I made sure she got in her car safely, and then I followed her home and waited for her to let herself in before I decided to come and search for you."

"Thanks, Jackie."

Jackie sat down on the little patch of grass next to Tucker. "You care about her, don't you?"

The silence stretched out all around them before Tucker answered. "I care for her a lot. But—"

"Tucker, cut the 'but' crap. You worry too much. One thing I know for sure, Leah cares for you, too. I know there's a lot going on right now, but having someone who cares deeply for you will help. Stop trying to shut Leah out."

Tucker turned toward Jackie, her face barely visible in the darkness.

"Cares deeply? Does Leah care deeply? Did she say those words?"

"She doesn't have to, Tucker. It's written all over her face when you two are together. She's smitten, and, by the way, so are you."

Tucker looked down at her hands—hands she barely saw in front of her. "Am I?"

"Yes, Tucker, you are."

They sat listening to the crickets for a long time before Tucker spoke again. This time, she spoke so softly, she thought Jackie might not have heard her. "I know."

When she said it, even in the black of night, Tucker saw her white, wide grin.

"That's my girl," Jackie said.

TUCKER AND JACKIE sat on Tenderfoot Hill for a while longer. Tucker told her about the puzzle pieces and how she figured out her error—falling through The Charlie's front door—and how she now suspected she was never inside at all but was dropped there by someone who drove her from somewhere else.

"Dropped off? Somewhere else? Tucker, you need to tell this to the sheriff."

"Jackie, calm down. I didn't share this with you to make you upset."

"But you don't know what happened out there. You could have been—"

"I wasn't raped, if that's what you're thinking."

Jackie stared at her before asking, "How do you know? You can't remember."

"I can't remember the details of what happened, but somehow, I can't explain it, but I know this—whatever it was—wasn't rape. It's about something else."

"What? What's it about, Tucker?"

"If I knew the answer to that, I would have fewer problems, wouldn't I?"

"Then how can you say for sure you weren't sexually assaulted?"

"It's instinct or something. I can't explain it. Besides, I have no sign whatever that anything like that happened. You have to trust me on this one, Jackie. I am positive nothing like that happened. This is about something else entirely."

Jackie blew out a breath. Tucker could tell she was finally calming down.

"Don't you see, I'm remembering. It's just a small piece, but I'm finally figuring it out. It's a good thing. I'm putting the puzzle together. If I can fit more pieces together, I might actually see the whole picture."

"Okay, I see what you're saying about fitting pieces together." She smacked Tucker across the arm. "But there better not be any little Tuckers running around here in nine months."

"Trust me, my friend, that's not going to happen."

WHEN JACKIE YAWNED, reflecting the weariness Tucker

realized she too felt, Tucker said, "We should probably go back to town and get to bed."

"I agree. If we don't leave soon, I may be sleeping here tonight."

Tucker stood and held out her hand to help Jackie up.

"If you do, you'll need a chiropractor in the morning. Did you drive up here?" Tucker knew Jackie would have to leave her car at the bottom of the hill because only a narrow path took them to the top where they sat now.

"No. After I made sure Leah got home, I drove to my house and left my car. I decided I'd take a walk to try to get a handle on my concern for you. Leah was concerned, too, but she wouldn't have known to come after you up here. I was pretty sure I'd find you here."

"And so you did," Tucker pronounced.

"So I did."

"I'm glad you came, Jackie, and I appreciate your help and support."

"For the revitalization project."

Tucker looked at her and said, "Yeah, for the project, too."

She barely made out Jackie's smile in the darkness.

They walked back into town in silence, hugging when they reached Main Street. Then they each walked in opposite directions. As Tucker strode back to the hotel, she thought about puzzles, and about the new information she put together, which only produced more questions for which she needed answers. Who dropped her off, groggy and hurt, in front of The Charlie the night this all started? And what happened to her before she got there? If she found answers to those questions, she might be able to fill in a vast section of the puzzle.

THE NEXT MORNING, as Tucker, Leah and Jackie sat eating another tasty breakfast Leah cooked, Tucker filled Leah in about puzzle edges and on her new insights. She pulled out the now crumpled list, flattening it with her palm against the kitchen table and enumerated what she knew.

"Dunbar and this guy Notch are one and the same, I'm positive of it," Tucker said. "Once I figure out how I know Notch, I might be able to discover why he's a part of all this."

"I'm starting to think Olivia Justice and Lily Hart are my brain's way of telling me this all means something. After all, if a bunch of strangers invaded my mind, I might think of it as a bad dream. I'm not sure whether it's a dream or reality, but I'm realizing it actually means something important."

She indicated the next item she'd written on the piece of paper. "*Why does Dunbar want to kill me?* I'm not sure about this one. Maybe I'm being warned off. Whenever I feel like I'm getting close to remembering something, I keep hearing the word 'forget.' I also get these feelings of being afraid of something, but I have no idea what it is that's causing the dread. If it's a warning, I have no idea what I'm being warned against.

"Although the fire in the jail back in 1873 held the potential to harm me, someone set it outside the jail. It was started in a pile of rubble. Maybe the jail caught on fire in error. I don't know for sure, but I'm starting to think so. Maybe it's another edge to the puzzle."

Leah and Jackie listened intently.

"Finally, what do this guy Notch and his missing groupie have to do with any of this? This is the one I must find the answer to. It might be a key piece. If this has something to do with the missing girl, I might have information the police need. The problem is I don't know if I'll ever be able to access the knowledge I might have buried deep within my subconscious. Until I make some progress, I've got to go about my business and hope something happens to help me make some sense of it all."

Leah pointed toward the paper on the table. "What about the whole thing about feeling beat up and confused and not remembering anything when you came out of The Charlie?"

"I don't think I came out of The Charlie at all. I realize now, I stood there with the wall holding me up, afraid of collapsing, but I never remembered coming through the door. And there's something else—the time. I got back to the hotel after three o'clock in the morning. The Charlie looked closed when I was in front. I also think I remember a car—and being dragged from a vehicle. I think someone dumped me there."

Leah wrinkled her brow. "Then where were you before you found yourself in front of the saloon?"

"Ah," Tucker said, "there's the question, wouldn't you say? And I'll bet it's a big section of the puzzle—if only I can find the pieces and link them together."

Chapter Ten

TUCKER THOUGHT LEAH looked sexy in her tight jeans with her hair pulled back in a ponytail, ready to work. She extended an invitation to Leah to join her as she did a cursory inspection of the outside of the mine. After she picked Leah up at her house, they struck out, clipboards in hand, to evaluate what they could so Tucker could meet with the mayor to give him a report.

As she and Leah walked the road to the mine entrance, Tucker said, "I contacted a firm from Sacramento to evaluate the condition inside the mine. Once we get access, I'll firm up an appointment with them. They're going to give me a written report on what might need to be done to ensure people touring the mine are safe. They gave me an estimate on what the initial assessment will cost with some contingencies, so I'll get the mayor's approval once I meet with him."

"So what's the purpose of our visit today?"

"Just to have a look around the outside. The last time I was here I think I was a freshman in high school. I just wanted to see if anything's changed, like road access, and get a feel for what the place looks like from the outside. There used to be thick wooden doors on the mine entrance with iron braces bolted to the wood, holding the planks together."

Leah double-timed it to keep up with Tucker's long strides. When Tucker realized she was having trouble, she slowed her pace.

"I've heard it was a rite of passage to come up here and try to get into the mine."

"Yep, I guess we all tried it a time or two. Some of the kids I came out here with only wanted to see it from a distance. Others scrambled all over these hills with me to try to find a way in. Jackie's been out here with me."

"Did you ever figure it out? How to get in?"

"Nope. Never did." Even all these years later, she felt the disappointment of a failed adventure.

They reached the door and saw that it was just as Tucker described. A large old, rusted padlock held the doors firmly closed.

Tucker walked up to the lock and pulled on it. When it didn't budge, she looked at Leah and shrugged. "A girl can try."

"A girl can try, but she didn't succeed."

Tucker said, "You can wipe that smirk off your face now."

Tucker jotted some notes about the trail leading to the mine and the condition of the doors and the lock.

Below those notes, she scribbled, Leah's name, followed by the two-word comment, "like her." She added a smiley face.

As they headed back toward Tucker's truck, Leah said, "Can I take a look at your notes? I can see if I have anything to add to help out."

Panic oozed up Tucker's spine and she felt her face redden. "Oh, nobody can read my chicken scrawls. That's why I do most of my writing on my laptop. Besides, I just put down that the place would be accessible to equipment trucks and the doors were locked up tight with that padlock and pretty secure because of the thick wood and the iron bars. That's all."

Tucker saw Leah look down at the clipboard in her hand. Before she tried to gain access, Tucker decided she'd better add, "If you saw anything else you want me to add, just let me know and I'll put it on the list." She switched the clipboard out of the hand nearest Leah and waved it around where she was sure she couldn't see it.

Leah gave her a perplexed look and said, "I don't think your writing is all that bad. I could read the list you made at my house just fine. But, no, I don't have anything else to add. I think you've just about covered it."

Tucker ignored Leah's comment about her writing and they continued back up the access trail until they reached Tucker's truck and drove back into town. Once she dropped Leah off, Tucker went back to the hotel to get cleaned up for her meeting with the mayor.

When she reached his office, she found him sitting at his desk, working on some paperwork, waiting for her. They discussed the estimate, her observations about access, and the state of the entrance to the mine.

"All we need now is access to the place. You don't happen to know where the key to that lock is, do you?"

The mayor said, "You'd think with all the talk about the mine, someone would have told you by now if they knew the whereabouts of the key. I don't know where it is, but I'll ask around. See if anybody around here knows where there's one."

Tucker said, "I'll put out the word at our next community meeting to try to find out who has access."

As they walked toward the hall, he added, "You've done some solid planning here, Tucker. I appreciate all the work you're doing. The mining firm's estimate for the evaluation looks reasonable. Hopefully, we won't have too big an expense once they get in there and complete it, but right now, I think we're good to go."

As they entered the corridor, they saw Joe Dawson, kneeling a few feet away.

The mayor said, "Joe? Is that you? Do you need something?"

Joe stood up and faced them. "No thanks. Got a loose shoelace. Darn thing won't stay tied."

Tucker wondered what he was doing there, but Joe shrugged and walked off, leaving the mayor and Tucker with furrowed brows.

THE NEXT TIME Tucker saw Joe Dawson, he stood at the back of his beat up old Toyota truck, struggling with a large antique bureau, trying to get it into the truck bed. Tucker approached and offered to help. He thanked her and hopped up into the truck bed, asking her to steady the piece as he tipped it up onto the floor of the truck. Once he got it into position, they wrestled it into place.

"Where are you headed with this thing, Joe?" Tucker asked.

"Someone over in Portero wants it. Paying a good price, too," Joe said.

It was the most she'd heard come out of Joe's mouth since her return to Elder Creek. "Good for you," Tucker said. She thought about broaching the subject of his objection about the mine, but as he was focused on the job at hand, she decided not to say anything.

Joe jumped over the side of the truck and thanked her. Then, he took her by surprise by adding, "Hey, Tucker, I heard you're going to open the mine."

Well, she thought, he made that decision for me.

"Don't think it's a good idea."

She stepped toward him and said, "Tell me what the problem is, Joe. I think you might be the only one left in town who doesn't think it's a good idea. I'd like to understand what issues you have with it."

Joe wiped his brow with the sleeve of his shirt. "I don't think it's a good idea, is all," he said. "Might be more trouble than you can handle."

Tucker's anger bubbled to the surface. "How do you figure, Joe? It's sure to be a money maker for the town. We'll all profit from it in the end. If there's good reason not to do it, I'd like to hear it."

"Oh, there's good reason for it. The reason is you'll be sorry if you do it." He stopped and looked down at the ground. When he looked up, he said, "What about the ghost?"

It took every ounce of self-control for Tucker not to laugh. "A ghost is your reason? It's kind of a silly one, don't you think? You're a grown man, Joe. The ghost story is for little kids."

Joe scowled at her. "Watch your mouth, Tucker. I don't think it's silly and you shouldn't either. You're asking for trouble if you open the mine. There're things you know nothing about."

"Then give me something better than ghost stories, Joe. I want to understand, but so far, I haven't heard anything good enough to convince me."

He remained silent, glaring at her.

She'd heard enough. He didn't have a thing to offer. She finally recognized him as merely another inhabitant of Elder Creek, entrenched in his ways, not willing to budge. She'd probably engaged him too much over this topic already.

"Well, Joe, I'll take your warning under advisement, but I've still got a job to do and getting the mine opened is part of it."

She turned and walked away. By the time she put a block between them, Joe started up his truck and took off in the opposite direction, toward Portero. Tucker froze, hesitating before taking her next step, not knowing why. Uncertainty bubbled up within her as she turned and watched the truck take a left off Main Street and disappear around a corner.

Forget.

A small dust cloud settled back onto the street in the truck's wake. The cloud of confusion settled with it. As it evaporated before her eyes, she wondered what happened.

WHEN TUCKER PUSHED open The Charlie's front door later in the afternoon, she found Jackie standing at the community bulletin board, putting up a large poster with the picture of a young blonde woman. The big, bold letters across the sign read "Have You Seen Me?" and gave details about her and her disappearance. Almost a month passed since she'd been reported missing.

"Hi, Tucker," Jackie called.

Tucker moved closer and did a double-take, struck by how much the young woman in the picture resembled Leah. She looked younger than college age, more like a sophomore or junior in high school. "That's the missing woman, isn't it?"

"Yes. Apparently the search for her is ramping up again. They distributed small posters a few weeks ago." Jackie indicated the bulletin board. "But they're asking us to change to these larger ones in the hopes they'll get more notice. Her parents and friends have promised to be out every weekend, searching the area and distributing flyers. They're asking all the merchants to post these. I've got another one to put in the window, too."

"I suppose finding her car must have a lot to do with it. They don't think she's a runaway anymore, I presume."

"Her parents have never thought she ran away. She's never done it before, and they insist it isn't something she would do. I think the police know it now, after finding her car the way they did."

Tucker stared at the picture, tilting her head one way, then the other.

"It's uncanny, isn't it," Jackie said.

Tucker gave her a questioning look.

"She could pass for Leah's kid sister don't you think?"

"Yeah," Tucker replied.

"It's kind of unsettling, actually."

Tucker agreed. "I think I'd better keep a closer eye on her — Leah, I mean."

"Maybe we both should," Jackie added.

Once Jackie returned to the bar and served Tucker the beer she'd ordered, Tucker told her about the meeting she set up for the following week with the engineering company.

"I'd like you to go with me to the mine when they do their initial investigation. The project engineer said he'd come out and take a look to see what equipment they might need and get the layout of the place, and we'd take it from there. Once he's done, he'll bring a team back, and they'll do the full evaluation and give us a written report. But for his first visit, since there won't be any report, I thought it might be good if I have your ears and eyes, too."

"Sure, Tuck. What day and time? I'll make sure either Tracey or Denise can be here so I'll be free."

"He's scheduled for next Thursday at eleven o'clock."

While Jackie agreed, noting the date and time in her phone calendar, Tucker's phone rang. She broke into a broad smile when she saw the caller ID.

"Hi, there."

"Hi, Tucker."

The sound of Leah's voice reminded Tucker of rich, creamy vanilla ice cream with flecks of the dark bean running through it. "I'm on my way home from school and I thought I'd give you a call. I've got something interesting to tell you. Do you want to come over for dinner tonight?"

"I'd love to, but you know, you can't keep feeding me like this."

"Sure I can. Meet me in about an hour, okay?"

"Will do. Say, what's this information about?"

"I'll tell you later. One of the students at the school and I were talking and something interesting came up in the conversation I want to share with you."

"Mysterious," Tucker said.

"You don't know the half of it. See you soon."

"I'm looking forward to it."

"So am I, Tucker."

Leah's phone ID disappeared from Tucker's screen, and she shoved her cell back into her jeans pocket.

Jackie walked down the length of the bar from where she chatted with another customer and stood facing Tucker again.

Tucker said, "Got a decent bottle of wine I can buy from you?"

Without question, Jackie pivoted on the spot and pulled a bottle of red from the built-in wine rack. "Where are you going? Or might I be able to guess?"

"Leah invited me to dinner. How much do I owe you?"

"Nothing. I'll put it on your tab."

Tucker chuckled and shook her head. She never tired of the on-going joke between them — this non-existent tab. "Thanks."

She winked at Jackie and started toward the door. After a few steps, she stopped and said, "By the way, just so you know, this is all a part of my plan to keep an eye on Leah."

As she walked out the door, she heard Jackie say, "Ri-i-i-ght."

WHEN LEAH OPENED the door Tucker greeted her with a bottle of Napa Valley Cabernet in her hand and a silly grin on her face. She acknowledged this new plan to keep an eye on Leah made her feel giddy inside.

Leah looked down at the bottle and back up to Tucker's face. Tucker said, "Something wrong?"

"No, but from the look on your face, I thought perhaps you'd already gotten into your wine bottle."

"Nope." She held out the offering and Leah took it from her. "Aren't you going to invite me in?"

Leah jumped back, saying, "Oh, of course. I'm sorry. Please." She gestured her into the front room.

Tucker passed her in one long stride. When Leah closed the front door, Tucker bent toward her and gave her a peck on the cheek. Leah gave her a wary look.

"What are you up to Tucker Stevens?"

Tucker put her hand over her heart. "Me? Whatever do you mean? I'm not up to anything. I'm here for the company and to hear what it is you wanted to tell me."

A brief pause followed. Then Leah began laughing. "Okay, Tucker, whatever you say, but I still think you're up to something."

When they entered the living room, a savory aroma of herbs and spices met Tucker's nose. Her mouth started to water. "Something smells wonderful," she said.

"Thank you, I've got a chicken and some veggies roasting in the oven. They probably won't be ready for another twenty minutes or so. Shall we enjoy a glass of this wine while we wait?"

Tucker agreed. "And you can tell me your story."

The smile disappeared from Leah's face. "I'll open this and bring some glasses. Have a seat. I'll be right back."

Leah returned with wine glasses and the opened bottle of wine. She poured. They sipped and sat in companionable silence while half the liquid in the glasses disappeared. Finally, Tucker said, "So, what about this conversation between you and your student?"

Leah pursed her lips before speaking. "You have to understand this may mean nothing at all. It did strike me as a little strange and I thought I might need to share it with you."

Tucker raised an eyebrow. "What's it about, Leah?"

"The mine."

Tucker sat up at attention. "Go ahead." Tucker's voice reflected caution. Would she tell her about some new opposition to going ahead with the plans for the mine or something else entirely?

"We have a few freshmen who help out in the library on Friday afternoons. We organize and re-shelve books, sweep and clean. The kids start out doing it because it gets them out of class early on Fridays when they're chomping at the bit to start their weekend. I like to think it gives them a chance to interact with someone who is more mentor than taskmaster, as they often consider their teachers, and they learn a lot about the library by doing simple things to keep it in good shape. After a month or so, they usually start opening up and talking to me more, which I think is a good thing for them."

"What you're telling me is nice, Leah, but—"

Leah held up her hand. "Let me finish. A couple of the boys were talking about going somewhere this weekend. It sounded like they might be planning something with potential to get them into trouble, so I tried to engage them about it. At first they were pretty vague. Then they finally admitted they were going to go out to the mine on Saturday night. These particular kids are too young to drive, but one of them has an older brother with a license who is willing to join them in their little adventure."

Tucker chuckled. "Kids have been going out there forever. It's almost a rite of passage. When I was a kid—heck, long before I even reached high school age—I used to go out there with Jackie and we'd climb all over the area, trying to find a rumored secret passage into the mine—"

Leah broke in. "But these kids were there two weekends ago. Apparently they got an older kid with a car to take them over there. They were making their way to the mine after being dropped off, walking a narrow path through some brush, they said. Fortunately, they were still well hidden because someone arrived by car and went into the mine."

"How in the world did someone get into the mine?" Tucker asked, distracted from the story and wondering who gained access. "Did they have a key to the padlock?"

"Apparently."

"Did they see the person? I need to locate whoever's in possession of it before next Thursday so I can take the engineer in to do a preliminary assessment of the place."

"The kids never saw the person's face. It was past dusk—too dark—and apparently their line of sight wasn't very good. There was nothing familiar about the guy. All the boys are from Portero, so if it was someone from Elder Creek, they probably wouldn't have known him anyway. Even if it was someone from Portero, it's a town of over five thousand people. What are the chances they might have known the person even then?

"Anyway, they said the guy disappeared inside the mine for

quite a while. The kids said they almost got tired of waiting. Kids don't have a very long attention span, especially when they're doing nothing. However, as they were debating what to do next, the person came out of the mine, got into the car and backed down the path at top speed. The car disappeared before they got to a place with good visibility without being seen themselves. About the same time, their friend showed up from his errand in Elder Creek to pick them up, and they went back to Portero without getting to explore or without seeing anything else. It's why they were planning to go back this weekend."

They sat in silence, drinking the last of the wine in their glasses. Leah finally said, "What do you think about all this, Tucker. Any ideas?"

Tucker shook her head. "No idea at all. And without identifying the guy, I don't know how we'll ever find out. Any information on the kind of car? License number? Anything to help?"

"A four-door, with dark color paint, but they didn't have any other details. From what they said, it was pretty dark out there and it was difficult to see through the brush where they hid."

Tucker said, "I don't know what to think. It's curious to think someone has such easy access to the mine and hasn't come forward. Those kids didn't see anything to indicate anything malicious going on, so I think there's nothing to do but put out the word, again."

"Maybe so. I think I discouraged the boys from going back, though. I pointed out the danger of going out there. I'm afraid I went a little 'taskmaster' on them. I hope I didn't destroy the relationship I've been building all these weeks since school started."

Tucker laughed. "I'm sure fourteen-year-old boys worship the ground you walk on, Ms. Hudson." *I know I'm starting to.* "I'll bet you have nothing to worry about."

"I hope you're right," Leah mumbled. "With someone who can drive them up there and take part in their explorations, my admonitions might not work. We'll have to hope for the best."

The timer went off in the kitchen and Tucker's stomach growled. Leah popped up from her seat and said, "Bring the wine, Tucker. Dinner is served."

Tucker tried to stifle her smile as she watched Leah walk into the kitchen in front of her, hips swinging sensually, beckoning Tucker to follow. Tucker realized, then, she would follow Leah Hudson anywhere.

AS PEOPLE GATHERED for the meeting, Tucker stood with

Leah and Jackie discussing tonight's agenda. Jackie would give her proposal about people adopting historical characters' personalities, and Leah would give a brief summary of the most colorful ones she found. They'd then find out if people were interested in following through with the idea as a way to give Elder Creek some color. If the idea appealed to them, then Leah would do more in-depth research and see what else she'd discover, so they would have enough characters to go around. Tucker would report on the engineering company they were about to engage and announce there would be a preliminary visit to determine what equipment they might need to bring in to do a full analysis.

At Jackie and Leah's suggestion, they decided not to announce the date of the visit in case there might be a problem with the unknown person with access to the mine. Finally, Tucker would ask the question about the key. Hopefully, whoever controlled the key would come forward. Then they'd see what would happen next. Because of Tucker's conversation with the mayor and the city attorney, she confirmed the mine was declared eminent domain by the city years before, so the city attorney said, whoever went into the mine almost two weeks ago would be subject to prosecution for trespassing on city property. Tucker felt emboldened by this new information.

The meeting went well. People were excited by Jackie and Leah's proposal to adopt characters and stay within them during their encounters with the tourists they expected would come to town. When Tucker announced the engagement of the engineering firm, no one voiced opposition. People either sat and stared or acknowledged agreement with the information she gave them.

Finally, Tucker asked about the key, telling the attendees about rumors of one existing.

"Does anyone know who might have it? We'll need it before the engineering company comes in. If we can get it, it will make things much easier."

People looked around at one another and a soft murmur ran through the crowd.

Tucker continued, "I don't know how many of you have been out to the mine—" Tucker noted lots of head-shaking. "—but there's a big-ass old iron lock on those thick wooden doors. Excuse my French, folks, but I'm a little frustrated with this. If we can't find the key, we'll have to take bolt cutters to it, but it sure would be nice to preserve the lock. After all, it's part of the mine's history and atmosphere, too."

Tucker noted a lot of shrugs while she waited for another murmur to quiet down as people discussed who might have the key. When no one added anything, Tucker said, "Well, pass the word around. You never know who might know something. Someone must have the key or know where it is. If anyone can let me know who has it, I'd appreciate it. Now, if no one else has anything to add, I think we can adjourn this meeting."

As soon as she said it, people were on their feet. Some mingled and talked in small groups and others headed for the door.

Jackie came up behind Tucker and said in her ear, "Now, we wait."

Tucker sighed. "Indeed, now we wait. And someone has very little time to produce that key."

Chapter Eleven

SEVERAL NIGHTS LATER, Tucker sat at her computer in her hotel room. Light from the desk lamp shone in a diffuse circle on her desk. The curtains remained open, and outside her window she spied the sooty night sky. No stars tonight, only dark clouds shadowing any light from above.

She refocused on the work on her computer screen where she defined the beginnings of a timeline to implement their plan for becoming a living history town over the next eighteen months. The mine details would have to be filled in once the engineering company completed their evaluation. She sat back, pleased with her work, smiling. This project would succeed. Even if it took longer to get the mine opened, they'd put all their other plans in place and build up the mine as a coming attraction.

When her phone rang, she hoped for someone with information to allow them access to the mine. Her grin widened when she saw the caller ID. No, it wouldn't be information about the key, but it pleased her as much—maybe more.

"Hi, there, Leah. How are you?"

"I don't know, Tucker." Her voice sounded unsteady, spooked.

Tucker sat up straight in her chair, her heart rate speeding up, anxiety clawing up her back, settling at the base of her skull. "Are you okay? You sound rattled."

"I am, a little, I guess."

"What happened?"

"I think someone tried to break in here. I heard noises. When I checked the back door where I heard them, I found scratches all around the doorknob and the lock. I'm frightened, Tucker."

"Hold on, Leah, I'm coming over. I'll be there in a few minutes. Make sure everything's locked up and don't open the door 'til I get there."

When Tucker drove up to Leah's, she found the house lit up like a Christmas tree with every light in the house on in spite of the late hour. She parked at the edge of the dirt and gravel strip bordering the yard and headed for the porch. When she reached the front door, Leah pulled it open. Her face was ashen. Tucker stepped inside, pushed the door closed and engaged the lock. Then she grasped Leah's shoulders and pulled her into a hug.

Tucker felt her tremble. She kissed the top of Leah's head and rubbed her back, trying to offer comfort. "It's okay, Leah, honey. I'm here now. I've got you. Everything's going to be all right."

Leah pushed into Tucker's body until Tucker almost lost her footing.

"Let's sit down in the living room and you tell me everything, okay?"

Leah sniffled and smashed herself up against Tucker's side as they walked into the living room and sat down together on the couch.

"When you're ready, you go ahead. Start at the beginning and don't leave out any details, okay? I'll listen."

Leah pulled a tissue out of a box on the table in front of them and dabbed at her eyes. She blew her nose, crumpled up the tissue in her hand, took a deep breath and began. "I finished getting ready for bed."

Tucker noticed Leah's street clothes.

"I went back into the bathroom to hang up my towel and I thought I heard something at the back of the house. I figured it might be a raccoon rooting around back there so I didn't think much of it. All the lights were off except my bedside lamp because I planned to head to bed to read for a while—a nice, relaxing evening, you know?"

She paused to compose herself. Tucker tried to encourage her with a smile. Leah twisted a corner of the tissue in her hands.

"My bedroom's at the back of the house."

Tucker considered the back bedroom, her mother's old room.

Leah continued, "I went into the bedroom and shut off the light because I figured I'd be able to see into the dark yard better, but between the screen on the window and angle in trying to look down the length of the house to the back porch, I wasn't able to see much, but as I tried to change my perspective, I saw movement. Maybe my imagination playing tricks, I thought, but I saw a dark figure hunched over at the back door. I heard the scraping sound all the way down the length of the house."

Leah shivered against Tucker's body. Tucker put her arm around Leah's shoulders and pulled her in closer.

"I froze for a few seconds. Then I thought, what am I doing? Am I going to stand here while someone breaks in and does god-knows-what to my home? To me? So I tiptoed into the kitchen and picked up my cast iron skillet off the stove and went to the back door with it raised over my head, ready to smash the bastard's head in."

Tucker smiled against Leah's hair where she laid her head, comforting her. Tucker knew Leah well enough now to know she wasn't the type to swear a lot—or to threaten violence. It sounded comical coming from her—until the seriousness of the story settled in on Tucker again.

Leah continued, "I don't know if he saw me coming and ran, or what happened, but once I got to the kitchen door and peeked out the window, everything was quiet. I saw no one. I opened the back door and I found the scrapes. I know they weren't there before. I slammed the door shut as fast as possible, locked it, and ran and called you. Then I went around the house turning every light on and waited for you to come."

"And you got dressed," Tucker added.

"I got dressed before I wielded the frying pan. I'd never open the door in my nightgown."

Tucker imagined Leah in a nightgown. She sighed and pushed the image away. *Not appropriate, Tucker Stevens.*

Leah sniffed again. "It didn't take you long. Thank you for coming so quickly."

Tucker pulled Leah closer again. "You're welcome. It didn't take me long because I've been up working on the timeline, which I've finished as much as I can, by the way. After you called I grabbed my keys and took off. It only takes about two minutes by car."

They sat together, Leah leaning her head against Tucker's shoulder, Tucker's arm wrapped around her protectively, for a few more minutes.

Then, Tucker said, "Now, how about we both go take a look at your door together? Then we'll decide if we need to call the sheriff."

LEAH GRASPED TUCKER'S hand as they approached the back door. Tucker switched on the porch light and peered out the small window set into the door. The tiny back porch shone in an amber glow, lighting the four-foot square and the single step down to the backyard. Tucker and a neighbor added the overhanging roof, supports, and a railing the summer before she left for college. Her mom liked to throw out stale bread from the porch for the birds. Tucker tried to tell her other varmints were attracted to the bread, too, but her mom insisted on doing it, so Tucker wanted her to have a little protection from the sun, which beat down pretty mercilessly in summer, and from winter precipitation.

Her examination of the porch through the window tonight didn't show anything out of place. When she reached for the lock, she heard Leah, now standing behind her and no longer tethered to Tucker, take in a breath.

Tucker gave her a reassuring smile. "It'll be okay."

Leah's shoulders relaxed.

Tucker twisted the knob and pulled the door open into the kitchen. Fresh gouges in a haphazard pattern marked the door around the handle and the lock. Tucker tilted her head, contemplating the marks. Could it have been a bear? Maybe, but she didn't think a bear would concentrate its scratching to so specific an area as the door knob.

A bear would have clawed at the whole door, wouldn't it? She didn't know for sure. The gouges didn't look evenly spaced enough to have been made by bear claws. They looked more like random chisel marks, made from positioning a tool at different angles. Maybe she should keep the information to herself right now. Maybe she'd say... "I think we should err on the side of caution and call the sheriff."

Tucker saw Leah's eyes widened and she hastened to add, "It might've been a bear, but, you know, just in case. And if a bear is roaming around here, the sheriff should be alerted anyway. The neighborhood should be notified."

THE SHERIFF'S CAR parked in front of Leah's house caused a bit of a stir in the neighborhood. Some of the neighbors came out and stood around on the gravel path for a while. One or two of them must have gotten bored when nothing exciting happened and wandered off to The Charlie, perhaps thinking a bottle of beer might be more interesting. It didn't take long before Jackie knocked on the front door.

Leah and the sheriff were finishing up with her statement, so Tucker answered.

Jackie's face, flushed from her sprint up the hill, looked drawn with worry. "Tucker, what's going on? Matt Chandler came into the bar a while ago and told us about trouble here at Leah's." She scanned the room. "Is she all right?"

Tucker noticed the remaining bystanders all shifted a little closer to the house, presumably trying to catch a bit of the conversation. She motioned Jackie in and closed the door, saying, "She's fine. Everything's fine. I called Sheriff Baker as a precaution." Tucker looked back over her shoulder through the front window and watched people milling around in the front yard. "Damn gossip-mongers," she muttered.

"Well, what happened?"

Tucker filled her in while trying to emphasize the marks may have been made by a bear trying to get to food or water. She knew Jackie wasn't buying it.

"What's the sheriff going to do to the bear, Tucker? Arrest him—or her?"

"No, but I thought he should know, in case, you know, he—or she—comes back—or harasses someone else in the neighborhood."

She glanced out the window again. There were only a couple of people left standing around. "Although I can think of a few nosy people I'd like to sic a bear on about now."

Jackie lost control and let out a belly laugh. Leah and the sheriff wound around in their seats at the kitchen table to see what was so amusing. Tucker shrugged at them, and she and Jackie went back to their conversation. Finally, Leah and the sheriff got up from their seats and walked into the living room.

Tucker noticed the color returned to Leah's face. She and the sheriff acknowledged Jackie, then he tipped his hat, saying, "Don't worry Ms. Hudson, we'll patrol the neighborhood and keep an eye on you. Make sure you keep the doors and windows locked."

Tucker said, "I'll keep an eye on her, too. I'm staying tonight."

Leah raised an eyebrow at Tucker.

In response, Tucker added, looking at the sheriff instead of Leah, "I'll be sleeping right here." Tucker motioned toward the couch. She caught Jackie's smirk out of the corner of her eye and turned to give her a glaring look in return.

Tucker walked Sheriff Baker to his patrol car.

"So what do you think, Sheriff?"

"I'm pretty sure it wasn't a bear, Ms. Stevens."

"I thought so, although I'm sorry to hear it confirmed. A bear would be less scary at this point."

"I understand. I'm glad you'll be staying here tonight. We'll be driving by, too." He hesitated before he added, "It's all the more concerning because of the missing girl over in Portero. I'd hate to see something happen to her." He dipped his head toward the house. "One night might not be enough for someone else to be in the house with her."

Tucker grinned. "I'll talk to her, Sheriff." She thought for a minute, then added, "I'm getting mighty tired of staying at the hotel. Maybe it's time Miss Leah took in a boarder."

The sheriff smiled. "Maybe so, Ms. Stevens. Maybe so. But I have a feeling it won't be easy talking her into it. She's pretty independent."

Tucker's grin widened. "We'll see."

As Tucker watched Sheriff Baker drive off down the street, she whispered into the night, "We'll see, indeed."

As she walked back toward the house, she glared at two hangers-on from down the street. They glanced down at the dirt walkway, trying to avoid eye contact with her.

"Go home," she ordered. "There's nothing going on here. Go home."

They slinked back in the direction of their own houses. As Tucker watched them walk out of earshot, she spat her words at their backs. "Nosy, small-town bastards." It made her angry to think rumors would be flying all over town by morning. Most of them wouldn't be true.

WHEN TUCKER ENTERED the house, she found Leah standing alone, staring out the kitchen window. Careful not to scare her, Tucker called her name softly. "Leah."

Leah turned and faced her. She gave her a weak smile. "The first time I walked into this house, it felt so much like home. I've loved living here."

"I'm glad. I want you to be comfortable."

Leah hesitated before she spoke again. When she did, Tucker faced eyes filled with apprehension—and questions. "I hope I still can be."

"Leah, look, this has been difficult for you. We can hope this bear or maybe kids making mischief is a one-off, never to happen again. I understand your unease, though, I do. So I have a proposal for you."

Leah looked wary, making Tucker hesitate. Maybe it's not such a good idea after all, Tucker decided. Maybe, but it wasn't safe to leave Leah alone, at least until they figured out what's going on.

If it turned out to be as she suggested, some kids messing around, everything would go back to normal quickly. If it were kids, then the sheriff's car out front and all the commotion it caused would probably put the fear of the Almighty into them and there wouldn't be any more trouble. Eventually, they'd both feel more comfortable about Leah living here alone again. Hopefully. Maybe by then, Tucker would buy a small trailer and live up on Tenderfoot Hill until her place could be built, presuming the approval for the sale of the land happened as she hoped.

"I'm waiting," Leah said, probing Tucker's eyes with her own look.

"Well, now, Leah, let me put it to you this way. I've been living at the National for over a month now. It's starting to get a little old, living in a hotel. So, I thought, maybe, just temporarily you understand, I would come and stay here for a while. Until we're sure everything's okay around here. What do you say?"

Tucker blew out her breath. Making her case proved tougher than she imagined. She didn't want to impose on Leah. She did, however, want to watch over her, protect her. She struggled with the dilemma. She didn't want Leah to feel incapable of taking care of herself, either. On the other hand, Leah did call her when she felt threatened. So maybe she wouldn't flat out say no. Maybe.

Leah watched Tucker with intense concentration.

Tucker knew her inner turmoil must have shown on her face. It usually did. Her mother used to say she "wore her heart on her sleeve." She hated it about herself. She never played poker because of it.

"Well?" Tucker asked. "What do you think? Help a girl out?" One side of her mouth rose ever so slightly as she tried to project a smile full of charm.

It worked. Sort of. Leah looked at her, a stern expression painted on her face, and she pointed toward the living room, "Are you saying you're prepared for an extended stay on the couch? Because you know I've converted the second bedroom into an office. Or do you want me to take my stuff out of there and we can bring in a cot?" She poked a thumb over her shoulder, in the general direction of the bedrooms.

"The couch will be fine. I've slept on it lots during my lifetime. And this is a temporary arrangement."

"Until..."

"Until everything settles down. Until we know the bear—or whatever appeared at your back door—" She regretted the last part as soon as she said it, especially when Leah's eyes widened. She began again, hoping to do better the second time. "Until we know the bear isn't going to come back."

"Then what?" Leah asked. "Back to the hotel?"

"No. I think I told you about Tenderfoot. I'm trying to

negotiate some land up there. Maybe by the time we decide everything's back to normal around here, I will have acquired the parcel up there, and I can get a trailer and stay there while the contractor starts to build. I'm hoping anyway. We'll see."

Leah stood, pursing her lips, staring at Tucker. "What's so special about that place, anyway?"

"I don't know. It's always meant something to me. It's beautiful up there, quiet, away from town enough so you feel like you're out in the country."

Leah laughed, "Tucker, we *are* in the country. This is the foothills of the Sierra Nevada Mountains. Elder Creek has a population of twenty-three hundred people. This town is pretty countrified if you ask me."

"I know, I guess I mean, well, it's really special up there. Peaceful. And the view's spectacular. You can see three-hundred and sixty degrees. You can look up at the mountains on one side, and see the lights of Elder Creek at night down below on the other side. And the night sky—it is so amazing. The stars are so bright. There's nothing like the view up there."

When Tucker looked at Leah again, her eyes were dancing.

"Will you take me up there sometime? To your *Shangri-La*? I'd love to see it."

A wide grin spread across Tucker's face. "I'd love to, Leah."

They stared into one another's eyes, and Tucker felt her spine tingle like a hundred tiny fingers were massaging her. It felt good to look into those sparkling blue eyes. Tonight, right now, they were deep and dark, almost denim colored. They were— beautiful, breath-taking. As she watched Leah's face, her lips drew Tucker's attention. Those soft, sweet lips. Those lips that kissed her. Those lips, she would love to feel on hers again.

Leah cleared her throat. Tucker shook off the sensation of a swarm of bees buzzing around her head.

"I'll get some bed linens for you. Do you have something to sleep in?" Leah blushed a little at her question.

Tucker said, "I always keep a case in the truck. I've done it for years. When I lived in Phoenix, on my own, and I plunged into the midst of writing a story, I'd just take off and go somewhere quiet. Change up the scenery. Sometimes I'd stay overnight, so I took to carrying a change of clothes and some other necessities. I'll be right back." She headed for the front door. Before she stepped outside, she said, "Oh, and by the way, this month's rent is on me. I haven't deposited your check yet. I'll give it back to you tomorrow."

Leah laughed heartily now. It pleased Tucker to know she caused it.

WHEN TUCKER RETURNED with her bag, she asked Leah when Jackie left. Leah told her Jackie said she needed to get back to the bar to help close up about the time Tucker walked with the sheriff to his car. "She said to tell you she'd see you tomorrow. Well, us, actually. She invited us to The Charlie to have dinner before the meeting tomorrow night. I've got some work to do on those character studies to be ready, though. I'm going to try to get to them during lunch tomorrow."

"And while you're at work, I'll check out of the hotel and store the rest of my stuff over here."

"I should clear out some space in the office so you have a place to put things."

"Don't worry about it, Leah. I don't have much. I've been living pretty simply these past few weeks. I can keep most of my stuff in my truck."

"No, Tucker. If you're going to stay here, I want you to be comfortable. You need at least a little space." Leah looked down at her hands as she twisted and untwisted her fingers. "I'm grateful for—you know—you wanting to stay. Thank you."

Tucker smiled and pulled Leah into an embrace. "Think nothing of it."

Leah looked up into her eyes, "Tucker?"

"Yes, Leah?"

"Kiss me?"

Tucker didn't think about it. She kissed Leah softly. They deepened the kiss and Tucker never wanted to stop. Apparently, Leah didn't want to either. When Tucker finally mustered enough willpower to pull away, absence, emptiness quickly replaced the fullness of the emotion she felt while kissing Leah. She thought about pulling her into another kiss, not stopping this time, touching in places Leah might not want to be touched. She smiled apologetically for thinking things she shouldn't.

Leah gave her a bashful smile. "I'll go get those bed linens," she said.

As Leah walked down the hall, Tucker watched her go, appreciating the view. *Good grief, I've got to stop this. All I'm doing at this point is torturing myself.*

She chuckled and, from down the hall, Leah poked her head out from the linen closet and asked, "What are you laughing at?"

"Irony," Tucker said.

Leah approached her with a stack of linens in her arms. "What's that supposed to mean?"

It means, a couple of weeks ago, you were the aggressor in this relationship. Apparently, the tables have turned. "Nothing," Tucker replied, "It's my mind working out a paradox."

The couch felt a lot less comfortable than Tucker remembered. Of course, the last time she fell asleep on it she was a college student and probably a lot more fit than she was these days. A sharp pain radiated from her left hip down the side of her leg, but she tried to ignore it. She shifted her position and willed herself back to sleep. The pain subsided after a while. The charcoal dimness of early morning surrounded her. Tucker pulled the blanket up over her exposed ear and drifted back to sleep.

Chapter Twelve

TUCKER WALKED DOWN Main Street watching her boots scuff little clouds of dirt as she took each step. She'd have to clean all the dust from her boots before she went out to dinner with Leah tonight. Then, it hit her.

She stopped mid-stride and looked around. No pavement. It meant only one thing.

The groaning sound coming from deep in her chest expressed her frustration. Why the hell did she end up back here? She didn't want to come here anymore — shouldn't come here anymore. She might be a fugitive. If so, would she be thrown back in jail as soon as someone recognized her? She looked around again, trying to get her bearings.

Strains of "Oh! Susanna" rode on the air from The St. Charles Saloon down the street behind her. She didn't dare go in there. She risked her life in an encounter with Dunbar or Notch, or whatever name the guy went by. She glanced down the street trying to decide what to do next.

Olivia. Maybe she'd be of some help. Then again, maybe not. Who knew? It might be worth a try. She needed to do something. Obviously, coming back here again meant something. Maybe there was some piece of information to glean from the goings on here in the last vestiges of the Old West of her town.

Tucker's stomach rumbled, giving her more impetus to march toward Olivia's. She hoped once she got there, she wouldn't be apprehended by someone. She looked around the Main Street again. Deserted. She looked up and saw blackness dotted with stars as bright as those visible only up on Tenderfoot Hill in her time.

Her time. She wished herself back there to no avail. She didn't care for this time very much anymore. Not since the jail incident. Not since the fire. She shivered and willed her legs to keep going toward Olivia's. As she approached, she observed the few small oil lamps burning inside and Olivia's form as she stood working at the stove at the far end of the room. Tucker stepped through the doorway and found the room empty except for Olivia.

Olivia turned toward the sound of the footsteps behind her, her mouth drawn into a small "o" in surprise when she saw Tucker.

Tucker smiled at her weakly. "Am I too late to get something to eat?"

Olivia concentrated on the contents of the frying pan as Tucker drew closer and peered over her shoulder. The aroma from the mixture of potatoes, onions and spices wafted under Tucker's nose, and her stomach growled again.

"I'm making myself a little something before I go home," Olivia said. "If you don't mind the simplicity of it, I'll share it with you."

"I don't want to take your meal from you."

"Don't concern yourself. There's plenty. No charge tonight."

"I can pay, Olivia."

As soon as she said it, Tucker wondered if she could pay. She plunged her hand into her jeans pocket. At the bottom she found the coins she hoped would be there. She smiled at the discovery. "I will pay. No arguments."

"Suit yourself," Olivia said.

She focused on the cast iron frying pan, scooping the contents onto two plates with a large metal spoon. She carried them over to one of the tables and set them down. Tucker followed her and pulled out Olivia's chair for her. Olivia gave her a wary look before she sat. Tucker joined her.

An oil lantern lit the surface of the bare wood of the table, casting its light on the plates of food. They sat facing each other and began eating. Tucker savored her first bite before shoveling in the remainder of the potato concoction. They didn't speak. Tucker didn't know what to say. Should she refer to Olivia's kindness at bringing her a meal while she sat in the Elder Creek excuse for a jail? She decided she'd better wait to see if Olivia brought up the topic first.

She wanted to ask Olivia if she thought she was in danger of being thrown back in jail if she was discovered. Again, she thought it better not to bring it up. What if it never happened? What if her mind continued to play tricks on her and this was all nothing more than her brain's twisted fantasy? But didn't she already realize this whole experience was more than that. It contained truths and she needed to mine them in order to shed light on what she needed to know.

As if reading her mind, Olivia said, "What are you doing back here? You shouldn't have come, you know. It's dangerous."

"I have no idea what I'm doing back here, Olivia. I wish I weren't here, but apparently there is something for me to learn. I need information—information I can only get here."

"What information is it you're looking for?"

"I have no idea. If I knew, I probably wouldn't need to come back. I'd be better off going to the library to look it up."

Olivia looked at her, eyes full of questions. "What a silly thing to say. First, the closest library is hours away in Sacramento. Second, if you want to know something from this place, you've got to be here, not in some library."

Tucker stared. "You know, Olivia, you're probably right. But I'm not even sure where I should look for what I need. Not only that, I don't know what questions to ask."

Olivia's look felt as if it penetrated into Tucker's soul. "If you want answers to your questions, the first answer is obvious. You've got to knock on the right door."

Tucker recognized the answer as soon as she heard it. She repeated it over and over. If she wanted the solution to her problem, she'd have to knock on the right door. It escaped her how she knew this to be correct, but she understood it as truth without question. "The right door," she said aloud.

Olivia nodded once. Then, she disappeared right before Tucker's eyes as if she were an apparition.

Tucker blinked and looked around the room. She found herself, no longer in Olivia's place of business, but in Leah's living room on her couch with the first gray light of dawn breaking, visible through the living room window.

She mumbled to herself. "I have to find the right door." She blew out her breath in frustration. "What the heck does it mean? Which door? Where?" The certainty faded as her frustration increased.

She closed her eyes and drew in a long, slow breath, filling her lungs, hoping to fill her mind with answers. By the time she exhaled, she could think of only one more question. It boiled down to this: what question would the door — or perhaps what existed on the other side of the door — answer?

Before she pondered any further, she drifted off to sleep again. This time, she slept the sleep of peaceful dreamlessness, without encounters with Olivia, or anyone else.

THE NEXT TIME Tucker woke, the light shone so brightly, it penetrated through her closed eyelids. She thought about how much it might hurt when she opened them, but she knew it was necessary. She opened one eye a crack and found it not quite as blinding as she thought it would be. She opened the other eye slightly. Okay, this works. She opened both eyes a little more and Leah stepped within her field of vision.

At first details were impossible to decipher as light from behind Leah gave her body an angelic aura, making her appear in silhouette. Then the sun's rays shifted behind her and she stood in a gossamer gown, allowing the outline of her whole body to be silhouetted from within the garment.

Tucker felt the saliva stick in her throat mid-swallow. She tried to smile, but it felt like a grimace. Holy shit, she thought. What's going on? She didn't know how she'd manage all these mixed messages from Leah.

Passionate kisses and instructions to sleep on the couch were one thing, but standing before her like this? Tucker didn't know if she'd be able to resist scooping her up in her arms and carrying her off to bed. She thought she would call out Leah's name, to reason with her, to tell her she couldn't come and stand before her looking like *that* and expect her to be able to control herself. How much willpower did she think Tucker could muster, anyway? However, when she tried to speak, nothing came out but a dry, raspy sound.

Leah extended her hand to Tucker without uttering a word. Tucker grasped it firmly and allowed Leah to pull her up to a standing position. Still holding on to Tucker's hand, Leah led — no, dragged — Tucker down the hall. Where were they going?

Uh-oh.

When they reached the doorway to Leah's bedroom, Tucker tried to clear her throat to say something. Uncertainty filled her. Should she protest? Challenge her actions? Express caution? Give consent?

Tucker didn't succeed in finding her voice, so she tried to buy some time by pulling Leah to a halt. Leah resisted, but finally stopped and looked at her. However, something distracted Tucker now, because, set into the closed bedroom door, right above Leah's head, bold black characters caught her eye. They glowed with bright white light around them.

Tucker struggled to make sense of them. Letters? What did they spell? What she saw didn't make sense.

Her mind cleared. No. Not letters — numbers. Tucker blinked several times, trying to bring them into better focus, to make sure she understood what she saw. One...eight...seven...three.

Eighteen-seventy-three? Was it possible? Could the date on the newspaper not be a year at all, but instead be —

Forget.

A whooshing sound, like a gale force wind, echoed in her ears with the word embedded within it.

Forget.

The wind tried to carry this new realization away, pulling it from her mind.

As if clinging to a tree in a tornado, so as not to blow away, Tucker tried to hold on to this new awareness—1873 might not be a year at all. It might be an address.

The wind picked up, pummeling her, clothes snapping against her skin, her hair like tiny whip ends beating against her face.

Forget.

The wind pried at her grip on Leah's hand. Tucker grasped it tighter.

Forget.

Like Dorothy in the *Wizard of Oz*, she felt as if she'd be blown away to a land with experiences stranger than anything in L. Frank Baum's imagination. She held onto Leah's fingers with the tips of her own, barely clinging to her. One more gust and she'd be gone. Maybe she'd be blown back to 1873. But now she knew 1873 wasn't a year. The conviction of this new knowledge filled her. Not a year at all—an address.

Forget.

The wind picked up and raged one more time and Leah's fingertips slid from hers. The wind swirled around her. Tucker watched as Leah rode the cold blast upward, she heard her laugh, but this time the sound gave Tucker no joy. It didn't sound like Leah's laugh at all. As Leah disappeared, she thought she saw the angry face of Nigel Dunbar supplanted on Leah's body, white, gossamer tendrils of the garment flowing all around his menacing form. She squeezed her eyes shut against the image.

TUCKER OPENED HER eyes to an eerie quiet, the storm dissipated. The sun shone through the windows, everything appeared normal in the morning light. Down the hall, she noticed Leah's bedroom door ajar, but she heard no sounds.

The bedroom door...she threw off the covers, sprang from the couch, and ran down the hall. The familiar word floated around her, but this time it sounded weak, distant.

Forget.

Its power was gone.

She examined the door. It appeared as she remembered it

from years ago, painted in a glistening white enamel, without numbers.

"Leah?"

No answer.

Tucker called louder this time. "Leah? Are you in there?"

Nothing. She pushed open the bedroom door with one finger, her heart thundering in her ears.

The bedroom was awash in bright morning light. Leah's bed stood in the center of the room, crisply made up with a white bedspread embroidered with tiny pink flowers. Everything in the room looked neat and tidy.

Her heart slowed down a little, but she still didn't feel completely at ease. Where was Leah?

She walked back down the hall and entered the kitchen. On the table, she found Leah's note.

When she found Tucker sleeping so soundly this morning, it read, she didn't want to wake her. She needed to get to school early for a staff meeting. She'd meet her at The Charlie for dinner at five. She signed it with a little heart cradled in the angle of the letter L.

Tucker's heart slowed to a more normal rhythm. Leah was okay.

She looked at the clock on the microwave. Nine-fifteen. It was odd for her to sleep so long and why didn't Leah's stirrings wake her? A barrage of emotions thrashed against her mind, all centered on Leah's safety. She'd be at work by now, surrounded by people. She thought about the strange dream. Leah's coming to her, looking very sexy, very alluring. She'd never have been able to resist her, the way she looked, the way she dressed. She would have been willing to go into the bedroom...

The door appeared in her mind's eye. She visualized the numbers as if she saw them in the dream.

Forget.

For a second time, she realized the word lost some of its influence on her, confirming the memories were more likely the true ones. She remembered. The number, 1873, wasn't a year at all. Perhaps it explained why the newspaper contained all the wrong information in it. Even the errors contributed to the clues.

Instead, 1873 might very well be an address, but an address where?

She walked into Leah's office, hoping to find information using Leah's laptop, but she found the spot it usually occupied on the desk empty. Leah probably took it to school with her. She sighed. She'd have to go back to the hotel and get hers.

Just as well, she thought. She wanted to go pack up and check out anyway. She smiled at the thought of sharing this, her childhood home, with Leah, at least for a while.

She shivered with pleasure when she thought about seeing Leah in the nearly see-through nightgown. Then she quivered again as she recalled it wasn't actually Leah. Because in the end, the person's face became the man she dreaded most, Dunbar, and he didn't look at all pleased. Bile raised in her throat matching the feeling of pressure in her chest caused by the fear Dunbar evoked in her. Now, if she could only figure out the connection between Dunbar and Demetrius Notch.

TUCKER SAT AT a table near the door of The Charlie drinking a Twigs. She wanted beer but thought she'd better have a clear head for the upcoming meeting. She tapped her finger on the wooden surface, anxious for Leah to appear.

Jackie came up behind her and said, "You know, you remind me of Rusty."

"Rusty? Who's—oh, you mean the dog you used to have when we were kids?"

"Yes, him. Rusty."

"Why's that?"

"Because he worshiped the ground my father walked on. Every day, about twenty minutes before my dad would come home, he'd get up from his nap, stretch and shake, then go sit bolt upright about three feet from the front door, waiting for Dad to get home from work. He never wavered. He did it every day. He didn't lie down. He never waited one foot back or one foot closer. He always waited three feet away from the door, always sitting up straight as a pole, and always twenty minutes before dad came home. You reminded me of Rusty for a minute there."

Tucker chuckled at the comparison. "I'm worried about her, is all. I'll feel better as soon as I see her walk in here."

The reference made her think of her dream—or whatever the hell she experienced earlier in the day. She remained silent about it, deciding not to tell Jackie. She didn't want to tell anyone. It creeped her out the more she thought about it. She knew Leah wasn't the one trying to seduce her, but seduce her to what? More clouds swirled, blocking her ability to figure it out.

She checked out of the hotel and, having allowed the old self-locking Schlage lock to engage behind her at Leah's when she left, she returned using her landlord key. She knew Leah wouldn't mind, but she also made a note to have a deadbolt installed on both doors of the place as soon as possible.

Once she settled her belongings out of the way of traffic in the living room, she booted up her computer and searched online for an address in Elder Creek. It yielded no 1873 for any street in town or in the unincorporated outskirts. At a loss as to what to do next to try to solve the mystery, she started second guessing herself, wondering if her assumption about an address might be wrong, thinking her mind might be playing crazy tricks on her — again.

Jackie shook her from her musings as she patted her on the shoulder without saying another word and sauntered behind the bar. The front door opened. One of the townspeople walked in and sat at the bar. Jackie began pouring a draft beer. Tucker dug her phone from her pocket and looked at the time. Five-fifteen. Where was Leah? She should be here by now.

She began tapping the table again. Another five minutes passed while she sat there, sipping on the Twigs, tapping, staring, willing Leah to appear. Just like Rusty, she thought.

At five-thirty the door opened, and Tucker recognized Leah's blonde head. She blew out a breath and with her next intake of air, her world righted itself again. Leah approached, unwrapping herself from her wool coat and scarf.

"Sorry I'm late."

When Tucker looked into her eyes, she knew something was wrong.

"SOMEONE FOLLOWED ME from school tonight."

Jackie joined Leah and Tucker, bringing their dinner with her. "How do you know? Maybe someone happened to be coming to Elder Creek tonight."

"The thought did occur to me. So I sped up a little and they sped up, too. Then, I pulled into Snackajawea in Portero and the car went by me. I waited a few minutes. Then I headed here. A few blocks out, the car appeared again. I kept driving, knowing when I hit Elder Creek if I parked where people walked around, I'd be fine. When I reached town, I pulled into the first space I found near here and waited. The car kept driving out of town. As soon as they went by me, I jumped out of my car and ran in here, in case they decided to loop around, but I didn't see the car again."

"Did you get a license number? Maybe the car make and model?" Jackie asked.

"I didn't get a license number. We need better street lighting in this town." She glared at Tucker and said, "Can you do something about the street lights around here? Put it on your assistant's list, maybe?" She looked over at Jackie.

Jackie chuckled. "It's assistant flunky to you. Go on. Did you see the make of the car by any chance?"

"All I can tell you is it's a dark colored four-door. Oh, but I did notice the back bumper pulled out a little where it curved around the side of the car as it went past me. It looks like it might have gotten caught on something to pull it out of shape. Otherwise, I've got nothing."

Tucker tapped the table top. Jackie glared at her.

"Stop it. You drive me crazy with your tapping." Then, "Why are you so quiet. Don't you have anything to say?"

Tucker stopped tapping. "What I have to say is this sounds like trouble following Leah. I think we need to make another phone call to the sheriff." She looked at Leah. "And I think you need to take some time off from work."

"I can't take time off because of some unproven threat, Tucker."

Tucker resumed the tapping until Jackie stilled her hand by placing her own over it. "Tucker, please."

Tucker pulled her hand away and looked at Leah and said, "Please, Leah, how can I protect you when you're off in Portero all day?"

"You don't need to protect me. You have your own business to attend to. I can take care of myself. Maybe Jackie's right. Maybe it's a coincidence. Maybe the person needed to come to Elder Creek and happened to be behind me."

"Even after you pulled off the road for a while?" Tucker asked. "Not likely. Something's going on, Leah. Something serious. Who knows if it's related to all the things going on around here lately? Maybe I shouldn't be the one staying with you. Maybe I'm bringing danger to your door. Now I'm not so sure if I should have checked out of the hotel. And those crazy experiences I've been having, what about those? Until I can figure it out, maybe Jackie should be the one staying with you."

Jackie's eyes widened. "Me? What protection would I be? I'm here at the bar 'till late most nights."

"What about Tracey or Denise? Why can't they work the night shift?"

"Tucker, look, Tracey and Denise both have kids. I hired them specifically to give me time off during the day. Tracey's willing to work nights once a week to give me a whole day off, and they'll help out when we have a meeting, but neither one of those women would be willing to work nights regularly and I don't blame them. We didn't agree to those kinds of hours.

"Besides, I don't understand how those experiences you've been having back in days of old relate to whatever is going on surrounding Leah. A bear came to her back door, and she encountered someone who happened to be coming to Elder Creek from Portero at the same time she did. This unknown person also might have stopped off somewhere to run an errand at the same time Leah pulled off the road. Did that possibility ever occur to you? And maybe it's a coincidence the other person happened to finish his or her errand around the same time and pulled back onto the road behind Leah again. Stranger things have happened."

Stranger things could happen. "Okay, Jackie, if you say so," Tucker still didn't believe it was mere coincidence.

"Except," Leah chimed in, "we all know a bear didn't come to my back door, don't we?"

Tucker looked at Leah, then back at Jackie. "See what you've done?"

"What?"

"You've burst the bubble of illusion. We were supposed to keep the bubble intact and high in the air, so Leah wouldn't worry too much. Now you've ruined it."

"Why is it my fault? I'm the one advocating for the happenstance theory here."

"Yes, but by prolonging this conversation, Leah has been obviously ruminating on not only her most recent experience, but now she's back on the bear."

"Or the not-a-bear," Leah said.

"Oh. Sorry, Leah," Jackie mumbled.

"It doesn't matter, Jackie," Leah said. "The bubble wasn't working anyway."

They sat in silence until Jackie picked up her phone from the table and said, "Look at the time. The meeting starts in fifteen minutes." She gathered their empty plates and added, "Let's all take a deep breath and try not to worry about any of this right now. You can figure out if you need to call the sheriff after the meeting. You two go on. I'll meet you there."

THE MEETING WENT well. The crowd participated enthusiastically, but since their numbers were smaller than the previous meeting, Leah only gave out half of the character study sheets she compiled. The people who took them articulated their enthusiasm about playing their parts and it pleased Tucker.

When she asked if anyone heard any information about the mine access key, people stared at one another or shook their heads. A couple of people said they spread the word, but no one knew who might be in possession of the key. The consensus expressed was maybe no one did. Of course, Tucker knew better from Leah's conversation with those students from her school. They wouldn't get anywhere regarding the key tonight. Tucker knew it, so she adjourned the meeting.

"I hesitated to bring up the key again," Tucker said. "I thought someone might ask when the engineering company would be here for the inspection. I don't want the information out there. Better they should come for the initial look first. Then we'll announce what's happening when we have a better idea of the timeline involved. They said it might take a few weeks after the first visit before starting the actual inspection, especially if they need to bring equipment in."

"Well, it looks like you're going to have to get a very large bolt cutter to get into the place," Jackie said.

"What about a locksmith?" Leah asked. "Maybe someone can pick the lock for you."

"I guess it's a possibility," Tucker said. "I'll look into it. Although I'm not sure I want the locksmith from Portero to come over here and get into our business. I might have to look for someone farther out. Going out of town is going to cost more. And I have a feeling it can't be any old locksmith. It probably needs to be someone who specializes in antique locks."

"Well, in that case, you might have to cross that bridge—or should I say, open the door, unlock the lock, when you come to it."

Jackie and Leah laughed at the pun. Tucker didn't. The door to Leah's bedroom loomed in her mind. The numbers appeared. Then she heard the faint whisperings of the word again.

Forget.

"Speaking of doors," Tucker said, "I've got something to share with you two."

"Something about doors?" Leah said.

"That's right," Tucker said.

"Come back to the bar," Jackie said. "I need to get back on duty."

Tucker didn't want to talk about her experience and discuss what it might mean in public. "Come back to Leah's for a few minutes. It won't take long."

Jackie considered the request. "Okay, but I can only stay a few minutes."

Leah said, "Let's take my car. It's parked beside The Charlie."

They walked to Leah's car, piled in, and drove to Leah's. Once they were settled in the living room, now with Tucker's bags and belongings stacked in a corner, Tucker told the story of the door and the numbers and her theory it might be an address. She left out the part of Leah in a negligée and her form changing into Nigel Dunbar, convinced it wouldn't add any information, and it struck her as a little too personal to share with either of them right now. Personal—and still kind of creepy—thinking about it again. Maybe she'd never share it.

When she told them she searched for any Elder Creek street with an 1873 address and turned up nothing, Leah suggested they try Portero. They said good night to Jackie before they retired to Leah's office to do the search online.

THE LIGHT OF the laptop screen illuminated their faces as they sat in the darkened office at the front of the house.

"How did you look up the address information for Elder Creek?" Leah asked.

"I found this site called Melissa Data." You can put in an address number without a street, and as long as you include a zip code, it returns a list of street addresses for the zip. I tried it with the address of this house and it worked fine. It also gave me the same address number as this house for a place on Gold Street. I drove by it to check it out later in the day and found it. The address on Gold Street is a storage place. It's a row of cinder block garages with roll-up doors."

"Okay, let's try it for Portero, but let's try Google, too. It will help make sure we get a complete list."

To familiarize herself with the Melissa Data Web site, Leah entered 1873 into the address field with the one zip code for Elder Creek. The search returned no addresses. Then, Leah put in her address on Yankee Hill Road. As Tucker reported, it gave the Yankee Hill address and one on Gold Street.

"Let's try Google." She entered the Yankee Hill address number and "Elder Creek, CA" and hit enter. It returned the same two addresses. Then she entered 1873 with the Elder Creek information. The response read: your search did not match any documents.

Leah entered the number again, this time adding "Portero, CA." She hit enter. Three addresses appeared.

Tucker stood up, excited. "Can you print those?"

Leah gave her a confused look, "Sure," she said as Tucker strode away down the hall.

Leah plucked the sheet from the printer tray as Tucker appeared back in the doorway with her jacket and her cowboy hat on.

"Let's go."

Leah's coat and scarf dangled from her fingers.

"Where?"

"To check out those addresses."

Tucker bounded down the hall, then slowed to let Leah catch up. When she saw Leah struggling into her coat as she hurried behind her, Tucker walked back to her and helped her put it on. Then she resumed her sprint to the front door. When they reached it, and Tucker turned toward her. Leah slammed into her.

Tucker said, "Better make sure the back door's locked."

Tucker watched Leah retrace her route and head for the kitchen, coming back to report the door secure. Tucker bounded down the front stairs as Leah locked the front door. She sat in the driver's seat, waiting, drumming her fingers on the steering wheel as Leah negotiated her way down the porch steps.

Tucker sped off down the street before Leah finished securing her seatbelt.

As they drove out of town, Tucker leaned across Leah and retrieved her GPS from the glove compartment. She handed it to Leah. "Can you put in those addresses while I drive? I'll head toward the one on Broadway first. I think it's probably downtown somewhere. Once you get them programmed, let's head there."

It took Leah a couple of tries to get the information entered into Tucker's GPS. The computerized voice picked up the directions as they entered town.

After several blocks along Portero's main street, the voice instructed them to make a right onto Broadway. Another two blocks and the GPS told them they arrived at 1873. They saw a glass fronted shop, a gift boutique housed in one of the historic buildings of Portero's downtown.

Tucker stared, her mind quiet. After a few minutes, she pronounced, "This isn't it."

"It?" Leah said. "Tucker what are we looking for?"

"I don't know right now. But I'm pretty sure I will know it when I see it. Next address, please."

"Do you want Elm Street or Dover? I think they're both going to be residential. They're both in the neighborhood near my school, although Elm has a lot of Victorians converted into businesses. There's a whole section of the New Age folks there. Massage therapists, crystals and bookstores."

"Doesn't matter. The street names aren't speaking to me. I think the number is key. I'll leave it to you to pick one."

When they arrived at the address on Dover Street, Tucker parked in front of the structure and stared. The little craftsman house sported a well maintained façade and neat, tiny front yard. A dim light shone in the living room as if someone left it on for their return from a night out. A bright porch light also lit the entrance. Nothing—this place meant nothing to her. Time to go on. Leah selected the last address on the list: 1873 Elm Street.

THEY SAT PARKED ACROSS from the house on Elm Street.

"Can you read the sign?" Leah asked.

Tucker didn't look at the sign. She focused on the front door. The hair on the back of her neck stood up.

Forget.

The now familiar word echoed in her ear, no more than a whisper, its pull on her psyche almost non-existent.

Tucker sat, staring at the house across the street. The small pewter-gray Victorian huddled against the dark night as if trying to remain unseen in the shadows of the two larger homes on either side of it. Black shutters trimmed white framed windows. The small front porch sat engulfed in darkness, but the front door reflected what little light it grabbed from its nighttime surroundings with its white painted surface. Darkness from the porch overhang rendered the bold, black numbers high up on the door almost invisible.

The small sign Leah referred to hung from a wrought iron bracket at the edge of the tiny front yard. It suspended the sign perpendicular to the street, making it visible to anyone approaching on the sidewalk. The angle made it impossible for Tucker to read from her vantage point.

"No, I can't see it. And the cars in front of us and behind us don't give me much room to go forward or back. I'll have to get out."

"Why? Don't get out, Tucker. We can look it up online and see what the business is."

"I know we can, but I need to get a better look at the door. I can check out the sign while I'm at it."

"Tucker—"

Too late. Tucker jumped out of the truck and dashed across the street.

TUCKER TRIED TO look casual as she stepped quickly across the street. She took a diagonal path, away from the house. As she walked, she formulated her plan. Once she walked some distance down the street, she planned to stop and backtrack toward the house. Then she'd approach at a slower pace as if she were out for an evening stroll. This would allow her a good look at the front door and address numbers. Finally, she'd take a quick look at the sign before crossing back to the truck.

After walking for a few minutes, she took a deep breath and started back. She slowed to a leisurely pace, hands in her jacket pockets. All the while, her heart raced, and her neck still tingled. The prickling increased in intensity the closer she got.

With the house in full view again, she stared at the front door. Her steps slowed even more. She experienced the sensation of being dragged up the steps and thrown down like a sack of disjointed bones onto the porch. She heard the thud, felt the pain. She thought she would get up and run, but her legs wouldn't obey. Her body refused to do her bidding at all. As she lay there unable to gain any muscle control, her body slid down the porch support railing where she came to rest.

At first, her eyes wouldn't work properly. She blinked a few times and the scene began to clear. The white front door on the dark house came into focus. She opened her eyes wide, trying to keep them from blurring again. She saw thick black numbers— 1873. The white of the door almost glowed around them.

She shook off the image. She almost reached the front of the house now. She'd have to cross to the truck in another few steps, but she needed to get a good look at the sign. She found it difficult to look away from the door, but at the last minute, she glanced down and read the sign.

She felt faint.

Tucker stumbled toward the truck, staggering like a drunk. When she found her footing again, she continued, her face masked by the shadow of her hat brim.

When Tucker reached for the door handle, her ashen face glowed in the light of the street lamp.

Tucker wrenched open the truck door and hurled her body into the driver's seat. She slammed the door after her so forcefully she made Leah cringe. As she reached for the ignition key, her hand trembled.

Leah said, "Let's get out of here."

Tucker didn't argue. Somewhere in the part of her brain that monitored such things, she knew she drove recklessly, but she couldn't stop. She expected Leah to rebuke her for breaking the law, but she said nothing and Tucker felt relief.

She sent a silent prayer out to the Universe for their safety as they bumped along the road well above the speed limit while Leah gripped her seat. Tucker's heart continued racing. They rode on in silence, the truck cab crackling with unspoken fear.

Tucker pulled up in front of the house, dirt flying as she slammed on the breaks. They both leaped out of the truck and sped toward the front door. Once inside, Leah checked the locks on both doors, while Tucker walked quickly through the house to make sure they were the only ones in it. Satisfied, Tucker plopped down on the living room couch.

Leah charged back into the kitchen. Tucker heard a cupboard door open and glasses clink as Leah sat them on the counter. She heard more scraping. Then, Leah returned to the living room with a highball glass in each hand and the Bushmills 16 in the crook of her arm. She slammed the glasses on the coffee table and put the whiskey in front of Tucker.

"There is a god," Tucker murmured, as she reached for the bottle and poured.

THEY SLUGGED DOWN their drinks, then sat in silence for a few minutes before Leah said, "Okay, spill. Something spooked you back there and I want to know what it is. Was it the sign?"

Tucker poured another two fingers in each glass and swallowed the mellow liquid, letting it spill down her throat more slowly this time. The alcohol sent a shiver through her body finally chasing away the last of the electricity that coursed through her.

"It was more than the sign, but the sign was bad enough. I—I experienced something back there. I've been on that porch before. I think I may have been drugged or something. My legs wouldn't respond. I tried so hard and they would not do my bidding. When

I tried to pull myself up, I realized running wasn't an option. And my eyes wouldn't focus. It took a lot of effort to keep them open. When I finally could concentrate long enough, I got a glimpse of a white door edged in a little bit of the dark colored house and made out the numbers there. Eighteen-seventy-three, in black metal numbers. I've seen that door before—and not only in an apparition."

Tucker took a long sip of the Bushmills again before continuing.

"Something bad happened there. I can feel it. My body felt trapped, unable to do what I told it to, and it scared the crap out of me. I must have blacked out after that, though, because I don't remember anything else. I don't remember if I went inside, and I don't remember what happened to me other than the one brief moment on the porch. But I know I've been there before, and now all my experiences back in the Old West 1873 might be starting to make some sense. Puzzle pieces, you know?"

Leah gave her an intense look as she absorbed what Tucker told her.

"Somehow, my brain retained the number and tried to tell me what happened, but put it into the wrong context. In place of a house number, my brain interpreted the information as the year in a newspaper. Maybe it put the date into the paper but reported the stories all out of sync to get my attention and to identify the number as something especially important, I don't know. All I know is, my brain probably tried to give me a message—that address. There's no doubt now."

"Okay, but what about the sign? Are you going to make me look up what business is located at the address or are you going to make it easy on me and tell me what the sign said?"

Tucker stared at her. A debate raged within her and caused her stomach to cramp. The implications were devastating. After all they'd been through, Leah deserved to know the truth—all of it. Tucker drew in a deep breath.

"The sign," Tucker started. She pushed against her fear, her revulsion, in order to get the words out. "The sign read 'Professor Demetrius Notch, Spiritualist, Hypnotist' and for all I know, it might have said 'and teacher of the Dark Arts.'"

Leah's jaw dropped open. "Notch?"

"The very same."

"You mean the guy whose girlfriend has been all over the news?"

Tucker concurred again and added, "The guy who also works

as the bartender back in my 1873."

Leah's eyes widened. "Why would he want you, Tucker? Do you think he—Tucker, when you thought you staggered from The Charlie the night you were hurt, do you think you were dumped there, instead?"

"I've wondered about it myself. Now, it's a real possibility. But why? Why would this guy do such a thing to me? Why me?"

Leah took Tucker's hand and looked her in the eye. "Tucker, I think it's time we called the sheriff again."

Chapter Thirteen

SHERIFF BAKER SYMPATHIZED with Tucker and her story. He didn't discount her story, but without any specific evidence, his hands were tied.

"If you would have reported it right after it happened, Ms. Stevens, we would have tested you to see if you'd been drugged. It might have given me something to substantiate what you're telling me."

He held up his hand before she responded. "I'm not saying I don't believe you because I do. There have been too many strange things happening around here lately, and I won't discount anything anyone tells me right now. All I'm saying is your statement will be kept on file until we have some hard evidence to tie it all together. The police in Portero are already keeping a watchful eye on this guy Notch. Eventually, we might even figure out if what happened to you has any impact on the Hammersmith case. Believe me, Ms. Stevens, you have my support and my sympathy in this."

Tucker didn't doubt his compassion and she knew he believed her, but he needed facts and, without evidence, he might never be able to substantiate anything in her report.

At least she'd told her story, gotten it off her chest, gotten it on file. Not much else to do, at least not now, not tonight. When she walked the sheriff to the front door, she spied the usual suspects milling around on the path outside the house, drawn there by the presence of the sheriff's vehicle parked outside again.

She blew out a breath in frustration. "You'll excuse me if I don't walk you out, Sheriff. I can't handle those nosy gawkers tonight."

"Don't worry, Ms. Stevens. I'll tell them to go home—and we'll keep patrolling by here again tonight. Make sure you lock everything up tight when I leave, okay?"

"We will."

He said goodbye to Leah and Tucker. Tucker closed and locked the door behind him. Leah headed to the back door, then down the hall, turning off lights as she went. Tucker followed, catching up with her as she checked the window in her office. Tucker stood in the doorway. Leah stepped across the room into Tucker's arms.

They stood holding each other, silence surrounding them, until Leah said, "Stay with me tonight." It wasn't a question.

"I am staying with you. I live here now, remember? At least for a while."

"You know what I mean, Tucker Stevens."

Tucker smiled into Leah's hair at her use of the teacher tone.

"Leah, I don't think this is a good idea. I'll be right in the living room on the couch. I'll protect you. Don't worry."

"It's not me who needs the protecting tonight, Tucker." She stepped back and looked into Tucker's eyes.

Tucker felt the aqua-blue depths drawing her in the dim light. A shiver ran through her. Leah was so beautiful. She felt so good in her arms.

"I want us to be close tonight. I won't be able to sleep wondering if you're awake all night on the couch, worrying. Please. This has nothing to do with sex. I want you nearby so I know you're all right."

Nothing to do with sex? Tucker didn't think she could say the same thing. She weighed her answer. If she said no, she'd only make things worse for Leah, who might be awake all night worrying about her. If she said yes...she sighed. "All right, but this only has to do with comforting each other. I don't want you to think I'd ever take advantage of you in a situation like this."

"I know, my noble friend. I know it very well." Her look changed. She looked impish, filled with mischief. "Maybe someday I'll convince you to...maybe...not be so honorable."

Tucker raised an eyebrow and said, "Maybe. Someday."

She tightened her hold on Leah again. Maybe when all this craziness is over and life tilts back onto a more normal axis, she thought.

TUCKER AWOKE AROUND three in the morning to a dull scraping sound at the back door. She tried to slip her arm out from under Leah's body without waking her, but Leah opened her eyes and smiled up at her.

"Bathroom?"

Leah's sleep-tinged voice sent a pleasant shiver through Tucker.

Tucker whispered, "No. I thought I heard a noise out back. I'm going to go check."

Leah's eyes popped open wide. "Not alone, you're not," she whispered back. "I'm coming with you."

Tucker wiped her hand over her eyes in exasperation, knowing Leah would never stay put.

"You don't happen to own a gun, do you?"

"No!" Then realizing she might have said it a little too loud, she repeated in a whisper, "No."

"How about a baseball bat? Do you have one of those?"

Leah shook her head, her tussled hair bouncing on her forehead as she did so.

Her face brightened and she said, "Golf clubs."

"Golf clubs?"

"Yes. I used to play down in southern California."

She got out of bed and walked over to the closet and opened the door. Her head disappeared as she dipped toward the back of the small space, and when she emerged she held a driver with the biggest head Tucker ever saw. Tucker stood beside her now, smiling.

"This'll work," she said, her voice still quiet. "Got another one of these?"

"Not quite as big, but it'll do." Leah extracted another club with a smaller head.

They heard the scraping again as they stole down the hall.

Tucker put her lips up against Leah's ear and said, "You stay right here." She tried to convey it in as commanding a voice as possible, but concern filled her that Leah wouldn't hear the whispered message the way she intended it. "I'm going to go out the front door and come up behind whoever it is. If you don't hear anything in a few minutes, call the sheriff."

Leah opened her mouth in protest. "You can't—"

She gave Leah a stern look. "Got it?"

Leah looked deflated. "Got it," she said.

Tucker left her standing in the hall.

Tucker crawled to the front door, trying to remain invisible to the intruder at the back of the house, dragging the club with her. When she got to the front, she stood up, opened the door enough to slide through the opening and slipped outside.

When she reached the corner of the house she peeked around it into the back yard, trying to maintain her stealth. The porch was bathed in shadows, but it looked empty from her angle. She'd have to try to get closer to be sure. She flattened her back against the siding and slipped along the back of the house, crab-like, holding the club down at her side. When she got close enough for a better view of the porch, she confirmed no one lurked there. She stepped away from the wall and looked around into the darkness. No sounds. No movement. She let out the breath she'd been holding.

Thinking she should check the back door for signs of attempted entry, she slithered around to the porch steps. Then, she saw it. At the back door, through the window in the kitchen, a dark shape loomed.

Was the perpetrator already in the house? Her mind clouded with fear as she thought about protecting Leah. She skulked to the door, grabbed the knob and twisted. At the same time, the door gave way from the inside. Tucker raised her club and met—

"Leah, stop! It's me." Leah stood on the other side of the threshold, her own club held high, ready to bash in Tucker's head.

The surprise on Leah's face melted into an expression of horror, and she slowly lowered her weapon. "Oh, God, Tucker, I almost killed you."

Tucker dropped her club in the doorway and pulled Leah into a tight embrace. "Nah, you probably would have only given me a concussion. Maybe you'd have knocked some sense into me." She grinned at Leah.

"You're not even a little bit funny, Tucker Stevens."

Tucker turned Leah gently toward the living room. "Let's get inside and lock up again. If someone was out there, they're long gone now."

Tucker retrieved her golf club and locked the back door. When she went to the front door, she found Leah already locked it. Good woman, she thought.

They went back to bed, leaving their newly conscripted weapons propped up beside them at the ready should they need them again.

"Leah, did you unlock the back door just now?"

"Yes, I turned the lock very slowly. Thank goodness it's quiet. I wanted to be able to yank the door open and bash in the head of the person trying to break in."

Tucker debated her next thought but decided she needed to point out the flaw in Leah's reasoning, even at the risk of irritating her. "You do realize by unlocking the door, you may have allowed someone to rush you and get in, don't you?"

Leah sighed. "Well, I couldn't just do nothing. What would you have me do? Stand there while someone tried to force his way in. I wanted to be able to strike first. Therefore, the door must be unlocked."

Although Tucker couldn't agree with it, she could

acknowledge there was some logic to Leah's reasoning. Leah certainly wasn't put off by the challenge, even if it was dangerous.

As they lay in the darkness, Leah asked, "Did you ever see anyone out there?"

"Everything was quiet by the time I got there. I have a feeling whoever it was heard us moving around and it resulted in second thoughts about trying to break in."

A dog barked, the sound cutting through another pause in their conversation. Tucker drew Leah close.

"You know," Tucker said, "we'll have to call Baker again in the morning."

Leah groaned. "He's going to think we're a couple of crackpots."

"Welcome to my world," Tucker said.

TUCKER DREAMT OF searching for and trying to open doors all night long. When she found one unlocked, it revealed a deep, dark, swirling abyss. She knew if she crossed the threshold she'd be plunged into oblivion. Yet the swirling nothingness pulled at her, trying to suck her through the opening. When she thought the battle would be lost and she felt unable to hold back, the negative pressure drawing her toward the other side against her will, someone grabbed her from behind and pulled her back, out of harm's way. When she turned around, Leah stood there, smiling, saying she thought she'd return the favor. The clear message meant Leah would help and protect her as much as Tucker would Leah. She found comfort in the thought.

The dream continued, but she knew the danger no longer existed. The sky lightened. The sucking wind on the other side of the doorway died down. The door slammed shut, but the brightness remained all around her. The dream dissolved. She blinked her eyes open and found herself in Leah's bedroom, surrounded by morning light and Leah's side of the bed was empty.

Tucker breathed a sigh of relief when she found Leah in the kitchen, staring out the back door window, a cup of coffee in her hand. The aroma of the brew met Tucker's nose. It smelled heavenly.

She cleared her throat and Leah turned. Only it wasn't Leah. Leah's blonde hair framed the scowling face of Nigel Dunbar. Tucker felt the fear and confusion rise to her throat. Dunbar came at her, but when he put his hand on her shoulder to grab her, his touch felt surprisingly tender.

"Tucker."

He sounded like Leah, confusing Tucker even more.

"Tucker, wake up."

Dunbar's image faded with sparkling transparency in the sunlight streaming through the window.

"Tucker."

She felt a push at her shoulder, more insistent now.

"Tucker, wake up."

Leah sounded desperate. Tucker put every ounce of energy into prying her eyes open. When she finally lifted her lids, she saw Leah's worried face close to her own.

Leah let out her breath in relief. Then she smiled, and Tucker's fear and confusion dissipated.

"I was worried there for a minute, Tucker. I thought you'd never wake up. Are you all right?" The concerned look reappeared while she spoke.

"I'm okay," Tucker said.

Her voice cracked a little when she spoke, mostly from just having awakened, but some resulted from recalling Leah as she turned around in the kitchen to reveal Dunbar's face. She suppressed a slight tremor.

"Are you sure, Tucker? You're shaking."

"I'll be fine. Bad dream. Nothing to be concerned about."

She looked into Leah's eyes. The blue of them reminded her of the color of shallow water on a tropical beach. Emotion filled her. A warm glow followed as a thought hit her. She knew with certainty they should do it. "When this is over, let's go to Hawaii," Tucker said.

"What?"

Now, Leah wore the confused look. "How did we get from a bad dream to 'let's go to Hawaii'?"

The uneasiness melted away. The shaking stopped. Tucker smiled.

"Your eyes. They remind me of tropical waters, they're so blue."

Leah's cheeks flushed, looking as if they'd been splashed with Rosé Moscato. Tucker, unable to resist, pulled herself up on one elbow and kissed the pink tinged skin lightly.

Leah's chest rose and fell as if she were having trouble catching her breath. She held Tucker's gaze, the blue of her eyes darkening to deep turquoise. Tucker watched her pupils dilate and recognized her arousal.

Tucker threw off the bed covers and stood up, causing Leah to reel back. "I'd better go make us some coffee."

LATER IN THE day, Sheriff Baker arrived and scolded them, especially Tucker, for going outside with only a golf club for protection.

"But it was a really big golf club," Tucker said. She cupped her hands together in a circle to indicate the size.

The sincerity in her voice didn't dissuade Baker from admonishing them. "And whoever you heard out there could have been wielding a really big gun."

"Well, he didn't. Or at least he took off by the time I got there, with or without a gun," Tucker insisted.

Baker stared at her, then said, "I'll go have a look around. If we're lucky, this person may have been dumb enough to leave something behind to give us a better handle on who they are and what their motive was for coming here." He looked at them sternly. "You two stay put," he warned. "I'll be back in a few minutes."

Tucker raised her eyebrow at him. He sounded like he thought she'd interfere with his investigation if he didn't nail her to her seat with his words. Good thing she already liked this guy. She wouldn't take offense at his attitude.

He walked out the front door to retrace Tucker's steps to the backyard.

"He thinks we're taking things into our own hands," Leah said.

"Probably. You know how the police are. They don't want anyone compromising their investigation. They're kind of touchy about such things." Tucker grinned at Leah.

Leah cupped her chin in her palm, elbow resting on the kitchen table. "So tell me about this trip to Hawaii. When are we supposed to take this, now?"

"When all this is over and done with. When they figure out how Notch is related to all these strange goings-on. Maybe when they finally find out what happened to the Hammersmith girl..."

Her voice trailed off. She wanted to say more, but the timing was wrong. She knew Leah cared for her and she cared, very much, for Leah, too. She realized it with a clarity she'd never understood before—this relationship with Leah felt so completely different from anything she'd experienced previously. However, with all the recent events, how could she complicate their lives by letting her attraction to Leah propel them in a direction they might not go under normal circumstances? Besides, for all she knew, Leah liked flirting with her for fun. Maybe it's what got her into trouble with the woman down south. Maybe she attracted crazy people and stalkers, Tucker included among them.

As soon as she thought it, she recognized it as a defense mechanism. She liked Leah a lot. And not just to kiss, although her kisses were wonderful. She would find it so easy to make a life with Leah, and she definitely wanted to do more than kiss her.

"Tucker, are you okay?"

Tucker snapped back from her musings. "Yeah, I'm fine. Why?"

"Your face went from normal color to bright red in about three seconds. I watched it happen. Are you sure you're okay?"

Tucker gave her a grin tinged with embarrassment. "I'm fine," she insisted.

Rescue came when the sheriff returned.

"Got more looky-loos out there I'm afraid, Tucker." Sheriff Baker waved toward the front window. "I asked them to move on, but you know how people are. They took about two steps away from the house and called it good."

Tucker grunted her frustration.

"I'll be gone in a few minutes. Then they'll disperse, especially if you two stay put for a while."

Sergeant Baker reported he found nothing in the backyard or on the porch. "Too bad it's not later in the year," Baker said. "Since we haven't seen any rain, the ground isn't wet or I might have found something in the way of a footprint, but I didn't find anything, though. The ground's still too solid."

He walked the entire back yard, he informed them, all the way to the perimeter of the unfenced boundary, and found nothing out of the ordinary, nothing to indicate an intruder. He also checked both sides of the house and along the front. Again, he found nothing. Baker said. "I wish there was something to go on, but there's nothing to show anyone prowling around out there."

Tucker and Leah thanked him, and Tucker walked him to the door. As Baker put his hand on the knob, he said, "Make sure you keep the doors and windows locked." He gave Tucker a warning look. "And if you hear anything, anything at all going on outside, call. Don't do anything foolish."

More plea than admonition tinged his voice when he added, "Please."

"I'LL TELL YOU what, I'll make you a deal," Tucker said.

She struggled to make her last, best proposal acceptable to Leah on Sunday evening. They spent the weekend holed up in the house, avoiding all contact with the outside world except for a brief visit by Jackie, who came looking for assurance they were okay.

Later, Tucker and Leah discussed their plans for the next day, Monday, without conclusion. Tucker tried to encourage Leah to call in to school, telling them she came down with a bug. Leah insisted she needed to go to work. They went 'round and 'round as they finished the apple pie Leah baked earlier in the weekend. Tucker said the pie defined perfection, but the impasse continued until late in the evening on Sunday, when Leah eyed Tucker with suspicion and asked, "What's your proposal?"

"I'll take you to work. While you're there, I'll spend the day in Portero. I'll take my computer with me and stake out a table at the Cuppa Joe. It'll give me a chance to work on my novel without distraction. God knows I'm behind with it and need to concentrate on getting some work done or I won't meet my next deadline."

Leah considered the offer.

"What about lunch? They only have pastries at the Cuppa."

"Maybe someone I know can accompany me somewhere for lunch." Tucker wiggled her eyebrows.

Leah laughed.

Tucker's stomach did multiple flips at the sound. Days passed since she'd heard Leah laugh. The sound delighted her.

Silence followed, until Leah said, "I'm not going to win this one, am I?"

"I doubt it."

Tucker stared into those eyes—eyes as blue as a Mediterranean lagoon.

Leah sighed. "And what do you propose to do for the rest of the day, after lunch?"

Her eyes popped open wide. "Promise me you won't go near that house! Tucker, you have to promise me."

"Are you kidding? It's the last place I want to go. Don't worry. I won't go anywhere near that house."

A look of relief washed over Leah's face.

"No," Tucker said, "I'll probably go back and hang out at the Cuppa again until school's out. You can call me before you're ready to leave, then I'll swing by and pick you up at the door. Service with a smile, ma'am." She tipped an imaginary hat.

Leah raised an eyebrow. "You're sure it's not an inconvenience?" she asked.

Tucker identified the teasing in her tone. Invisible fingers tickled their way up Tucker's spine. She must stop looking into those eyes. She needed to stop thinking of all the things she might do with Leah if they stopped talking about tomorrow and came to an agreement.

Today, right now, they could be in Leah's bed, she might have Leah on her back, with her clothes off. Her mouth watered at the thought. She swiped her hand across her lips, trying to erase the thoughts.

"Tucker?"

"Leah, it's no trouble at all."

Best to keep to the subject at hand, she thought.

"And I'll feel better knowing you're not alone traveling to and from school. Please, let me do this."

She wanted her plea to mean something else entirely, but she knew it wasn't the time. She wouldn't allow it. Like a petulant child, she slammed the door shut on her thoughts of carrying Leah to her bedroom and making love to her, annoyed by her out of control fantasies.

Leah contemplated Tucker. Finally, she responded, "Okay. I'll take your deal."

Relief washed over Tucker as she felt the tingling dissipate and her body relax. Somewhat. Maybe she wouldn't need a cold shower after all. "Deal," Tucker said.

They spent the rest of the evening with Leah curled up on the couch, reading, and Tucker sitting in a chair, her feet on the matching ottoman, her computer nestled on her lap as she tried to concentrate on working on her novel.

Tucker made slow progress. She felt jittery, out of sorts. She couldn't put her finger on the problem. She felt incapable of settling down into the task in front of her. Something didn't feel right. When she looked up from her computer, she met Leah's eyes.

"Something wrong?" Leah asked.

"Yes, and I have no idea what it is."

She cocked her head and listened. Quiet permeated the house. No threatening noises could be heard outside. Still, she thought it better to have a look around. "I think I'll check to make sure everything's locked up tight."

Before Tucker could get up, though, Leah marked her place, put her book on the side table, and walked over to stand behind Tucker's chair. Every nerve ending in Tucker's body switched to alert as Leah placed her hands on Tucker's shoulders and began massaging.

It felt heavenly. It felt—

"Your shoulders are tight. This should help."

Tucker didn't believe it would. The tension increased. Leah's touch felt fantastic, sensual. Her kneading fingers sent prickling vibrations down Tucker's back—and her front. If Leah didn't stop, she couldn't be responsible for what she did next. All her earlier thoughts of Leah, the bedroom, clothes on the floor, caressing her, looking at her, wanting her, came flooding back.

It took every ounce of energy Tucker could manage to make her voice sound normal when she said, "We probably should do our check, then get to bed. It's getting late." She put her own hands over Leah's to stop the kneading motion. Leah didn't pull away, neither did Tucker.

The energy dispersed into the air around them. The moment ended. Leah shifted away and walked down the hall. "I'll check the back of the house. You check the front." Tucker heard a tremor in Leah's voice.

Leah met Tucker in the hall as she returned from checking the bedroom windows. They turned sideways to pass each other in the narrow space, brushing against each other. A shockwave pulsed through Tucker. Her face reddened. Leah took in a sharp breath.

Okay. The feelings from moments before still skittered within her.

"Will you come to bed with me tonight, Tucker?"

Alarm bells sounded in Tucker's brain. She knew if she walked into Leah's bedroom tonight, nothing would be the same in the morning. She also knew if she and Leah were going to embark on a relationship—a real relationship—she didn't want it to be with all this anxiety and uncertainty swirling around them, pressing in on them from every side.

"Leah." She tried to convey the tenderness she felt, tried not to sound as if she were rejecting Leah. "I think I'd better go back to the couch."

She didn't succeed.

"Fine," Leah snapped. She stormed down the hall into the

bedroom and slammed the door.

The force may have come from Leah's frustration, or her anger, or merely a result of an accidental expenditure of excess energy. One thing Tucker knew for sure. A long, restless night lay ahead of them.

Chapter Fourteen

THE TRIP TO Portero the next morning proved to be pleasant enough. Tucker drove her truck while Leah sat in the passenger seat, making casual comments as they made their way to Leah's high school. Every so often, a frisson of tension would flash through the truck, bouncing off the cab walls, only to dissolve into the air surrounding them. Neither of them spoke of it.

Leah pointed out the side entrance to the school. Tucker pulled up to the steps and stopped. Leah opened the passenger door. Before she got out, Tucker said, "Shall I wait for your call to pick you up for lunch?"

Leah smiled. "The library stays open for the kids during lunch time. Can you pick me up at one o'clock?"

"Sounds fine. I'll be right here at one, then."

Leah got out, but before she closed the door, she poked her head back in and said, "Tucker, everything's okay between us, isn't it?"

Tucker gave her a weak smile. "I hope so. Is it?"

Leah grinned. She looked determined as she said, "Yes. Yes, it is."

"Good."

She watched Leah walk up the steps and disappear through the door. God those hips drove her crazy. An image flashed through her mind. Tucker grasping Leah's buttocks, thrusting her body into Tucker's. Tucker grinding into her.

She took a deep breath and choked out a moan filled with frustration. Good thing the crisp fall day made her keep her windows rolled up. She wouldn't have wanted the two women walking across the parking lot to hear her mournful cry. She cranked the engine to life and sped off toward the Cuppa Joe downtown, trying to outrun her feelings.

TUCKER GLANCED AT the time on her computer before she shut it down. Four-fifteen. At lunch, Leah told Tucker some of the students would be helping her after class. She estimated she'd be done around four-thirty, so they decided Tucker would head over and wait for her in the parking lot. If Leah needed a few more minutes, it wouldn't add any stress, Tucker would be there, waiting. She told Leah to take all the time she needed.

They enjoyed a pleasant lunch with the tension between them completely gone. Tucker smiled at their conversation. Leah told her about teaching the freshmen how to do in-depth research to ensure they understood the internet didn't always provide the best source material and, if they wanted reputable resources, using the library would be a much more reliable way to support their essays and reports. Tucker realized the kids must love Leah. How could they not? And Leah loved teaching the kids, too.

Tucker wrote all morning, consuming more than one latte, and felt like she caught up to herself with her fiction deadline. That made her happy, relieved. In the afternoon, she continued writing, feeling the extra time would let her get a little ahead of schedule so she'd be able to devote more time to the next phase of the revitalization project without worry. She knew Thursday would be a loss because she'd be spending it with the guy from the engineering company. She wanted to hear the assessment about how much equipment would be needed and how long it would take to complete the full evaluation.

She made a note to set up a meeting with the volunteers to do an inventory of any contents of the mine once they had it open and knew if it was safe enough for them to take stock.

The ever-present question about who accessed the mine and how she was going to get in still existed, but she dismissed it. If someone came forward with the key, they'd use it. If not, she'd make sure she brought a beefy bolt cutter with her to give them entry.

With her laptop packed away securely, Tucker headed to her truck to make her way over to the high school. She checked her phone when she arrived. Four-twenty-six. No sign of Leah yet, so she put the windows down a crack to let in some air. While she waited, she checked her e-mail. Then she got lost in social media for a while. Next time she checked the time, her phone indicated four-fifty-two. Should she be concerned?

Nah, some teenager who needed someone to talk to probably chewed Leah's ear off. She wouldn't worry—yet.

At five-oh-five, she decided fidgeting while she sat in her truck did her no good. She needed to get out and find Leah, see what delayed her.

The parking lot emptied during the time Tucker waited, and held only a few scattered cars. As she reached the side door, a middle-aged woman with a tote bag and a purse over one arm opened it, obviously leaving for the day. The woman looked wary and asked if she needed help, and Tucker told her she'd come to pick up Leah.

In response, the woman broke into a smile and said, "Oh, you must be Tucker." She pointed out the library a few doors down the hall. The lights from the room shone onto the shiny wood floor in the hallway, creating a parallelogram of light across the boards.

Tucker entered the room with a smile on her face, but it disappeared when she found no one inside. She walked over to the desk in the middle of the room and spied Leah's purse sitting on the chair. Relief washed through her. Leah probably stopped by the women's room in preparation for the ride home.

A single closed door behind the desk made Tucker curious. Did Leah have a private bathroom in the library? Not very likely, she thought, but she tried the knob. Although a skeleton key stuck out from the old lock, it didn't need to be turned. The door opened easily. A light flashed on, automatically, revealing a small closet containing supplies. Opened boxes of pencils, scissors protruding from glass jars, stacks of three-by-five cards, and reams of paper sat neatly arranged on shelves. She examined the room again.

"Leah?"

Silence.

"Leah, are you here?"

No answer.

A boy Tucker found it difficult to believe was old enough to be in high school stepped into the room. A black instrument case dangled from his hand. He wore a large backpack on his back, which stooped him over. "Miss Hudson's not here," he said. He didn't smile.

Tucker scowled. "Where is she?" She tried to quell the new wave of panic rising up inside her.

"Don't know," the boy said. "I saw her leave, though."

Tucker's breathing quickened. She started to perspire.

"Was she alone?"

"She was with some guy. Maybe it's her boyfriend." He brightened at his creativity. Tucker tried to quell her annoyance at the assumption.

"What did he look like, this guy she left with?"

"I don't know. They were walking away from me. I only saw the back of him. I was coming in the side door." He pointed in the direction of the door Tucker entered earlier. "I have a music lesson at four-thirty. I play the flute."

Tucker tamped down her impatience at his meandering. "The man, what about him?"

"Oh." Surprise registered on his face at her impatience but he recovered to continue. "They were walking toward the front door." Now he pointed in the opposite direction. "He was holding onto her arm." The boy frowned and looked down at the case in his hand. When he looked up, he said, "I—I—think maybe I saw him push her a little. Maybe I should have told my teacher."

Tucker worried she might be sick, but she pushed herself to find out a couple of more things. "Was this guy tall?"

The kid acknowledged her question with a slight bob of his head.

"Did he have long hair, down to his collar, his shoulders maybe, and slicked back?"

He signaled his confirmation of the new fact.

Fear filled her. She knew who it was. She swallowed several times, trying to keep the bitterness from rising in her throat. She'd also be willing to put every cent she'd saved to put down on the plot of land atop Tenderfoot Hill on where he'd taken Leah. With absolute finality, she knew their destination—the mine.

She pushed past the boy.

As she rounded the corner, running down the hall, she heard the kid shout, "Maybe you should call the police, lady," but she knew she didn't have time.

TUCKER SWERVED TO avoid a car leaving the parking lot. A horn blared behind her and she waved her apology over her shoulder. Once out of town, she pushed the gas pedal to the floor. With less traffic to concentrate on, she grabbed her phone and hit speed dial. Luckily, Jackie answered after the second ring. Tucker spewed out her own words so fast, she stammered several times. She told Jackie what she knew and asked her to call the sheriff.

Jackie pleaded with her not to go to the mine by herself, but Tucker wouldn't listen. She needed to get there, confirm if her suspicions were true or not, if he took Leah. Most of all, her brain required assurance Leah was all right. If he hurt her, Tucker didn't know what she'd do. Agitated and desperate, she'd slowed the truck only enough to swing onto Gold Street. She took a right at Schoolhouse Road and sped toward the mine.

Upper Schoolhouse appeared deserted. She floored the gas pedal again and became airborne when she hit a pothole. The truck bounced back onto the road. She kept going, not caring about anything but finding Leah.

She left the truck on the access road and ran the rest of the way. When she broke through a thicket of tall brush, she stopped. Below her, a narrow gravel path ended a few feet beyond the mine entrance. A dark blue BMW with a deformed rear bumper sat parked only feet from the heavy mine doors. The big lock hung like a limp rag from the hasp ring, unlocked.

Tucker charged down the hill, losing her footing and sliding half-way to the soft embankment. She didn't take the time to brush herself off. She needed to find Leah. She needed to beat the crap out of Notch. If he harmed Leah, she would kill him—with her bare hands if necessary. She slipped through the opening between the two thick wooden doors and stopped, surrounded by blackness. Then she marched on, too impatient to allow her eyes a chance to adjust completely in the darkness.

Tucker thought Notch was sloppy for leaving the doors open, but then, maybe he didn't figure she'd know to come here. The dank smell made her wrinkle her nose. She wanted to sprint down the tunnel, but the darkness prevented her from doing so. She stilled and forced herself to wait for her eyes to adjust a little more. Off in the distance, she made out a faint dot of light. It might be coming from an intersecting passageway, but to get from here to there, she'd have to be careful. The path followed a downward slope and darkness swallowed everything as the tunnel descended. She could use the flashlight on her phone, but she didn't know where Notch was. She couldn't risk turning it on and giving herself away. But, if she tripped and hurt herself, she'd be no help to Leah and she might give herself away anyway. She chose to continue on in the dark.

With the faint light of the cracked entrance doors behind her, the details of the craggy walls materialized as her eyes adjusted. An outcropping, which might have tripped her up, loomed. She barely made out the features in the dirt floor under her feet, forcing her to take her first few steps tentatively. The smooth ground, probably worn by many feet over the years of mine operation, stretched out in front of her. She focused on the pinpoint of light off in the distance and headed for it. She felt the trail sloping away from her as she stepped along, full of caution.

A short way in, she realized she'd have even more trouble negotiating her way forward when she found ore cart tracks rising up out of the path. Now, she needed to step over or on the cross pieces holding the rails. It took a few strides, but she got into a rhythm and quickened her pace. She soon felt out of breath, panting. She tried to decide if she was out of shape or terrified she wouldn't get to Leah in time. Concluding it might be both, she pushed on.

The closer she got to the lighted area, the more carefully she stepped, trying to move quietly, not to give herself away. She quelled her desire to break out into a run, sure she'd tumble down the grade if she tried it.

The path she followed took an abrupt left. She stopped. Ahead of her, before the blackness refused to allow a look deeper into the tunnel in front of her, she surveyed support beams, thick wooden Tinker-Toy structures on walls and over her head, continuing into the darkness. To her right, a dimly illuminated, smaller tunnel would probably take her to Leah. She held her breath and poked her head from behind the wall.

She found herself peering down a short tunnel. It opened into a room-like feature, a small cavern perhaps. The ore cart tracks and the overhead supports didn't extend in that direction.

Through the small opening, containing a light source not visible from her vantage point, she spied dusty old crates and thick, dirty ropes. A rusted pickax rested against a wooden keg. It occurred to her, if she figured out how to get to it, she'd have some means of defense.

A shadow broke across the beam of light projected on the chamber floor. The person remained out of sight, but she recognized the voice as soon as she heard it. Nigel Dunbar-Notch.

"What's wrong with your girlfriend?" the last word pronounced in a pejorative tone. The disembodied voice echoed in the chamber. "Apparently, she's not as smart as I thought. She should have figured this all out by now. She should have showed up looking for you. I don't think you picked a very good one, do you?"

No response.

The sound of dirt crunching underfoot told her Notch was on the move. She sprang back behind her cover. When the noise stopped, she dared another look. She still saw no one. The silhouetted outline she saw earlier disappeared from sight.

Her brain urged, push forward get closer. How else would she know if Leah was all right? Oh God, let her be okay. But she must be. He must be talking to her.

She didn't want to think what Notch might have done to Leah. Instead, she focused on the short distance she'd have to navigate in order to reach the end of the tunnel and enter the room where Notch—and most likely, Leah—were.

As she lifted a foot to step into the dimly lit area, she heard it and froze. The muffled sound clearly conveyed annoyance, anger. There were no words, only an indistinct noise mimicking the cadence of speech. Leah—and even without recognizable words—she sounded pissed.

Relief washed over Tucker. At least she was alive. Hope and joy danced together in Tucker's chest. She took in a deep breath and stepped into the tunnel. Fortunately, Notch chose that moment to start ranting again. He remained out of sight. His voice masked any sound her footfalls might make as she advanced, hugging the wall.

"I should have known. You're all stupid cunts. You're all useless. What good is it to have come this far and not have her be able to figure out where we are? She's supposed to come. It's an important part of my plan." He paused, then, started in again. "If she doesn't show up soon, you will have outlived your usefulness, you know that? You'll be nothing but a millstone around my neck. I'll have to do something to remedy that situation."

When he stopped talking, Tucker stopped. Leah grunted again, her defiance and disgust apparent.

He resumed his rant, and Tucker stepped forward with more urgency now. He repeated his threat about having no reason to keep her alive if Tucker ended up too dumb to find them.

She arrived at the entrance to the cavern. Outcroppings jutted out on either side of the small opening. She stayed behind the one on her side, unseen, still with a clear view of the pickax.

She licked her lips. She needed that pickax. But without knowing where Notch stood and Leah's location, it was too dangerous. Fear and frustration overtook her, the hope and joy she felt earlier replaced by the awful, sinking feeling.

Should she wait? No telling when Notch would do something rash. The burning anger erupted within her. Unable to contain it, she pushed off, burst through the opening and lunged for the ax. She whirled around, letting the weight of it carry her until she came face to face with Demetrius Notch.

As she reeled on him, poised to strike, he looked stunned. He recovered quickly, pushed away from the crate he leaned on, and stood his ground.

"Well, well, well," he said. "It looks like she has some measure of intelligence after all."

Tucker wanted to slash the arrogant expression from his face. When he grimaced at her, she supposed he meant it to be a smile, but it didn't work, and it made him look even more like Nigel Dunbar.

The anger flared within her even stronger. As the fire in her chest burst into a blaze, he registered her fury and stepped backward, bumping into the crate. She realized he held no weapon. As he sidestepped the obstacle behind him, she recognized his attempt to slither toward the cave opening, to give himself an escape route.

"You son-of-a-bitch," she growled. "What gives you the right to kidnap people and drag them into a place like this?" Her anger roiled in her chest.

"You know nothing you stupid girl," he spat. "I am merely trying to scare some sense into your perverted girlfriend, here. She needs to be taught a lesson." His eyes glowed in the lamplight from a battery operated lantern on one of the crates.

"I think you'd better be careful who you call perverted, asshole. If anyone is depraved around here, it's you."

A smile broke across his face, but the look in his eyes didn't change. "I saw you, you know."

His remark filled her with confusion. "What? What are you talking about?"

"In her backyard the other night." He pointed toward Leah, bound and gagged, leaning against a large wooden box.

"I looked in the window." His face oozed smugness. "I saw you cuddled up in bed like two little lovebirds." His look darkened. "You disgust me."

A shock wave rolled through her. Notch saw them? The bastard. They weren't even doing anything sexual. In a moment of offering comfort and consolation, of trying to calm Leah's anxiety, this prick jumped to conclusions as he watched through the window? Who was he calling disgusting, perverted?

Revulsion filled her. It didn't matter what she felt for Leah. It didn't matter if she fantasized about making love to her. This bastard peered through the window at them while they held each other. He violated their privacy, sullied an intimate moment. Wave after wave of anger and loathing crashed through her. Her body coiled tightly and she squeezed the handle of the ax until her knuckles whitened, while a thought, a possibility loomed in her mind.

"Did you do something to me to make me think I'm crazy?" She needed to know. She wanted to hear it from his mouth. "Did you give me some kind of drug and mess with my mind?"

He sneered. "You foolish girl. You can't do anything right. All you were required to do was to *forget*." He rasped out the last word.

That word. The voice. It was him. His voice kept repeating the word she found impossible to switch off. He whispered it in her ear, in her mind. He was responsible for it. Her anger flared again. "What did you do to me?" she screamed.

He looked startled but recovered quickly.

"You needed to be stopped. You kept on and on about opening the mine. I couldn't allow it. I needed the mine to stay closed. So, you see, I didn't have any choice. I knew I possessed the power to influence you. I gave instructions for you to be shot." He sounded proud.

Taken aback, she questioned, did he shoot her? No, she knew that wasn't right.

"I think I'd know if I'd been shot. A bullet wound is kind of obvious."

Looking down his nose at her, he said, "Not a bullet, stupid girl, a dart. Tranquilized. You were tranquilized. Then you were brought to my office and I gave you a suggestion about forgetting everything about the mine. Forget opening it. Forget using it. Forget all about me and forget what happened to you. But you don't listen very well. You aren't a good subject. If you'd cooperated, none of this would be happening. Well, some of it may have happened anyway." He glanced over her shoulder. She knew his gaze fixed on Leah. She understood his implication.

"Did you kill the Hammersmith girl?"

He met her gaze again. "An unfortunate accident. If she did as I instructed her that night, it would never have happened. She made me lose my temper. I can't abide a loss of control. She needed to be put in her place. I never intended her to hit her head on the corner of that cabinet. It proved how unintelligent the girl was."

"So you did something to her, pushed her or something, she fell and hit her head and you think she's the stupid one?"

She found it laughable how twisted this guy's reasoning was—laughable, yes, but in more of an absurd way, rather than funny. No, it wasn't funny at all. Notch was a very dangerous man.

"And what did you intend to do with us?" she asked.

"Oh, you're easy. I need to put you out of your misery. My problem with the mine opening goes away, my problem with your perversion goes away, and all my problems go away. All I needed to do was grab your little friend here and I knew you'd come running to try to save her. For a minute there, I thought you wouldn't show up, thought you wouldn't be able to figure it out." He sneered at her, saying, "I'm so very glad you finally did."

He intended to kill her. She didn't find it surprising.

"And Leah?" She wasn't sure she wanted to know his answer. "What are your plans for her?"

"Oh, I have grand plans for her. She might be a little brighter than the Hammersmith girl. I might be able to work with her. A little tranquillization, a little power of suggestion. I might be able to bend her to my will."

Something snapped inside Tucker. Anger bubbled from the cracks inside her psyche. Who did this bastard think he was? Drugging, kidnapping, murdering, entrapping people? Her chest rose and fell as the pressure grew. He wasn't going to kill anyone else. He wasn't going to do anything to Leah. She refused to allow him to go near her, let alone touch her.

She took a step forward, he stepped back. His look changed from defiant arrogance to one of uncertainty, fear. Her rage shook him. She realized it now. He looked pathetic, impotent. He didn't wield any power. She was the one with it all. She took another step. He matched hers by moving back. If he thought he might escape, he'd better think again. She wasn't about to let him disappear out of this room, down the tunnel back to the entrance. She wouldn't let him run.

He pulled up to his full height, evidently trying to appear in command. He stiffened and stood in rigid defiance. "You can't hurt me. You're an irresponsible woman. Women are weak. Weak and rather moody, I might add." He gestured toward her, indicating her current state.

Fury raged in her. She raised the pickax. He looked surprised she would even be able to lift it. Or perhaps he didn't imagine she would continue to threaten him.

"You son of a bitch!" she growled and swung, letting the weight carry her, but he flinched, jerking his head as she thrust the heavy ax toward him. Instead of hitting him with the point, she made contact with the side of the ax head, hitting Notch in the temple. He crumpled to the floor in front of her.

She missed her mark. She meant to drive the rusty point though his head, but the weight of the heavy implement made it unwieldy, difficult to control. When he hit the ground, he curled up on his side in a ball. An image of a roly-poly bug appeared in her mind. She shook it off.

As she stood over him and raised the ax to strike another blow, he flinched and rolled tighter. The shot of adrenalin she experienced ebbed. The implement felt too heavy in her arms.

When she tried to strike at him again, she felt drained, weak. She brought the ax down and it flew out of her hands and hit the wall behind Notch. The rocky surface took the full force of the ringing blow. The shock wave reverberated around her as the ax bounced off the wall. The adrenalin coursing through her veins receded more. It would be useless to try to retrieve the tool. She knew she'd never be able to lift it again. Her arms dangled beside her like dead weights. She felt fragile, spent.

She stared at Notch's form, curled up on his side on the floor, and watched little mounds of dirt form tiny cones in a line along his exposed side. Steady streams of dust fell in thin, threadlike lines to build up the delicate structures. She followed the threads upward and squinted against flakes of fine rock dust trickling down from above in slow motion. Something was wrong.

She heard a crackling sound, then a sharp snap. She blinked against the dust coming from overhead. The rock didn't have any reinforcement here. She looked back down at Notch. He either passed out or she'd killed him. She didn't care which, as long as he no longer posed a threat, but now, she realized something else, something foreboding loomed above her.

Another crack resounded in the chamber, louder this time. She stepped back. They were in danger. The rock overhead wasn't going to hold. Maybe the blow to the wall compromised the cavern ceiling.

Notched moaned. Not dead. It didn't matter. Her immediate concern was to get Leah out of there.

Larger, fist-sized rocks fell over Notch, first one or two, then more tumbled over him, bouncing off his torso. He didn't stir.

She faced Leah, who sat ten feet from them, her eyes as big as dinner plates, blue pools in the middle of a churning white sea.

Tucker jumped out of the way as a rock the size of a softball fell from the ceiling and almost grazed her shoulder. She ran to Leah and fumbled with the rope around her ankles, finally working the knot out and unwinding the bindings immobilizing her legs. On the other side of the room, chunks of rock continued to fall every few seconds.

"We've got to get out of here, the rock is giving way. Can you stand?"

Leah nodded. Tucker helped her up and untied her hands.

Free from the ropes, Leah reached up and plucked at the wide duct tape across her mouth. When she loosened enough to get a good grip on it, she pulled, fast and hard. Tucker heard the tearing sound and winced.

"Ow, godammit!" Leah cried.

Her hand flew to her red, raw lips.

Rock pieces fell like rain above Notch now. He remained still.

As Tucker reached to guide Leah toward the cavern opening, she looked up to see a large forked crack zig-zag across the ceiling, dividing the room in two. Rock dust spewed from the cracks in streams like a roaring waterfall. The ceiling rumbled.

At the same time Tucker pointed toward the doorway, they heard a loud boom and a portion of the ceiling over Notch came down in several pieces, smaller debris followed.

Tucker tackled Leah like a linebacker and pushed her to the floor away from the compromised area. Rocks pelted them for what felt like an eternity as Tucker sheltered Leah. When the rocks stopped falling, Tucker pushed against a layer of debris to free herself. Pebbles tumbled from her back. She hoisted herself up to a kneeling position beside Leah. She felt wetness trickling down her temple. When she reached up to wipe the perspiration away, she came away with blood on her fingers. She wiped it off on the leg of her jeans.

"Are you okay, Leah?"

Tucker saw tiny crow's feet at the edges of Leah's tightly closed eyes. She thought the lines charming and pushed down a desire to kiss them.

"I'm fine," Leah said through swollen lips. She opened one eye. "That's not exactly the circumstance under which I envisioned having you on top of me, Tucker Stevens." Leah laughed.

Nervous laughter, Tucker recognized, but it thrilled her anyway. Butterflies tickled her stomach with their fluttering wings. The sensation dropped lower. She swam in a tropical blue sea, Leah's sea. Her swollen lips gave her a pouty, sexy appearance.

No, they didn't have time for this. They needed to get out. If Notch wasn't dead, they would need to get out in a hurry.

Tucker pulled herself up. Dust and debris fell from her head and shoulders. She brushed off what she could reach and held out her hand toward Leah, all business now. "Let's go."

Leah looked at her, growing concern on her face. "You're hurt. You've got blood—"

"It's nothing, just a scratch. We need to get out of here."

As Leah sat up and reached for the hand Tucker offered, she looked over Tucker's shoulder. Her eyes widened and "uh-oh" slipped from her lips.

Tucker followed her glance, fear rising in her, worried Notch might have freed himself. Instead, she saw something more ominous. A pile of huge boulders interspersed with smaller rock shards covered the entrance, blocking their means of escape.

Chapter Fifteen

TUCKER LOOKED BACK at Leah. "That's not good."

Leah shook her head and grasped Tucker's hand to stand. "Ow."

Tucker let go after she raised Leah up only a few inches, and she plopped back into a sitting position.

"What's wrong? Your hand?"

"My wrist." She made a fist and released it, grimacing. "I must have bruised it. I don't think it's serious." She looked toward the pile of rubble blocking their escape. "That's what I call serious."

Tucker eyed the rock pile. Beside the now blocked entrance, Notch lay buried in debris, except for an exposed hand and forearm. The weight of the rocks flattened him out onto his stomach. He didn't move. She surmised he no longer posed a threat.

She checked her emotions, wondering if she would feel bad. Nothing. She felt nothing for a mad man killed by an accident of falling rock. Some kind of poetic justice, she surmised. If it didn't happen, he would have killed her, and done something unthinkable to Leah.

She dismissed him from her mind. More pressing matters worried her. She looked toward the obstructed opening. They wouldn't be getting out anytime soon.

"I don't know if I can budge this stuff. Some of it's pretty big." She surveyed the rock ceiling overhead. When a large chunk fell, it left the rock above them with an uneven scar, the ceiling now higher than a few minutes prior. When she pushed Leah out of the way of the falling debris, they ended up inches outside the boundary where the rock had given way. Otherwise, they too might have succumbed to the same fate as Notch.

She listened for cracking sounds. Silence. The rock above them appeared to be stable for now, but she knew they shouldn't count on it staying that way.

She pulled the pickax from a pile of debris, and using the ax head as a lever, she pulled at a few medium sized boulders. They rolled down the pile. She found the larger stones impossible to budge.

"What do we do now?" Leah asked.

She thought for a minute. Circling slowly, surveying the cavity they were in. Her voice echoed off the ceiling as she spoke. "I think I told you as a kid, I always heard talk of a secret entrance to this place. We used to come up here all the time, sneaking around, hoping to discover the rumored hidden way in. Old timers acted like they were sure it existed, but no one ever divulged the location. If there is one, maybe we can find it and use it to escape."

She motioned toward a narrow opening in the wall opposite the blocked exit. It looked barely big enough for a person to squeeze through. "It'll be dangerous. It looks like it might be an exploratory tunnel. I'm pretty certain it won't be reinforced but it beats staying in here with him."

She pointed toward the pile of rocks covering Notch. The only evidence of his presence was his bloody hand protruding from the lower portion of his coat sleeve sticking out from the rubble.

"If we stay here, we're likely not going to find it very pleasant when he starts to decompose, anyway. It's hard to tell from here if that opening even goes anywhere, but there's only one way to find out. I'll go check it out—give you a chance to catch your breath."

Leah stared at Tucker. "Are you kidding me? You think I want to be in here with him?" She pointed at the disembodied arm. "No thanks. I want to go with you."

"Then I think we have no alternative but to see where the opening leads. You feel up to it?"

"I don't think I have a choice."

Tucker looked around at the rubble on the floor and picked up the lengths of rope Notch used to tie Leah. She wound them up into loops and helped Leah place one over her head. She pushed her unhurt arm through it, wearing it like a sash, from one shoulder to the opposite hip. Tucker did the same with hers. Leah lifted the lantern from the floor where it lay. It still gave off light, in spite of the crack in the glass.

As they set off toward the opening in the rock, Leah stopped and said, "There's a flashlight. Notch put it in his coat pocket when we got here once he lit the lantern."

"Good thinking. If I can get to it, it might extend our light if the battery on the lantern dies."

Tucker took a deep breath to steel herself against the thought of having to touch Notch. She used the tip of the pickax to clear some of the rock from around him in order to avoid contact for as long as possible. She estimated where his side pocket might be and found it only a few inches from her initial approximation. While pushing stones from Notch's side, she noted no movement or sound from him, convincing her he didn't survive the rockfall. She refused to think any more about his condition. There was nothing she could do and she knew her mission.

When she exposed the needed portion of his coat and located the pocket, she rocked back on her heels. She hoped he was right handed. If so, this would be the pocket into which he'd have pushed the flashlight. She didn't think she'd have the courage to keep at it if forced to look for the other pocket. She bent down, took a deep breath and plunged in her hand—and wrapped her fingers around the metal body of the small flashlight. After she extracted it, she faced Leah, a look of triumph on her face, and pushed the switch into the *on* position. The light sprang to life sending a strong, narrow beam across the room. Leah returned her smile.

Butterflies buffeted Tucker's stomach. She looked down at the light and tried to control the feeling as she pushed the switch to the *off* position. She dropped it into her pocket, attempting to block out the fact that she retrieved it from a dead man's pocket.

As she picked up the pickax again, she pointed with her chin toward the opening at the back of the cavity to what Tucker hoped would lead to the outside world. If not, there was only one remaining hope—Jackie, and the phone call Tucker trusted she'd made to the sheriff.

Chapter Sixteen

AFTER SQUEEZING THROUGH the narrow opening in the wall, they walked a level, narrow path without too much difficulty. When they reached a fork in the tunnel, they chose the wrong one first. Fortunately, it only spanned a few hundred yards before coming to an abrupt end. Both paths looked as if they might be exploration tunnels. They were so cramped, they needed to walk single file. In some places, they were compelled to inch their way sideways, skimming the walls, as they navigated.

Tucker wondered if the second fork would dead-end, too, terminating any possibility of escape, but when they backtracked and tried the other opening, they found it wider, and it took them on for quite a way before starting upward at a steep incline. As they labored up the slope, their hopes rose. They might be heading back up to the surface.

They walked, and sometimes scrambled, over debris. The tunnel widened and they walked side by side. After an hour, they needed to rest and sat on the path, leaning their backs against a small boulder near the jagged surface of the wall.

Tucker's mind kept pummeling her with questions, and she broke their silence. "I wonder why that jerk, Notch, thought involving me in this would solve all his problems. Didn't he realize if something happened to me, they'd only get someone else to take my place and continue on with the project?"

"You do realize he wasn't playing with a full deck, don't you?"

"Yeah, but it's still baffling why he wasn't capable of figuring it out."

They sat with their own thoughts for a few seconds, until Leah said, "You know, this is where he put Amy. If you kept going straight instead of veering off into the room we were in, she's in the other tunnel. He took me there, the bastard. He wanted me to see her. She looked pretty decomposed. He said he put some chemical on her to speed up the process. It was awful. He made me look at her, insisting I looked like her. I thought I'd throw up right there. He laughed and said I acted like her, no stomach, and no brains. I kicked him in the shin. I was trying to aim higher, but I lost my footing. He yelped, but he kept his damn grip on me. Then he retaliated, hitting me. Hard." She raised her good hand to her cheek, obviously remembering the blow. "It made me even more angry over the whole thing—me, Amy Hammersmith—everything."

Tucker didn't know what to say, how to respond. She thought it better just to let Leah talk.

"He bound her using duct tape and tossed it off to the side of the body. When I started swearing at him, he didn't like it very much. He dragged me into the other alcove and used the old ropes to tie me up. I kept haranguing him. He said he liked me when we were in his car. I mean, like, *really* liked me, so I thought if I acted like a bitch he wouldn't find me so appealing anymore and he might let me go. No such luck, though. He disappeared out of the cave room after tying me up, and when he came back, he held the last of the tape in his hand and used it over my mouth to shut me up."

Tucker noticed her lips were no longer swollen, but they still looked red, raw. Tears streamed down Leah's cheeks, leaving tracks in her dirt-smudged face.

"I'm so sorry, Leah."

Tucker wrapped her in an embrace. Leah leaned into her and put her head on her shoulder.

"I know. Thanks," she sniffed. "But now, we may end up stuck in here. We don't have any water. We may die like Amy. Not even at the hands of that monster, instead, in the belly of this whale, so to speak." She looked around in the dim light of the lantern.

Tucker blew out a breath. "Then we'd better find our way out."

She stood up and held out her hand. When Leah reached for her with her injured hand, Tucker didn't take it. Instead, she pointed to the other hand. Leah understood and changed hands. Tucker pulled her up into her arms. "We'll find it, Leah. I promise. This has to lead somewhere. It's gone on too long not to be the way out."

Leah tried to smile, unsuccessful in the attempt. Tears welled up in her eyes again. Tucker kissed her forehead then bent to pick up their gear. "Let's go, shall we?"

Leah agreed and they started toward the darkness.

As they trudged on, Leah offered, "Dawson is involved, you know."

Tucker stopped. "He is?"

"Yeah, Notch told me he ordered him to shoot you with enough tranquilizers to bring down a bear. The guy's certifiable,

Tucker. You should have seen his eyes. They glazed over as he bragged about what he did to you. He made Dawson drug you and bring you to his house."

Tucker said, "After he told me about tranquilizing me back there, I started to realize it's how come I recognized the address. I guess I revived from my drug-induced stupor briefly as somebody—Joe Dawson, probably—dragged me onto Notch's front porch."

Leah said, "Then, they took you inside and he hypnotized you so you'd forget about opening the mine and what they did to you."

"I'm sure it's why I kept hearing the word forget over and over, especially when I'd come close to recalling something."

"He used the power of suggestion. He's known—or he used to be known—for his ability to put people into a hypnotic state. It's how he got Amy to keep coming back to him. He obsessed over her. Look where it got her." She grew thoughtful.

"I'm afraid he started to transfer his obsession to me. My fate probably would have ended up the same as Amy's. He told me he sent Joe to get me—the first time I heard someone at the back door of the house. And obviously, from what Notch told us back there, he did a little creeping around himself." She shivered. "Joe might have been our bear. Notch got pretty angry at him for failing. He said Joe was next on his list after he took care of you."

Tucker stopped walking and pulled Leah toward her, wrapping her in a tight embrace. "Hey, it's all over now. Notch's dead. When we get out of here, we'll let the sheriff deal with Joe Dawson for his part in all this and I won't let anyone hurt you ever again."

Leah pulled away a little. "Don't make promises you can't keep, Tucker Stevens."

Tucker pulled Leah in closer. They stood embracing for a minute, until Tucker said, "We'd better get going."

TUCKER DIDN'T HAVE any idea how much time passed. Leah checked her watch and they estimated they had been walking for a couple of hours.

When the lantern finally gave out, they abandoned it on the path and took out the flashlight. At one point, they found their path partially blocked by a huge boulder. Tucker climbed up on top of it and shined the flashlight through to the opening down below. It looked like the path continued on, but to her disappointment, it plunged downward now. The light illuminated enough of the way for her to barely make out the path as it leveled off, but it was impossible to tell if it ever started to rise upward again.

"You'll need to climb up here, Leah. It's a steep drop on the other side, so we'll have to use one of the ropes so I can lower you down."

It took Leah a few tries to successfully climb to a level area half-way to the top. The low-heeled dress shoes she wore were now tattered and torn, and the climb proved difficult with only one hand to steady her. Tucker worried Leah's wrist was more than just bruised, but doing anything about it was impossible until they found their way out.

When Leah finally stood beside Tucker again, she said, "I'd give a year's salary for my hiking boots and some water — especially the water. If that idiot let me get my things before he dragged me from the library the way he did, I would have my purse. The one with a full bottle of water in it — and my phone."

"Don't think about the water. It'll make you thirstier. And your phone probably wouldn't be any good down here, anyway. No signal."

It gave Tucker an idea. She pulled out her phone and pressed the wake-up button. The phone sprang to life. She showed it to Leah. "No Service," it read. Tucker smiled.

"No service makes you happy?"

"No," Tucker said, "but an eighty-nine percent charge does. If the flashlight gives out, we can use the phone as another light source." Tucker shut the phone down to conserve the battery. She shoved it in her pocket and waved the flashlight back and forth across the rock on which they were standing, stopping in several places to examine it more closely.

"What are you doing?"

"Looking for a place to tie up, so I can get down after I help you."

She hit on a potential spot as she skimmed the surface of the rock with the light. A fracture off to one side left a spike-like protrusion sticking up. The large stone barb, about a foot long and almost as wide at the base, might allow her to cinch the rope around it firmly. As long as the protruding piece of stone didn't prove too brittle, it might hold her weight. She walked over to the spot, put her foot on the outcrop and pushed. It felt stable. Tucker surmised the rest of the rock to be solid. *Might work. If not, maybe it will at least break my fall if the spike doesn't crumble too early.*

Tucker strained to let the rope out slowly as and watched Leah make her way, carefully, to the path below. Leah helped by rappelling off the surface of the rock with her feet, the rope tied under her arms taking most of her weight, as Tucker grasped it from above, feeding it down, trying not to let the rough rope cause a burn.

When Leah reached the ground, Tucker breathed a sigh of relief. She tugged the rope already cinched around the protrusion, checking it one more time before edging over the side of the rock. As she worked her way down the rope, hand over hand, feet bumping against the rock, the rope slipped in her grasp a little each time she grabbed onto it, and it began to burn her hands. She tried not to think about it. She looked down. With only about seven or eight feet to go, she saw Leah looking up at her, an intense look of concentration on her face. Tucker slid her hand down the rope. A stiff, scratchy strand stabbed her already raw palm. Her brain reacted, sending the message to let go.

She hit bottom hard, the wind escaping from her lungs as she did. She struggled to get it back, but her lungs refused to expand. Her body wouldn't allow her to draw in the fresh supply of air she so desperately needed. Everything went black.

THEY SAT IN the dark to conserve the flashlight. Leah told her she was only out for a few seconds—long enough to scare the crap out of her, in Leah's words.

Tucker did a quick self-check.

"I'm okay, Leah. I just got winded from the fall. Couldn't take a breath in for a minute there, that's all. I might have a black and blue mark where I hit the ground. Maybe I'll have a little stiffness later, but I'm fine. No worries."

Most of the tension left Leah's face.

Leah said, "Tell you what. You sit here for a few minutes. I'll check the path to see where it goes."

Tucker opened her mouth to protest, but Leah held up her hand to stop her. "I'll just go a little way, just to get a feel for what's ahead of us. I won't be long."

"But the sooner we get up the trail, the sooner we might find the exit."

"No. Taking these few minutes for you to rest won't make that much difference, Tucker. Make sure you sit here until I get back. Promise me."

Tucker harrumphed and raised her right hand. "I promise.

But don't you go too far."

"I told you I won't." Before she left, she made Tucker promise not to move. Tucker repeated the oath, her tone grudging. Leah took the flashlight and marched up the path to see if it would make its way upward again.

Tucker estimated Leah to be gone about five minutes. When she returned, she wore a smile on her dirt-soiled face. She plopped down beside Tucker and quenched the light again.

"The path stays level for a while, but then ascends again. I didn't go too far once it started back up. There's lots of debris on the path in that area, so I thought I'd better conserve energy for the climb with you."

"Smart. Let's go."

She saw Leah's look of concern when she switched the light back on. She put a hand on Tucker's arm. "Are you sure?"

"Yes." She stood up, grunting against her body's protest. "We need to get moving."

They climbed at a steady rate. When the path leveled off for a short time, they stopped to rest. As they sat, their backs against the tunnel wall, Leah said, "I'm so thirsty, my tongue is sticking to the roof of my mouth. I so wish I had that bottle of water."

Tucker grasped her good hand and intertwined her fingers in Leah's. "It won't be long. Just hang on."

Leah said, "Give me a couple more minutes, then I'll be ready to go."

"No problem."

They sat in silence.

Tucker felt her shirt, drenched with perspiration, clinging to her back. Now, she felt cold. She said nothing at first because she wasn't sure what she perceived was real. When a slight breeze rippled across her skin, causing her to shiver, she knew without a doubt what it was.

She didn't have much energy left, but she mustered what she could and said, "Air."

"What?"

"Air," Tucker said, her excitement growing.

"Tucker, what are you talking about?"

"Shhh. Listen."

They quieted. Tucker heard a faint whistling sound.

"Hear that? The whistle?"

They listened again.

"Air," Leah said, her voice filled with awe. "From outside?"

Chapter Seventeen

THEY TRAVERSED THE remainder of their difficult trek toward freedom, made tougher by their physical condition. Lack of water and the strenuous activity took its toll. Tucker took the brunt of the rockfall back in the storage cavern and her free fall on the path left her feeling sore. Leah's shoes were in shreds, and her feet were blistered and bloodied. She finally admitted her wrist ached constantly now.

The last few yards proved to be a near vertical climb. Tucker heard voices in the distance and wondered if people were out looking for them. The sounds propelled them up and out of a hole only slightly larger than an average sized adult. Tucker emerged first, adrenalin allowing her to ignore the pain in her hands as she pulled herself up by scrub bush branches near the opening. Then she reached down and grasped Leah around her uninjured forearm and pulled. She popped out of the hole as if shot from a cannon and came to rest in Tucker's arms.

"Sorry," Tucker said when Leah made contact with the ground. "I think a final burst of adrenaline made me a little out of control."

Leah and Tucker stood together, taking in the clear, cool night air, listening to the faint sounds of a police radio and shouts from people in the distance, a search party Tucker now realized. Tucker felt as if she'd never clear the dirt and dust from her lungs, but they were free—and Leah stood safely by her side.

Tucker looked down at Leah's battered footwear. "Can you walk?"

Leah smiled weakly. "If it will take me to a drink of water, I'll walk anywhere."

They picked their way through some heavy overgrowth toward the direction of the voices echoing through the night. When they reached a clearing, they found themselves at the top of a hill overlooking a thin grove of trees.

Below her, Tucker saw Sheriff Baker and a group of people gathered in a tight knot. Tucker identified Jackie among them. Tucker waved the flashlight, now dim, its dying battery giving up the last of its energy.

Baker caught sight of it and pointed. He started up the embankment, others following behind him. When he crested the hill, Baker broke into a wide grin.

"Am I glad to see you two."

Tucker matched his expression. "And we're glad to see you, too."

Jackie crested the hill next and ran toward them, pulling them both into a tight embrace. Leah held her hand away from her body, so it wouldn't be crushed by Jackie's enthusiasm.

"I was so worried," Jackie breathed. "There was a cave-in. We didn't know if you were alive." Jackie's eyes filled with tears.

Tucker crooned, "Jackie. We're okay. It's going to be okay."

Jackie pursed her lips, and then she swatted at Tucker's arm.

Tucker grabbed the spot. "Ow. What'd you do that for?"

"That's for taking matters into your own hands, which was utterly stupid, Tucker Stevens. Don't you ever scare me like that again. Do you hear me?"

Tucker rubbed the sting from her arm. She knew it wouldn't do any good to try to reason with Jackie when she got like this. She wouldn't be able to hear her explanation. If she put off going straight to the mine, Leah might have met her end at Notch's hand.

It didn't matter right now. All that mattered was Leah's safety and their freedom. It was over.

Someone handed Leah a bottle of water and she swallowed half of it without stopping. Then, she handed it to Tucker, who finished it off and swiped her sleeve-covered arm across her mouth thinking it tasted better than the Bushmills.

Tucker looked down over the people still making the climb. She saw someone she didn't expect. She looked at Sheriff Baker and pointed down the hill, asking, "What's the Curmudgeon doing here?"

She didn't know if Baker would know who she meant, but he didn't miss a beat when he answered. "He was worried about you two." Baker chuckled. Then he added, "And, apparently, he's the only living person in Elder Creek who's ever found the secret entrance to the mine."

TUCKER SAT ON the bench seat of the ambulance guzzling a bottle of water. Leah lay on a gurney beside her. An EMT finished putting an intravenous saline line in Leah's arm and another one was splinting her wrist. They insisted she be carried by stretcher to the vehicle because of the condition of her feet, but they allowed Tucker to walk with the sheriff on one side and the

Curmudgeon, who insisted on taking the other side to steady her.

They rode to the hospital in Portero to be checked out, side by side.

As Tucker studied Leah, she said, "You know what I don't understand?"

Leah turned to meet her gaze. Tucker's stomach fluttered a little.

"What's that, Tucker?"

"How the heck did Notch get access to the mine when no one in town knew the whereabouts of the key?"

"Oh, Mr. Chatty told me about that, too. Honestly, Tucker, he wouldn't stop telling me about everything he'd done. He got the key to the mine from Joe Dawson. Apparently, Joe's grandfather was the last person to be a sort of caretaker of the mine. The key has been in his family's possession for years. When Notch lost his temper with Amy Hammersmith and knocked her against the edge of his kitchen cabinet, killing her, he called on Joe to help him get rid of the body. Joe suggested the mine. Then you started stirring up the citizenry to open the mine."

Tucker said, "I wonder what Joe Dawson's connection is with Notch in the first place. What hold did he have on him?"

"Family. Joe and Notch are cousins. Notch told me he bailed Joe out of financial trouble. Apparently, he almost lost his home last year because he couldn't come up with his property taxes for two years in a row and they were breathing down his neck and threatening foreclosure."

Tucker raised an eyebrow, surprised at all Leah knew.

"Like I said, I couldn't shut him up. Actually, I didn't try. When I realized all the valuable information he spewed, I encouraged him. I thought it might come in handy to use as evidence if I ever got out of the spot I found myself in. It also helped quell the terror. It kept my mind occupied."

When she paused, Tucker saw her take in a deep, shuttering breath.

"When he took me to see Amy—her body, anyway—ugh, creepy." Leah teared up and swiped at her cheek with her good hand. "He started telling me how much he liked blonde, blue eyed women. How he thought they were very pretty. Then he started saying how much he liked it when they allowed themselves to be bent to his will. How he liked to hypnotize them and suggest they—well, let's say, he liked to give them the power of suggestion and leave it at that."

Leah looked away. Tucker understood she needed a break

from the events of the past evening.

When the ambulance rolled to a stop and the EMT opened the back doors, Tucker's view beyond the covered carport showed dawn breaking over the hills. She marveled at the sky, dotted with billowing clouds, while the rising sun painted the puffs with the swirling reds and purples of a new day.

They rolled Leah out first. A nurse from the emergency room stuck her head around the door and said, "Hi, my name's Rachel. We're going to get you out in a second. You doing okay?"

Tucker smiled. "I'm doing fine. Take care of Leah first."

She barely finished the statement when the EMTs came back for her and helped her get out of the ambulance and into a wheelchair. They rolled her into the cubicle next to Leah's to be examined.

Chapter Eighteen

TUCKER BROUGHT THREE cups of tea into the living room on a tray. She balanced it carefully on her fingers, keeping her salved and bandaged palms free from pressure. Leah sat on her living room couch with a quilt tucked around her legs up to her waist. Her bandaged feet, treated in the same manner as Tucker's hands, stuck out the bottom of the quilt. Her wrist, in a bright pink cast, hung suspended in a sling.

Sergeant Baker sat in the chair to her right, informing her about their findings thus far.

"Bringing out the Hammersmith girl was fairly straightforward since the body wasn't in the collapsed area. We're still working on bringing out Notch. It's going to take a while to get the cave-in cleared away."

Tucker passed out cups and sat on the couch opposite Leah, careful not to touch her feet.

Baker offered his thanks to Tucker for the drink and took a sip of tea. "The man's got quite a rap sheet."

They knew he referred to Notch.

"He does?" Tucker said.

"Yep. He's quite the con man—has several aliases. Knox, Cox, Knott, Nunn. Even Notch is an alias. Apparently, his real name is Theodore Lithgow. Oh, and his degrees are fake, too."

The information didn't surprise Tucker.

Baker continued, "I thought you'd like to know we have Joe Dawson in custody. We've charged him as an accessory. He's been very helpful with details. He's likely to stay in jail, too. He can't come up with bail money. The shack he lives in isn't worth enough to put up for collateral and no one in town is willing to go to bat for him. Anyway, judge says he's a flight risk and he set his bail pretty high. He won't be going anywhere for a while."

Tucker fingered the steri-strips closing a gash at her temple.

Leah said, "Tucker, don't touch that."

Tucker jerked her hand away and smiled as if she'd been caught raiding the candy dish.

Baker grinned and shook his head. "Anyway, I wanted you two to know where we stand with everything. We have all the information we need from you. Let us take it from here. We've got your statements. All you need to do is get some rest and get better, especially you, Ms. Hudson." He gestured toward her cast.

"I'll be fine, Sheriff. It's only a hairline fracture. I'll be healed in about four weeks they tell me. And, by the way, don't you think you should call us by our first names? After all, we've been getting pretty friendly over the past several weeks."

Tucker agreed.

He chuckled. "All right, Leah, Tucker. If it's what you want. I'd be honored to call you by your given names." He took another sip of his tea. "Just remember, you two have been through a lot lately. Take it easy and do what the doctors say, okay?"

He looked at Tucker and said, "Oh, I almost forgot. Did you lose a denim jacket?"

Raising her eyebrows, she said, "I've been looking for my jacket for weeks now. I thought I left it at The Charlie. Do you have it?"

When he said he did, she asked, "How did you get it?"

"Evidence," he said.

His statement confused her. "How do you know it's my jacket?"

"This one has initials printed inside at the collar. TS."

Apparently it was her jacket.

"How in the world did it come to be evidence?"

"We found it at Notch's place."

Revulsion hit her as if she were punched in the stomach.

"You'll be able to get it back after the inquiry is completed since there won't be a trial. You know, since Joe's admitted to his part in the whole mess—and in the absence of a live criminal." His mouth twitched as he tried to stifle a smile, and she wondered if he was glad Notch didn't survive. "The investigation should go pretty quickly. We just have a few more details to wrap up."

"It's all right, Sheriff. I think I'll pass. You can throw the jacket out when you're done with it, as far as I'm concerned. If that man put his filthy hands on it, I don't want to touch it, let alone wear it."

"Suit yourself, Tucker. I certainly understand your feelings on the matter. I'll make a note of it."

He put his mug down and rose from his seat and looked at each of them. "Leah. Tucker. I'll be in touch again soon to let you know when we've completed the investigation. I don't think we'll need anything else from either of you, though. I hope you both can relax and put this all behind you."

Tucker looked back at Leah as she accompanied Baker to the

door. "Well, with Leah staying home to heal, and with the mine off limits, we've canceled the plans for the inspection and any work to open it, so I'll have some time on my hands to take care of her."

"Good," he said as he stepped toward the front door. Tucker followed.

When he pulled the door open, they found the Curmudgeon standing on the other side of the threshold, clutching a bouquet of bedraggled looking daisies.

TUCKER AND BAKER looked at each other in disbelief. As the Sergeant stepped around Ackerman, he tipped his hat in acknowledgment. Then he walked down the porch steps and went to his car.

Over the Curmudgeon's shoulder, Tucker noticed the walkway conspicuously empty of snooping neighbors. No doubt the news Baker relayed to them circulated all over town by now. The neighbors probably didn't need to snoop around their front porch in order to glean some tidbit of information.

Facing the Curmudgeon, Tucker hoped she succeeded in trying to hide her surprise at his appearance.

"Hello, Mr. Ackerman. Come in."

She turned back to the living room and saw Leah's wide-eyed look.

"Look, Leah, Mr. Ackerman's here."

She glared, trying to will the astonishment from Leah's face. Leah got the message and her expression changed from disbelief to an angelic smile as he entered the room behind Tucker. His grip on the flowers reminded Tucker of someone strangling a handful of snakes.

Leah peered around him. "Isn't Mrs. Ackerman with you?"

"No," he said. "She told me to come by myself. Sends her regards, though. Told me to give you these." He held out the raggedy flowers.

Leah grasped them in her good hand, holding them as if they were hundred-dollar long-stemmed roses. "Why, thank you, Mr. Ackerman, and thank your wife, too."

She thrust the flowers toward Tucker and asked, "Would you please put these in water? There's a vase under the sink."

Tucker took them from Leah and disappeared into the kitchen. When she returned with the flowers in the vase, she found Leah and Ackerman chatting away as if they were old friends.

Ackerman said to Leah, "I heard about your problem with your back door. Doris and I were talking about it and she said you probably shouldn't have to look at something to remind you of these unfortunate incidents of late. I've got a spare door that might fit. If you want, I can measure it and see if I can replace it for you." He gave Tucker a hopeful look and added, "Tucker, I know it's your property, so I'll need your permission along with Leah's."

Tucker pursed her lips, trying to hold back a smile as she thought, okay, who are you and what have you done with the Curmudgeon? She said, "That's very kind of you, Mr. Ackerman. And thank your wife for thinking about us. I'll pay you for your trouble, though."

Ackerman waved the comment away. "No need. It'll keep me out of Doris's hair for a few hours. She says I'm always banging around working on some project or other and she can't get a moment's peace. And, yes, in spite of her complaints, my Doris is a fine woman."

"Well, thank you, Mr. Ackerman. If you're sure I can't pay you — for the cost of the door at least?"

"No, no, I've got it covered," Ackerman said. "And, by the way, why don't you two call me Phil, okay?"

Tucker looked at Leah. She still wore the cherubic smile painted on her face. Tucker wondered if it masked more surprise. Did she feel as thunderstruck by the change in this man as Tucker did?

Tucker responded, "Sure Mr. Acker — I mean, Phil."

Leah's smile widened and she agreed to do the same.

Phil Ackerman stood and pulled a small metal tape measure out of the front pocket of his overalls and indicated the opening to the kitchen. Tucker waved him on, telling him she appreciated the help, once again, and he walked out of the room.

As soon as he left, Tucker said in a low voice, "What's gotten into him?"

Leah mouthed back, "I have no idea," adding a shrug for emphasis.

In a few minutes, he came back, grinning widely. "All set. I think the door I have will fit fine. I'll be back with it tomorrow if it's all right with you two. I want to put a fresh coat of paint on it and give it time to dry overnight."

They thanked him again. Tucker closed the front door behind him and watched him walk down the porch steps. She said, "I think our new best friend, Phil Ackerman, has been taken over by aliens."

Leah giggled.

Tucker acknowledged if she wasn't afraid of hurting Leah, she would have picked her up and carted her off to her bedroom.

Instead, she picked up her tea mug and said, "I need a warm-up." More like a cool down. "Want me to put yours in the microwave, too?"

Leah handed the cup over, a pained look on her face. Tucker didn't think her injured wrist was the cause.

Chapter Nineteen

Two months later...

JACKIE AND TUCKER sat at a table at the back of The Charlie as they waited for Leah to join them. They were celebrating several things. First, with Tucker's acquisition of the property up on Tenderfoot Hill, construction on the new house would start in a couple of weeks. Also, Sergeant Baker called them to let them know they completed the investigation over the incident at Elder Creek and the killing of the woman in Portero. Joe Dawson confessed to his part in the whole thing and, with his sentencing scheduled, they were ready to close the case.

As they waited for Leah to return from the women's room, Jackie said, "We're celebrating something else tonight, too, I see."

Tucker looked confused. "What's that?"

"You've done it, haven't you—you and Leah?"

Still perplexed, Tucker said, "Jackie, what the heck are you talking about?"

Jackie wiggled her eyebrows and said it more slowly this time. "You—and Leah." She lowered her voice before adding, "You've done the deed, haven't you?"

The light went on. Tucker's expression changed. A bright red tint crept up her neck. Through clenched teeth, she said, "Don't you dare say anything to Leah, Jackie O'Malley. If you do, I'll never speak to you again."

Jackie's laughter melded into the din from the crowd populating The Charlie tonight. "It's about time, too. I don't know what took you so long. Don't worry. Your secret's safe with me. I'm the model of discretion."

Tucker sneered at her. "Yeah, right."

Tucker took a sip of her beer. Without looking at Jackie, she asked, "How'd you know?"

Jackie waited a beat. "Leah's face," she said. "She's glowing. So are you, actually. And I'm not talking about the red glow of embarrassment you're wearing now."

Tucker reddened at this new comment—and just as her discomfort started to dissipate, too.

"Tucker." Jackie reached out to place her hand on Tucker's as it rested on the table. "I'm so happy for you. Really. You two are good for each other. You deserve each other."

Tucker smiled but continued to stare at the table. "Thanks."

Leah appeared around the corner. As she approached, Tucker shot Jackie a warning look. Her face still glowed pink.

"Remember," Tucker warned, "you are the model of discretion."

Leah pulled out her chair and settled herself. She looked at Jackie, then at Tucker. When she saw the color in Tucker's face, she gave her a questioning look. Tucker shrugged, so Leah dismissed it and looked around the room at the throng.

"So Jackie, it looks like Tucker's predictions came true. The revitalization project has brought in a lot more business, hasn't it?"

Jackie smiled. "Indeed. Some of the merchants were hesitant about closing Main Street to motorized vehicle traffic, but it's only helped with the setting and attracted more people to come and check us out. Everyone's very enthusiastic about it now."

"Wait 'til spring when the stagecoach starts running," Tucker added. It's going to be so great. People will be able to buy their tickets at the Wells Fargo office at the end of the block and ride the stage. I'll let you in on a little secret. Once the stage is out of town, it will be stopped by robbers and they'll put on a show the passengers won't forget. It's going to be very entertaining, I hear. Of course, no actual robbery will occur. From what I'm told, the passengers will merely be victims of the robbers' charms."

They laughed at Tucker's description. Leah leaned over and kissed Tucker on the cheek. Jackie raised her eyebrows, forcing Tucker to give her a stern look of warning. Leah looked from Tucker to Jackie, a puzzled look on her face, but said nothing.

Jackie said, "So, Tucker, how long will it be before you're no longer imposing on Leah by camping out at her house?"

Tucker squinted at her across the table. She wouldn't leave this alone, would she? Tucker attempted to deflect her by saying, "It'll take the better part of a year to get the new house built, maybe a little longer. However, Leah has assured me I am not a burden to her."

Leah agreed.

Jackie shook her head. "If you two say so. Far be it for me to suggest you two aren't compatible."

Leah's surprise registered. Tucker knew she recognized Jackie comprehended the full measure of their relationship. All three of them lifted their beers at the same time. Jackie thrust her glass in toward theirs. "To new beginnings," she said. Jackie winked at them and they all swigged their beers.

Eighteen months later...

TUCKER AND LEAH sat on the wrap-around porch of the newly finished log cabin high atop Tenderfoot Hill. Tucker just finished putting together their new porch swing, and they were testing it out to make sure they placed it in the perfect spot to watch the sunset. With the house finished for only a few days and the newly surfaced driveway in place, the movers would deliver the furnishings they picked out together the following day.

They faced west, watching the sun sink over the town of Elder Creek. The bright orange orb would eventually plunge into the ocean, hundreds of miles away, but here, within their sight, it would put on quite a show, painting purples and tangerines in streaks across the sky. The colors were already starting to materialize and tonight they promised to be spectacular.

They sat admiring the view as the cool night air circulated around them, one of the things Tucker liked about this location. In the evening, even on the hottest days in the foothills, this place always caught a cool breeze as it blew off the mountain.

Leah pulled something out of large tote bag she brought with her. Bushmills 16. When Tucker saw it, she broke into a wide smile and indicated the bottle in Leah's hands.

"I thought we finished that."

Leah's mouth drew up into a smile. "This is a new one. No past attached to it. New beginnings, new Bushmills."

The look on Tucker's face changed to one of concern. "Kind of expensive on a teacher's salary, isn't it?"

Leah's smile warmed her.

"You're worth it."

The grin returned to Tucker's face.

Leah handed her the bottle to open while she pulled out two objects wrapped in kitchen towels. After removing the wrappings, she held out two crystal glasses for Tucker to fill.

They toasted their new home, the settling of their lives, and the new beginning of the life they would start together in this house.

Tucker's thoughts drifted to the first bottle of Bushmills Leah once took from her cupboard in the house on Yankee Hill. "Can I ask you a question—about the other bottle?"

Leah knew what she meant. "Yes, you may."

"She gave it to you, didn't she? The woman you were trying to get away from."

"Yes." The answer came in a whisper.

"Why did you keep it?"

"I didn't, actually. When I decided to relocate, my friends helped me pack up. Someone else did the kitchen, not me. I didn't remember about that bottle. It was pushed to the back of some cubbyhole so I wouldn't have to look at it ever again. I knew it was good stuff. I just didn't know how good. I felt it was awfully wasteful to throw it away, even if it did have unpleasant memories attached to it.

"The friend who packed up the kitchen didn't know that bottle carried so much baggage. They put it in a box labeled 'miscellaneous.' My friends all know I'm a lightweight drinker, so I guess they thought I wouldn't need it any time soon. I didn't discover the box until after I settled in Elder Creek and I found it in the garage where I shoved it in a corner and forgot all about it. When I discovered the box, I wondered if it even belonged to me. I thought it might be a box you left stored there, but then I realized the writing looked familiar, so I decided I'd better open it. When I pulled the bottle out, it no longer evoked the strong emotions it once did. Maybe enough time passed, or maybe it was the hundreds of miles I put between the bottle and its source. I laughed at the irony of it making the trip all the way from LA and decided I must be *really* meant to have it, so I took it into the kitchen and put it in the cupboard."

Tucker chuckled. "It certainly saved me that day."

"Yes, and that morning, when I pulled it out of the cupboard, worried about you, what happened to you, I never gave a thought to all those unpleasant memories with more important things to think about.

"By the way, I heard from one of my old LA friends the other day. She told me she heard Kaz moved to Florida a few months ago. She's been in therapy. She's changed a lot, my friend said. That brought the final feeling of closure for me. All that old history is behind me. It's done."

"I'm glad, Leah."

Leah sighed and leaned against Tucker. As they continued to savor their drinks, Tucker set the swing rocking gently by pushing off with one foot. Her hand went to Leah's and their fingers intertwined.

"The mayor is talking about reviving plans for opening the

mine for tours again," Tucker said. "He asked me if I'd lead the effort."

"What did you tell him?"

"I told him I'd think about it, but only after I told him my concerns about whether or not there was enough time, you know, since the incident."

"Well, I guess you have to consider the majority of the people who'll come for the tour probably have no history with the mine. It'll only be the locals who know what's happened there recently."

"Yes, but people from Elder Creek will have to take them in for the tours, and what happened there over a year ago will still be pretty fresh in their minds."

"You're right, but you'll know when it's right."

Tucker continued the gentle swaying of the swing. The nervousness she managed to keep at bay since they arrived at the house started to rise to the surface. She knew why.

Leah broke through her thoughts. "Do you miss them?"

Tucker furrowed her brow, confused. "Miss who?"

"Olivia. Lily Hart."

Tucker chuckled. "No. Not at all. Besides, I see Lily every day." She wiggled her eyebrows at Leah. "I see plenty of her."

Leah blushed. She didn't mind being so closely linked to Lily. She came to understand Lily as part of her.

Tucker added, "And I see Olivia most days, too."

Leah smiled, understanding she meant Jackie.

Tucker fidgeted. She let go of Leah's hand.

"Tucker, are you okay? You're kind of antsy all of a sudden. Is anything wrong?"

Tucker looked into Leah's eyes, saw her concern. She didn't want Leah to ever have to worry about anything ever again. She knew her thought unrealistic, but she still couldn't help but wish it.

"No, nothing's wrong. Everything's great. What could be wrong? We're all packed up for the move. The new furniture and appliances will be delivered tomorrow. We're as organized as we can be. Everything should go like clockwork. I'm glad it all worked out so this happens during your summer vacation, too. With my book finished and you off from work, we'll both have plenty of time to settle in, get everything in place and be able to enjoy this place before we get busy again." She couldn't help it— the babbling. It happened when she felt nervous. She knew she needed to stop.

"Well, I've got a surprise for you," Leah said.

Her statement made Tucker more nervous. She hoped it didn't impact her own plans. She pursed her lips. When she spoke, she tried to keep her voice calm. "What surprise is that, Leah?"

"I signed my contract with the school yesterday. I told you they were looking for ways to cut back due to budget cuts. We've come to a mutual agreement. I'll only work four days a week next term. They jumped at the idea. I'll train some of the seniors to do checkouts and check-ins on Fridays, and I get three day weekends when I go back to school in the fall. I'll only have to commute four days a week, and it'll give me more time to work in the garden we plan to plant and maybe do some other things I never have the time for."

No, it wouldn't impact her plans. Tucker smiled at Leah, relieved. "Terrific news. I'm glad your idea worked out, about cutting back, I mean."

"Well, you're the one who helped me figure out the proposal. I think the idea of having students work on Fridays so the library remains open clinched the deal. The school is satisfied with the new arrangement. The seniors will be happy. They'll be able to get out of class for two hours at a time."

Tucker kept up the gentle motion of the swing, trying to suppress the urge to fidget again. If she did, she knew Leah would get concerned. Now was the time. She put her empty glass next to her on the porch.

Looking out into the hills, trying to keep her voice steady, Tucker said, "You know, before I get involved in the town project again, there's something we still need to do."

"Sounds like you've already decided about the project, then."

Tucker smiled. She looked down at her hands clasped tightly in her lap, trying to keep them still. "Yeah, I guess I have."

Leah said, "So what is it we still need to do?"

"We need to go to Hawaii. Remember that conversation?"

"Yes, I do. We never finished it, did we?"

Tucker stretched her long legs out in front of her and shifted on the seat as she plunged her hand into the side pocket of her jeans. The look on Leah's face changed from curiosity to wariness. Tucker knew she shouldn't delay any longer. She took a deep breath and shoved aside her nervousness.

She fished something out of her pocket, closing it in her fist with a firm grip. Then she took Leah's hand in her empty one, looked into the blue reminder of warm tropical waters and said, "Here's the completion of our conversation, not the way I would have finished it then, but how I want to finish it now." She took in another deep, calming breath, and knew what she planned to say felt so right.

"Leah Hudson," she opened her hand to reveal a diamond ring. "Will you do me the honor of marrying me?"

Leah gasped. Her hand flew to her cheek, her eyes filled with tears, making the blue look even more like a tropical sea. She struggled to find her voice, but finally whispered, "Yes. I will marry you."

They sat gazing into each other's eyes. Tucker continued to hold out the ring in the palm of her hand.

"Tucker?"

"Yes, Leah?"

"Can I have my ring, now?"

"Oh." Tucker twitched. The ring bounced in her hand. She caught it, enclosing it in her fist again and breathed out a sigh, relieved it didn't drop. She opened her hand again, picked up the ring and slid it onto the ring finger of Leah's offered hand.

"I love you, Leah Hudson. You make me feel free, sane, and so very happy. And you make me feel a little crazy, but it's a good crazy, you know, like we can have fun and enjoy life, enjoy this." She waved out toward the scenery before them. Nervous energy coursed through her again. She felt like a runaway truck. "I want to spend my life with you. You've made me so happy these past mon—"

Leah stopped her by placing a finger over Tucker's lips. With a sharp edge to her voice, she said, "Tucker."

Tucker sat up straighter.

Leah softened. "Shut up and kiss me."

The grin appeared slowly, lighting up Tucker's face. Her body relaxed. Then she pulled Leah to her and kissed her—hard—thrusting her tongue into her mouth with the urgency she felt. Leah matched her enthusiasm, allowing her in, capturing her, claiming her. Their chests rose and fell, their breathing increased as passion coursed through them.

Leah pulled away. Panting between her words, she said, "Let's go inside."

Tucker mumbled around her next kiss, "We don't have a bed."

"Let's. Go. Inside."

"Why? We're in the middle of nowhere up here." Tucker wore a teasing smile.

"That may be true, Tucker Stevens, but you know, there are

bears around here. I'd hate to be caught with my pants down."

Tucker stood and pulled Leah from the swing. "You say the most romantic things, Leah Hudson."

Leah laughed. The butterflies fluttered down to Tucker's center, the feeling so powerful, she worried her legs wouldn't hold her. She felt an irrepressible need to get inside — to get Leah inside. Now.

She pulled the thick fabric-covered cushions from the swing, stuffing them under one arm. She pulled Leah along with her free hand. If she didn't make love to this wonderful woman, she would burst — this woman who would soon be her wife — the love of her life.

Leah opened the door to their new home and they stepped into the empty living room. The muffled sound echoed off the walls as Tucker threw the cushions onto the floor. They knelt on them, facing each other, caressing each other, learning each other all over again in light of their newly established commitment, in their new home.

"They're calling what happened at the mine the incident at Elder Creek," Leah said between kisses and gulps for air.

"Oh?" Tucker said, barely catching her own breath.

Leah touched Tucker's nipple through her clothes and felt it pucker in her hand. She shivered in response.

Tucker pressed her palm to Leah's stomach. Her breathing quickened. Tucker slowly glided her hand down between Leah's legs. They were still fully clothed, making the touches all the more sensual, titillating.

"I've got an idea," Tucker said between labored breaths.

Leah put her hand over Tuckers and increased the pressure. She moaned.

"What?" Leah breathed the word like a sigh.

"Let's make this another incident — a better incident — at Elder Creek." Tucker stroked Leah again.

"Oh, yes!" Leah shouted.

Not a comment on Tucker's statement, she knew.

Tucker smiled against Leah's lips. "Oh, yes, indeed," she whispered.

More Books from Anna Furtado

The Heart's Desire
Book One of the Briarcrest Chronicles

Travel back in time to the early Renaissance town of Willowglen Township. Catherine Hawkins, a spice merchant and healer, prepares for the autumn faire when she is captivated by a woman with the most beautiful eyes. Join Catherine as she struggles to come to grips with her feelings for a mysterious noblewoman and against those who mean to keep the two women from their 'heart's desire.' Can they overcome these obstacles? Find out in Book One of the Briarcrest Chronicles: *The Heart's Desire*

ISBN: 1-932300-32-5
eISBN: 978-1-935053-81-1

The Heart's Strength
Book Two of the Briarcrest Chronicles

Travel back in time to the early Renaissance and revisit Catherine and Lydia as their story continues...

Lydia and Catherine have become the caretakers of Briarcrest. When a letter arrives from Catherine's old friend and former assistant, Sarah Pritchard, Catherine sets out on a journey that is both dangerous and embroiled in conflict.

Catherine encounters an old friend in Willowglen and forges a friendship with his daughter, Fiona. The tall, blue-eyed, raven-haired beauty becomes an important ally when two churchmen from Spain set the town in turmoil claiming the authority of the Inquisition.

Suddenly, friends and neighbors are under suspicion. Lydia joins Catherine, and the two women find that they and all whom they love are at the center of a terrible struggle. One of the priests, the Dark Monk, has long harbored a wicked secret and possesses ulterior motives. Catherine and Lydia are beset by danger at every turn. Each must dig deeply to find strength of heart in the battle against the injustices they encounter. But with religion and society at odds, will they all survive the ordeal?

ISBN: 978-1-932300-93-2
eISBN: 978-1-935053-82-8

The Heart's Longing
Book Three of the Briarcrest Chronicles

Trinn Wells is an award-winning chef in one of the finest hotel restaurants in Boston. She should be content, but she's not. She hates her boss, her ex-girlfriend has left her in debt, she finds it impossible to meet her mother's expectations, and she's having strange dreams that disturb her sleep.

Sidney Wycombe is a prestigious London solicitor driven to preserve the memory of a place that no longer exists. When she tries to convince Trinn to help her in her efforts, Trinn hesitates, but finally arrives in London looking forward to an all-expenses paid holiday, a respite from her troubles.

As Sidney reveals the knowledge and lore of Briarcrest, Trinn's dreams become an alternate reality where she meets a man known only as Catty. As Trinn becomes more involved in Catty's world, she discovers that not everything is as it seems at the Briarcrest of old. When she learns that Catty is involved in some very dangerous activities, the two women from the future begin to worry for Trinn's safety.

While the women try to unlock the secrets of the past, they battle their growing feelings for one another—feelings that neither one of them is prepared to deal with, but which, in the end, neither of them can deny. Will Sidney be able to let down her guard as noble protector of Briarcrest? Will Trinn let go of living up to other people's expectations and express her true feelings for Sidney?

The women of Briarcrest live! Travel back in time to find what the future holds for those who love the great castle and its inhabitants.

ISBN: 978-1-935053-26-2
eISBN: 978-1-935053-83-5

About the Author

Anna Furtado lives in the San Franscisco Bay Area with her wife, where she travels from this home base, writes, and enjoys retirement from the corporate world. *Incident at Elder Creek* is her fourth book. Contact Anna at wordweaver47@yahoo.com.

OTHER REGAL CREST PUBLICATIONS

Brenda Adcock	Pipeline	978-1-932300-64-2
Brenda Adcock	Redress of Grievances	978-1-932300-86-4
Brenda Adcock	The Chameleon	978-1-61929-102-7
Brenda Adcock	Tunnel Vision	978-1-935053-19-4
Pat Cronin	Reflections of Fate	978-1-61929-224-6
Sharon G. Clark	Into the Mist	978-1-935053-34-7
Moondancer Drake	Natural Order	978-1-61929-246-8
Moondancer Drake	Ancestral Magic	978-1-61929-264-2
Jane DiLucchio	Relationships Can Be Murder	978-1-61929-241-3
Jane DiLucchio	Teaching Can Be Murder	978-1-61929-262-8
Jane DiLucchio	Going Coastal	978-1-61929-268-0
Jane DiLucchio	Vacations Can Be Murder	978-1-61929-256-7
Dakota Hudson	White Roses Calling	978-1-61929-234-5
Dakota Hudson	Collateral Damage	978-1-61929-270-3
Helen M. Macpherson	Colder Than Ice	1-932300-29-5
Kate McLachlan	Hearts, Dead and Alive	978-1-61929-017-4
Kate McLachlan	Murder and the Hurdy Gurdy Girl	978-1-61929-126-3
Kate McLachlan	Rip Van Dyke	978-1-935053-29-3
Kate McLachlan	Rescue At Inspiration Point	978-1-61929-005-1
Kate McLachlan	Return of An Impetuous Pilot	978-1-61929-152-2
Kate McLachlan	Ten Little Lesbians	978-1-61929-236-9
Kate McLachlan	Alias Mrs. Jones	978-1-61929-282-6
Kate McLachlan	Christmas Crush	978-1-61929-196-6
Paula Offutt	To Sleep	978-1-61929-128-7
Paula Offutt	To Dream	978-1-61929-208-6
Kelly Sinclair	Getting Back	978-1-61929-242-0
Kelly Sinclair	Accidental Rebels	978-1-61929-260-4
S.Y. Thompson	Under Devil's Snare	978-1-61929-204-8
S.Y. Thompson	Under the Midnight Cloak	978-1-61929-094-5
S.Y. Thompson	Woeful Pines	978-1-61929-220-8
S.Y. Thompson	Destination Alara	978-1-61929-166-9
Barbara Valletto	Pulse Points	978-1-61929-254-3
Barbara Valletto	Everlong	978-1-61929-266-6

Be sure to check out our other imprints,
Blue Beacon Books, Mystic Books, Silver Dragon Books,
Troubadour Books, Yellow Rose Books, and Young Adult Books.

VISIT US ONLINE AT
www.regalcrest.biz

At the Regal Crest Website You'll Find

- The latest news about forthcoming titles and new releases

- Our complete backlist of romance, mystery, thriller and adventure titles

- Information about your favorite authors

- Media tearsheets to print and take with you when you shop

- Which books are also available as eBooks.

Regal Crest print titles are available from all progressive booksellers including numerous sources online. Our distributors are Bella Distribution and Ingram.

CPSIA information can be obtained
at www.ICGtesting.com
Printed in the USA
LVOW10s1002311217
561401LV00030B/1474/P

9 781619 293069